KATHRYN TROY

I0524614

DREAMS OF ICE AND SHADOW

FROSTBITE BOOK TWO

This book is a work of fiction. Names, characters, places, and incidents either are products of the author's imagination or are used fictitiously. Any resemblance to actual events or locales or persons, living or dead, is entirely coincidental and not intended by the author.

DREAMS OF ICE AND SHADOW
Frostbite, Book 2

CITY OWL PRESS
www.cityowlpress.com

All Rights reserved. Except as permitted under the U.S. Copyright Act of 1976, no part of this publication may be reproduced, distributed, or transmitted in any form or by any means, or stored in a database or retrieval system, without the prior consent and permission of the publisher.

Copyright © 2024 by Kathryn Troy.

Cover Design by MiblArt. All stock photos licensed appropriately.

Edited by Tee Tate.

For information on subsidiary rights, please contact the publisher at info@cityowlpress.com.

Print Edition ISBN: 978-1-64898-465-5

Digital Edition ISBN: 978-1-64898-466-2

Printed in the United States of America

BOOKS BY KATHRYN TROY

Curse of the Amber

The Shadow of Theron

A Vision in Crimson

Dreams of Ice and Shadow

PRAISE FOR KATHRYN TROY

"Exciting and engaging from the first page to the last, *The Shadow of Theron* is a high fantasy filled with romance, magic, and twists and turns that will keep the reader enthralled from beginning to end." — *Elayna R. Gallea, author of Tethered*

"Major Zorro vibes... excellent writing with gorgeous vocabulary." — *R.M. Krogman, author of The Keepers of Midgate*

"A vibrant, vivid world with a rich culture and complex religious system that draws the reader in... *The Shadow of Theron* is an exciting and riveting fantasy novel with an intriguing plot and well-developed characters that will keep the reader engaged until the end." — *Briar Boleyn, USA Today Bestselling author of Queen of Roses*

"Brimming with pulse-pounding adventure and sweet romance, this retelling of Zorro was such a joy to read." — *Olivia Wildenstein, author of House of Beating Wings*

"A wonderful book, fantastic action, a detailed and rich living world, and full of a passion you don't see too often in the genre. A can't miss!" — *Joshua C. Cook, author of Blood of a Fallen God*

"The heart of *Curse of the Amber* has the ability to steal the reader's breath and not return it until the very end. With the amount of details, as far as not only the story but also the glance into archeological procedures, the audience often feels they are living a different life rather than merely reading... There is a solid hook from the very start that no one is able to resist- pulling one in and giving them the ride of their lives." – *InD'tale Magazine*

To Annabelle & Adrian:
"I'm going to live as like a Narnian as I can even if there isn't any Narnia.
— C. S. Lewis, The Silver Chair

AUTHOR'S NOTE

This book is intended for a mature audience. It includes instances graphic violence, self-harm, suicidal thoughts and ideation, ambiguous consent, sexual assault and child abuse.

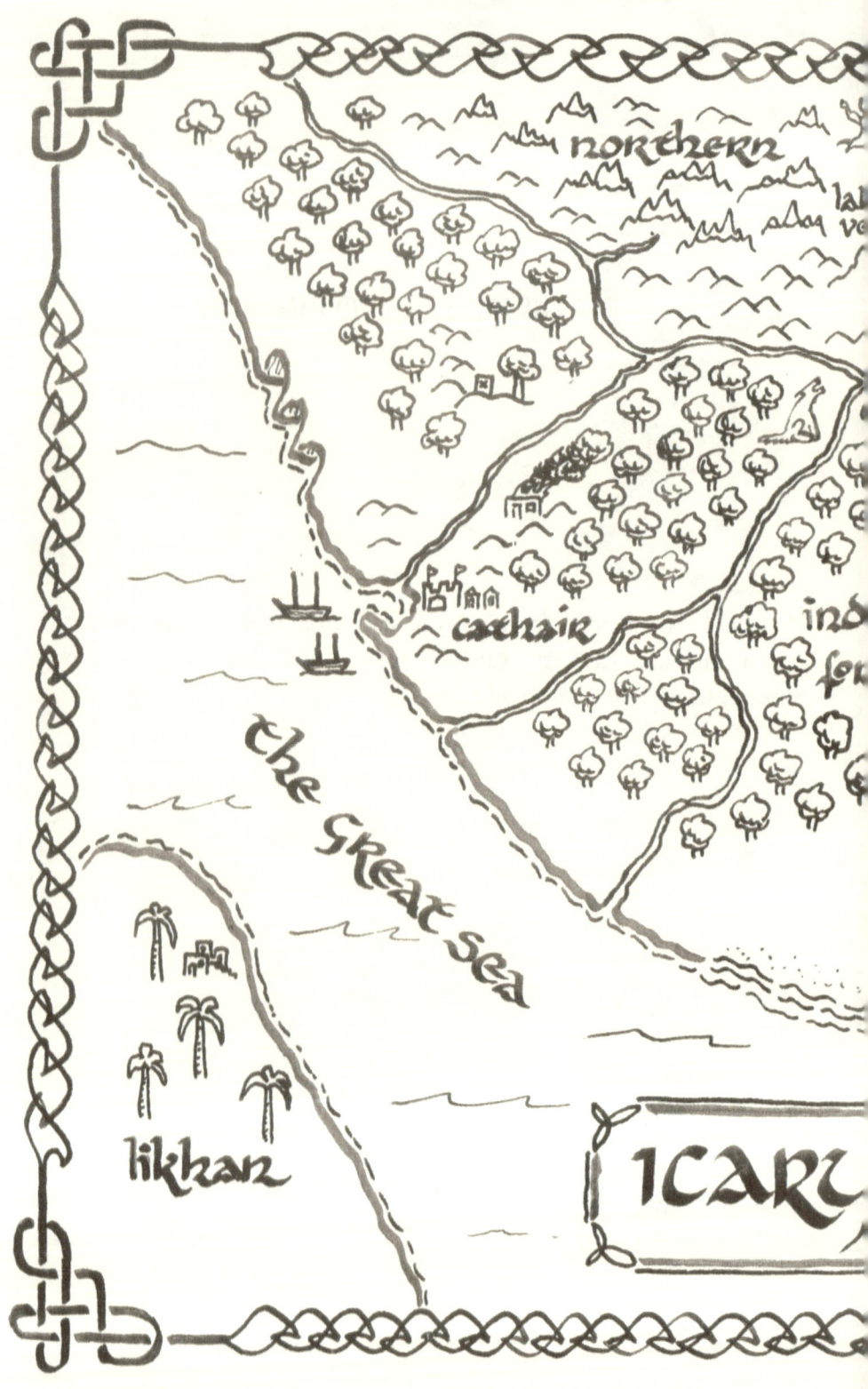

northern

cathair

the Great Sea

likhan

ICAR

1

The Indigo Forest was steeped in shadow as the sun sank, staining the waters beyond the cragged slope leading to Cathair. The canopy of the trees pulled closed, a tightly woven net drawing the darkness into its dense center. There, a shape blacker than the forest's deepest shadows lurked. Two bright lights ringed with a searing, luminescent red darted between thick trunks. Elongated paws crept through the underbrush without the resounding crunch of dried leaves and dead grass. The beast stopped in a small clearing and rested on its powerful haunches. Baring its extended canines, the wolf brought its front paw up to its face. The paw separated into pale, prehensile fingers midair and reached into the mouth of a human face. The menacing canines remained. The lycanthrope's clear eyes, straight nose, and thick, dark brows made him the mirror image of Luca. Or rather, this visage had been Luca's inheritance. The sole difference was the cold, calculating countenance that was permanent on the shadow's face.

He retrieved the crystal orb he had carried in his lupine mouth and examined it. He had taken the orb from an abandoned campfire to uncover its secrets. He sensed its untold power with every fiber of his undead existence.

Dracula had searched for days and nights without end for the clue that would unlock the magic trapped inside the crystalline sphere. Just as he felt he was nearing a breakthrough, his hideaway had been discovered by his son, born of a human mother, and razed to the ground. Luca had also succeeded in destroying Rene, the only consort Dracula had taken since tracking his son across the universe and into the magical realm of Icarya. His seething anger was mitigated by his pride.

Despite the setback, the vampire lord seemed to have stumbled upon the very answer he sought. Before Rene's house had collapsed, the orb had soaked in blood and grown before his eyes. His piercing gaze dissected the orb now, sifting through its murky contents for an explanation. His pupils caught the impression of a quick, slight movement. He rotated it in his palm, but its center remained inscrutable, hidden by a pale cloud of plasma.

Tempting fate, the dark prince brought his index finger to his mouth, punctured the tip, and dropped a small quantity of blood onto the orb. The crimson droplet ran down the curve of the orb, filling in a crease in his palm. A moment's disappointment was stymied as the line written in blood shrank, pulled into the orb by an unseen force. It took a breath. A sound like ice expanding issued forth. Dracula peered again into the milky obscurity. This time, he spied an impossibly small, humanoid form.

Elated, Dracula laid the orb at his feet and pulled a small, sharp dagger out of his singed coat. He dug the point into the palm of his hand, feeding the orb a continual stream, eyes gleaming as he watched it grow.

Sensing his son's nearness, he withdrew his blade suddenly. Their fated reunion, the meeting that Dracula had planned with such diligence for millennia, was rapidly approaching. Father would soon be ready to face his formidable son. But not yet. He grabbed the sphere, grown too large for him to close his fist around, and evaporated. The cells of his body transformed into waterlogged air, spreading a thick blanket of fog throughout the forest, looking for refuge.

LUCA CLOSED HIS HEAVY HEART OFF FROM KATE AS HE PUSHED THE BOAT headed toward Castelmor into the Great Sea, with Kate and a flabbergasted sailor inside it. She would have never gone willingly, leaving Luca alone to deal with his father. Not after the murder of a dear friend. But as much as her kingdom needed her to be strong, they needed her to be alive. So did he.

The prospect of Kate perishing had been unbearable since their chance meeting several months before. It was even more devastating now that he had come to know bliss with her. Luca bore the weight of his father's threat on his own shoulders. He needed to focus, or all would be lost. So he pushed her away into the deepening twilight. The pain that burst forth from her heart he felt as his own. Their psyches, their very souls were bound together. Having drunk her life force, they existed on the same plane, one he had abused for the sake of her safety. That bond was now in danger from betrayal and heartbreak. His soul cried out to her across the sea. His words flooded her shocked mind as he stood on the docks, the lone stationary figure amid the cacophony of the portside village falling easily into its nighttime routine.

I fear for your life, and it drains me of my strength. Please.

She stood in the boat and tossed something in his direction through the cool, sweet air. Luca closed his hand around a golden disk embossed with the figure of a tree, its roots spread endlessly over the emblem and forming its decorative border, ensnaring small creatures of all kinds in its branches. Her voice was cold as stone in his ears.

My seal. If you need help, you'll have it.

Thank you. Kate, my love, I—

Be swift.

He nodded, wiped the moisture from his eyes, and flew through the village to the hills beyond as Kate's boat faded into obscurity.

Rene's cottage was still in flames when Luca dove headlong into the forest to its rear, following the rabid howl that had turned every head in Cathair in its direction. Luca darted silently through the trees, his long, thinly curved blade in his hand. His heart raced with a supreme urgency to come upon Dracula in flight, to force a speedy confrontation and an instant end. As he reached the center of the forest his steps slowed, growing more cautious as the night thickened, closing in on him. His prey made no sound. He did not know what form to expect his father to be in, causing him to scan the ground in front of him, the trees, and even the sky. Feeling frenzied, Luca stood still and closed his eyes, ceding primacy to his other senses. He saw and heard nothing. The stillness was so complete it was like standing at the cold edge of the universe. His hair bristled on the back of his neck. The grip on his sword tightened. He sensed a cold spot, something breathing very near. He took two steps ahead to the right and lifted his sword above his head. Poised to strike, his blade was in one moment edged in darkness, and bathing in thick white mist the next. Luca's eyes peeled open. He rushed into the mist, hoping for some way, any way, to pull Dracula back into a physical form and compel him into battle. Alas, his sword cleaved blindly through the water-laden air. The fog spread in every direction, stretching murky tentacles into wooded footpaths. Luca swore at the faint echo of a snicker. His eyes blazed red, the only light visible through the impenetrable fog.

It moved without any seeming preternatural sentience, spreading toward the village and out into the sea. In a fit of anger, Luca swiped at the nearest tree, felling it in one stroke. He stepped into the clearing as the nexus of low-laying clouds dissipated outward, leaving nothing but curling wisps. Luca swatted away a thin tendril of mist with his hand as he knelt down, studying the paw prints on the ground. The lingering scent of vampire blood filled his nostrils, but the soil had absorbed only an infinitesimal amount.

Was he injured? Luca wondered. His father would heal as rapidly as all vampires did, which would account for the scant traces of crimson in the dirt. But the amount he saw spilled did not match the rankness that was unmistakable now that Dracula's heavy presence had lifted. The inconsistency puzzled him.

Where did the blood go?

Luca had missed his opportunity. That much was certain. His father could be anywhere within the growing fogbank's extended reach. He turned his attention toward potential hiding places as he emerged from the forest. The passing cloud had extinguished the ravenous flames that consumed Rene's cottage. Smoldering embers hissed upon extinction, submitting to the light drizzle that had begun to fall. Luca combed through the blackened ruins of Rene's home. The destruction he had unleashed upon the cottage in his fury seemed untouched. There was nothing here Dracula had been compelled to retrieve. Ashes of magical treatises lay undisturbed in every corner. Yet it was clear that they had been collected with care, acquired for some purpose. That Dracula might be adding a new form of magic to his already formidable arsenal unsettled him. Pointedly so, considering Kate's own abilities and the havoc they wrought on her. He pushed the possibility of a standoff between his father and his lover, and what price Kate might pay for her talent, to the deepest recesses of his mind. He was desperate to cling to the conviction in his own skill.

Luca passed the night drifting through the streets of Cathair, a silent sentinel. He limned a wide arc around the town's perimeter, keeping close watch on the docks and passing through the slumbering streets. The bluster from the tavern reverberated in the stillness. The village shielded itself in frivolity. Luca's dejected steps guarded the port until the sun rose. He tried not to think of the absence of Kate's voice in his head, the love that normally wrapped itself tightly around him.

In an ironic way, the fog's persistence lifted his spirit to no small measure. As long as the fogbank remained, it signaled Dracula's failure to secure safe passage away from the danger waiting at the edge of Luca's sword. Night slipped away into morning without another victim being taken. It was a small, but not insignificant victory.

NOT A SINGLE WORD PASSED BETWEEN KATE AND THE MAN ROWING HER boat in the long journey from Cathair to the smaller port that led to Castelmor's southern gate. The fog that had obscured their first night at sea had been replaced by a freezing aura, surrounding Kate in a twinkling white mist. The only time she opened her eyes or lifted her head was to exit the boat upon reaching the shore. She had just enough sense to pay the man generously for the awkward silence she had kept. The frozen mist dissipated as she ascended the stairs in the southern tower, her lonely stride echoing in the hallway to her suite as she shed her clothes in favor of a flowing silk sleeping robe and crawled into bed. She drew tight the midnight red curtains surrounding the frame of her resting place.

She ignored the light's attempt to steal a glance at her tear-stained face and the scurrying whispers of servants outside her door. She was unmoved by the scraping sounds of two meals being set out and taken away untouched.

It was Allistair who brought dinner to her room the following day on a burnished silver platter. He made a deliberate clatter as he picked at the miniature bowls and serving spoons holding supper's accompaniments and poured two glasses of a dark, robust wine. His stern voice pealed through the room.

"You're scaring people. Now get out here and eat."

The only response was the muffled rustling of sheets. It had been encouraging at first, until Allistair realized she had settled back into a comfortable ignorance. He took a draught of the wine and stood up, walked over to the bed, and slipped into its darkened space. Her back was facing him, unaffected by his intrusion. He laid down atop her bedcovers as she pulled them over her shoulders. He hugged his sister, and would not let go.

Kate twisted away from him, but Allistair held fast. He said nothing. Allistair could barely detect her breathing as she turned over, buried her face in his chest, and sobbed uncontrollably. The sound of her pain brought tears to her brother's eyes.

Kate's only solace was the silent compassion of her brother's embrace. Her chest was wracked with despair, and the back of her throat burned in unrestrained torment. When she could cry no more, Allistair succeeded in emerging with her into the quiet comfort of her room, and seated her in one of the high-backed upholstered chairs facing the tranquil crackling of the hearth before bringing his own seat as close as possible.

Without further prompting, Kate relayed the events leading up to Luca casting her off into the Great Sea—the distraught arrival of Rene's wife to her country cottage, the discovery that the friend and captain had fallen victim to Dracula's predation, the hunt that sent Luca careening headlong into the forest on his own.

"He pushed me away. His life is in more danger than it's ever been, and he pushed me away," she finished. Impossible tears welled from her emptied font, shocked into rage at her brother's unbridled relief.

"Thank god for that," he sighed.

She shot him a sharp, hateful glance, but Allistair countered it with an earnest expression.

"He loves you, Kate. Any man would have done the same."

"Any man would have betrayed a trust?" She turned her face away from her brother, unconsoled.

He narrowed his eyes at her stubbornness. "He put your safety ahead of his own needs, his own happiness. You wanted someone who could be your partner, who could share in the sacrifices you make. What did you think that would look like?"

She squeezed her eyes shut. She knew, all too well, that Luca shared in her soul-rending agony. "If he doesn't come back...I'll never be whole again."

"Don't I know it." Allistair swallowed hard, having never accepted his role of widower.

Kate looked up at her brother, astonished by her own foolishness. "Oh, Al, I'm—"

He shrugged off her embarrassment. "It's alright. We're not like Ted, sharing his bed with a different girl every night. We're peas in a pod, you and I."

A fraction of a smile tempted the corners of her mouth. "Yeah, I guess we still are."

"We always are," he corrected her, folding his fingers over hers. She kissed her brother's hand in gratitude.

"Thanks, Al."

He smiled and pressed his lips to his little sister's forehead before drawing her attention to a thick envelope tied with a familiar green ribbon.

"This arrived not long after you departed on your little honeymoon," Allistair said. "I was told it's for your eyes alone. I trust you'll relay what's pertinent to me."

She stared at what promised to be an interesting read with hesitation.

"It may be the distraction you need," he prodded, "to keep your mind off less pleasant things."

She brought the wine to her lips, deliberating as Allistair bade her goodnight. Returning the goblet to the platter, she reached for the cheese knife, wiped it on a cloth napkin, and broke the letter's seal.

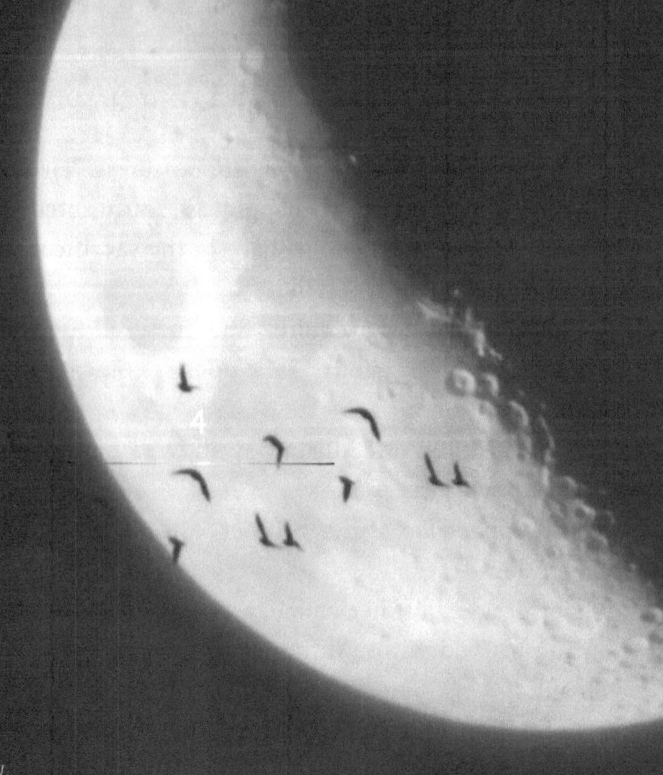

MY BELOVED QUEEN,

I arrived safely in Likhan a week ago, in time to partake in the grand feast enjoyed by the whole city, which marks one of the final stages of Likhanni mourning rituals. The entirety of the population under Reza's command prepared for the extended fast they would suffer starting the following day.

I made my way through the sea of mourners flooding the open plaza toward the royal family. I admit to being spoiled by Icaryan light, as the dim flames that stood vigil every few feet in tall, wrought-iron rows were a strain to my eyes. The city is sincere in its sorrow over the loss of their seht. At length I approached the edge of the procession that began at Reza's doorstep. Mehmnet made it his business to be first in line to grieve for his brother, and yet the man cannot stop smiling. His grin only broadened when he recognized your seal at my hip, and he insinuated upon our introduction that a beauty such as mine— that would be, Christine's—would fetch a fair price on his prized auction block. I gave him leave to try, though he abstained, as he said, for the sake of not appearing "unfriendly," and offered to put me up in his own home. How much, he asks, are you willing to pay for the freedom of your protectorate? Ever the pragmatist, rather than risk his own neck he would be perfectly content to extort you. With your permission, I vow to wipe the smug grin off that sagging bag of skin permanently.

For a flicker of time, you and I were more than lovers—we were confidants. I hope I do not overstep my bounds when I express myself in a way I have not done with another soul before or since. Seeing Reza's gilded face, carved in peaceful slumber into the inlaid gold of his death mask, grated on my soul. In the passing years I have felt the weight of the bodies on my shoulders. I am often absent in times of mourning, the phantom who never hears the cries of the bereaved. Doing Reza this long neglected honor was a terrible burden, but I lingered, distraught, near his house of death. It didn't feel like punishment nearly enough.

The one who seemed to suffer most from Reza's loss is our young friend Darien, who surprised me by seeking me out. He smiled graciously, flashing a bright countenance and sparkling eyes—one green, one blue. A beauty such as mine should be celebrated, he responded, to his uncle's unkind and provocative words, not caged. He defended you when Mehmnet reproached your absence, and was rather moved by the gesture of honoring Reza at all. He is a self-made student of Icaryan technology, and he made clear his particular interest in our light, inquiring whether it is a resource we would be willing to share. He has an inkling that its power could be channeled into more than its present applications.

Once Darien caught sight of me, I was not permitted to leave his side. I was restrained by a tender grip around my waist, and his soft voice in my ear. Insisting I address him informally, his flirtations were a perfect façade. His wandering eyes and hands suggested to all who beheld us that the grieving nephew's interest was keen, and yet he spoke of nothing but science, policy, your whereabouts and whether I have your ear, and can be made to influence you. Under the pretext of romance, I am staying at Darien's house, connected to the suites of Mehmnet and Reza's widow Haydee by a large open-air courtyard. He kindly informed me that if I wished to live through the night, I should under no circumstances have submitted to Mehmnet's proposal for accommodation.

Darien's generosity made me the fast enemy of the widow Haydee, who shot murderous barbs in my direction throughout the meal. She tempered her wrath by clinging closely to her aging brother-in-law in her grief, who made overtures to marry her. Darien has given her all his assurances. I have never, nor would I ever kiss my mother like that, through marriage or otherwise.

After her furious departure, Darien's confidence instantly dissolved. He fears for his life. Mehmnet is getting bolder in his language, more aggressive in his ploys. The world has fallen into his lap—and I put it there. To hear Darien tell it, the Hi'dinn Reza built, from the best minds and the greatest houses, are divided. Under Reza's guiding wing, Darien was working toward major reform in class structure. He pointed out with prideful conviction that no service is provided under his roof except by those that are paid. He envies your successful reign, remarking that there is an optimism in Icaryans that is only reflected in the eyes of the Likhanni in his dreams. Mehmnet and his coterie are at complete odds with Darien about Likhan's future. The oldest, wealthiest families side with Mehmnet, believing he will secure what they see as theirs. Younger generations are eager to expand the city's economy for greater opportunity. To increase Darien's suffering, Mehmnet has enlisted him as the one to pass him the chain of the new seht when the time comes.

Some good may yet come of my blunder. The ceremony to pass power from Reza to Mehmnet is postponed due to the violent nature of Reza's death. The people fear Reza's return as a vengeful ghost, so they will wait until the next moons to proclaim the new seht. This provides us the protection of little more than a season.

The rumor among Darien's friends is that the only reason he accepted Mehmnet's request is because he intends to withhold the chain—a challenge for power. Darien confirmed this with his own lips. He informs me that while his uncle is a renowned swordsman among the Likhanni, Darien's primary weapon is his tongue. He implored me to serve as his champion. He is desirous of building new and more complex alliances, with you especially. Our freedom would be guaranteed, certainly, but beyond that he wishes for cultural, technological exchange. Open trade. He does not hold great wealth on his side, but he believes he can successfully mobilize the general populace. They wish to uplift the city in which they and their fathers have toiled—nothing more. A people drawn to tradition.

On his side, Mehmnet's plan is to use the money he anticipates extracting from you only to better arm himself. He expects you to fund your own demise. Your presence, even through a representative, will make a powerful statement in the arena. I gave Darien to understand that your wish is for him to succeed, but I confessed to not knowing your mind on the matter of a challenge. If it is your wish, I am ready to serve.

There has been no intimation, no hint of knowledge pertaining to Darien's lineage. If it is known, he hides it well.

My Queen, I am honored to continue here as your faithful servant, anxious for a reply. You made yourself perfectly plain at our long sought after, bittersweet reunion, yet I wish to express my sincerest hope that, should the man who is most assuredly reading over your shoulder ever cease to bring that carefree smile to your lips, one that my harsh treatment and stubborn distance failed to do, that I may humbly request an opportunity to correct my error.

Yours, Alaric.

KATE LAID THE MANY FOLDED PAGES IN HER LAP, SENDING THE VERMILLION liquid in her glass into a whirling vortex before pouring the scant traces of wine past her lips. The final draught was unexpectedly salty, tainted by falling sadness, knowing that the sweetness of Luca's mouth had at last faded, and might not ever grace her lips again.

Her breath caught in her throat as Luca tugged at the edges of her mind. She was still so enraged by his surprise maneuver that the moment his head entered hers was robbed of its joy. She shut him out, unwilling to let him feel the extent of her torment, but regretted it almost immediately.

His consolation thrummed dolefully between her ears.

You didn't do anything wrong. I did. Forgive me, my love.

She set her glass down again, and closed her eyes. Her breath slowed, her heartbeat no more than a murmur. She heard familiar voices jeering, the creak of the sodden wood table, the deep clink of foaming mugs. The distinctive smell of fish and ale alerted her to Luca's location. She sat silently in his shadow while he supped, drowning his own sorrow in his dinner. She wallowed in the feel of him, so close and yet, impossibly far.

Kate rose from her seat as he retired, gripping the wooden claws framing the chair and struggling to maintain her balance before drifting to the open window. She leaned far out onto the ledge, her lungs gulping greedily at the night air. The hawk who had delivered Alaric's message perched on the sill beside her.

"Will you be requiring a return message, My Queen?"

Her response came slowly. "No. I thank you for your service."

"I'm pleased to be of assistance, Your Majesty. Sleep well." Off he fluttered. With the billowing air still streaming past her face at the hawk's departure, Kate drew closed the window, and went not to bed, but deeper into her suite, where her masques were kept.

DARIEN PACED HIS ROOM, HIS GLOSSY DARK CURLS RISING AND FALLING ON his shoulders and unraveling his impeccable grooming. He clasped his hands, the skin like that of a pale god's touched by caramel, behind his back. The traditional black of his lightweight garments followed his tall, slender frame, trailing down to the marble floor and circling him in his nervous pattern.

The man he knew as Christine sat in a large wide-backed wicker chair with his fingers folded calmly in his lap.

"Why hasn't she answered? She would have said already if she was planning to help me," Darien said, his steps echoing off the floor.

"She would not leave you stranded without good reason," Alaric reassured him.

"What reason?" Darien stopped mid-stride to face the woman he had taken as a confidant for the past several weeks. He had entrusted his life to her and her alone, solely on the reputation of Kate's power and mercy.

Alaric pursed his lips, averting his sour gaze. "The queen has been swept up in romance, and may have been indisposed. On my life, she would never willingly ignore my letter. I must conclude then that she has not received it."

The pair shared a quiet, tense dinner. Darien took sudden note of the young girl with short, plain brown hair, not yet an adult but no longer a child, pouring his wine. He stopped her.

"Where's Aggis?"

"She's sick, My Lord. I'm her niece. It's my honor to serve you while she recovers," she explained. Eyes down, head bent forward. Perfectly deferential. Before partaking again, Darien spoke into the head servant's ear to confirm the girl's story. He was wary of new faces in his house, so close to the impending day of reckoning. The girl turned her body to Christine, and lifted her jug.

"Do you require anything, My Lady?"

"No," Alaric answered.

"You didn't ask for assistance?"

"No, girl, I didn't—" Alaric snapped his neck in the servant girl's direction, grabbing her chin and leveling her eyes with his own. The girl, shaken, turned her gaze to the floor. The handle of the jug shuddered under her tightening grip.

"Look at me," Alaric demanded.

Feigning reluctance, the girl drew her eyes slowly to Alaric's, then met them with a knowing glance. He released her immediately.

"What? What is it?" Darien cried.

"Nothing. Everything seems to be in order," Alaric answered.

The servant resumed her bow.

"Yes, so I've just heard."

She bowed lower.

"The decanter in my room is nearly empty. I may require a replacement," Alaric suggested.

"Yes, Your Grace," the girl said, her voice barely above a whisper. She retreated backward to a corner and waited to be beckoned.

Alaric tried hard to hide his obvious distraction. He offered his hasty excuses at the conclusion of the meal and rushed to his chambers, the masque of Kate's emissary fading just as he extended his feet to reach the heavy wooden bar bolting the door. He whispered in his own voice before turning to look at the person he had sensed upon entering the room.

"It's about time she sent someone, Darien is losing his mind. But what good can a half-pint like you possibly—shit!" He leapt in surprise, bracing himself against the wall.

Kate sat on the edge of his bed, legs crossed at the ankles, leaning backward into palms that squeezed the end of the bed. Her hair fell past her shoulders in an effortless wave, radiant against her black garments, embellished with only the slightest hint of silver to flatter her svelte curvature. She wore a blank expression, tinged only by a hint of impatience.

"The servant girl?" he asked.

She raised her eyebrows, but remained silent. The supreme fashion in which she'd assumed another identity was so complete, it jarred him. His gaze darted left and right, even behind him toward the locked door. After the shock he'd just had, he took nothing for granted.

"Where's your other half?" he grunted.

Her tightly pursed mouth twitched, and her head listed to the side. Her expression hardened.

Alaric's eyes gleamed, and he pounced on the bed. Kate dodged, rising from her place and ducking out of his way as he crashed onto the mattress.

"That's not why I'm here!" she hissed.

"Look, I know I was rough with you before. I've always regretted that. Let me make it up to you," he said, rising from his place to stand next to her, inhaling the intoxicating fragrance of her tresses that had caused him to lose his mind so long ago. His fingers trailed up her arm and he craned his neck, his lips dangerously close to her skin. "I promise, after tonight, you will not even remember his name." His oversized frame shook with uncontrollable anticipation. Brain hazy, he felt he had slipped into a perfect dream.

She shoved him hard, sending his absurdly pronounced erection careening back into his leg.

"We don't need to do everything together to be together. Luca's handling another threat to Icarya."

"What threat?"

"That's not your concern."

Alaric snorted. "The hell it isn't. There's no reason to lie if he left you."

"He has never left me!" Her eyes burned. "He is always present in a way you couldn't possibly understand. You asked for my help, and he's acting elsewhere on my behalf. The end."

"Fine," he spat. Huffing loudly to disperse his rage, he settled himself upright on the bed. Kate waited for Alaric to regain his composure. Once he did, his eyes seemed dimmer, shallower.

"The passing of power is in two days," he said. "Darien is about to erupt. Am I fighting for him?"

"Tell him there's no need to seek an alternative."

Alaric took a deep breath. "That will be a great weight lifted."

"Have there been any actions against him?"

"Nothing overt. Mehmnet and his cronies seem willing to let him roll over. They're military men, and this kid can barely lift a sword, let alone swing one. They underestimate his bravery."

"We'll have to find him something lighter. You trust him?"

He nodded. "Everything he's told me appears genuine. He wants change, and others do too. But they're scared. *He's* scared. Mehmnet holds all the power."

"He *thinks* he does. Let's keep it that way, for now. Under no circumstances is Darien to tell anyone he's planning to challenge Mehmnet, or that we're backing him. One whiff of my presence and he'll suspect my motives immediately. What about the widow?"

"She sneaks through the complex into this wing most nights, has been since before Reza's death. Just with more frequency now. He loves her."

"And the other nights?"

"What?"

"Is she fucking Mehmnet?" she insisted.

"I'm fairly certain she is."

"*Fairly* certain?"

"Well, she sneaks into his suite just as often as she does Darien's and stays just as long, but I haven't *seen* them together. A pretty little thing like her with…" He shuddered in disgust. "I didn't want to go blind."

A mischievous smile played across Kate's lips, pressed into a thin straight line. She sat beside him, nudging his elbow as they both faced the barricaded door. He ignored it.

"Darien suspects nothing. He fears for her life as well as his own."

"I'm sorry if I frightened you." Her tone was softer now.

"Mehmnet's another story. I've gotten close enough to him, but definitive proof was not forthcoming."

"I did not intend to mislead you."

"The two of us might be able to cover more ground and learn something useful."

"Before Luca came into the picture—"

"Stop."

"I *did* think about you."

He met her sincere gaze with ire. "I'm tortured enough by my own mistakes. You're unbelievably cruel."

"I don't mean to torture you. I know how that feels, and I truly am sorry you're unhappy. But you deserve to know."

He pouted.

"I don't hate you, Alaric," she said. "But I don't love you. Though that isn't any reason why we can't work together now, is it?"

He swallowed hard. "No." He shook his head, his mouth twisted in a wry smile. "Why is it that every time you see me, you're tough as nails, and tender only after?"

"Force of habit."

They both laughed under their breath. "Life is interesting when you're around, if nothing else," he said. He pulled her hand from her lap onto his own, and folded his fingers in hers. She squeezed back.

A brief silence passed between them.

"You didn't have to leave," he said in a quiet voice.

"I couldn't possibly have stayed."

Alaric closed his eyes, feeling that old familiar pull that had urged him on so many occasions to pay her a visit, only to be severed by self-doubt and his ever-distracting choice of career.

"This always ends the same way, doesn't it?" he asked.

"I guess."

He drew in a satisfied breath and sat up straight. "Ready to call on Mehmnet?"

She nodded.

6

THE FORMS OF CHRISTINE AND AN ADOLESCENT SERVANT GIRL SLUNK OUT
of Christine's window, crawling through the potted foliage and sliding
down a marble column marking the edge of Darien's suite. Their feet
reached the tiled floor of the courtyard in silence. Squeezing into a
crack in the wall, they hid from the guard pacing back and forth,
waiting for the end of his shift. As a new guard appeared from a rear
gate to relieve the old one, Kate crept brazenly close in his shadow,
shielding herself from view of the guard facing her. As they reached the
center of the courtyard, she scampered away from the guard's leg
unseen and into the underbrush of a large fruit tree set next to a
glittering stone fountain. She settled into position as she eavesdropped
on the guards' conversation.

"She come through yet?" the new one asked.

"Not yet. Think luck is with Mehmnet tonight?"

"She's been at Darien's the past *four* nights. Luck's got nothing to do
with it. Gotta keep up appearances." They chuckled.

Alaric and Kate stared at each other across the way.

"How much do you think Mehmnet would pay for that kind of
information?" the new one asked as he assumed his post.

"Not half as dearly as *she'd* pay," the other replied, a deep voice trailing off as he drifted toward the spired gate defending Mehmnet's abode. Kate peeked her head up to watch as the soldier undid the complex latch to reveal an impossibly small keyhole. The soldier pulled a matching silver needle out of the chainmail poking out of his sleeve cuff, opened the gate with a resounding click, and disappeared behind a gilded door.

Kate and Alaric remained in their hiding places as the soldier completed two full rotations around the courtyard. Once Kate understood his routine, she swiped silently with a blade at the tangle of roots blocking her view, returned the severed branches to their place, and jostled the trunk, rustling the leaves as she resumed her crouch.

The guard turned his head in her direction. He scanned the area as he approached the tree, drawing his broad sword. Alaric retreated deeper into the wall's recess, hiding directly in the soldier's view, bathed in shadow. Incredulous, his stern gaze hardened, but she gestured with her hand that he should stay where he was, then pointed to herself. The guard was hers. The soldier's footsteps slowed as he approached, but his eyes showed no hint of suspicion as Kate, disguised as a mere girl, sprung from her refuge and stabbed a thick dagger up through his jawline and into his brain before he had a chance to understand what was happening to him. She'd given him no time to scream.

Alaric sprinted from the shadows as the guard crumpled on top of her. Kate struggled with the dead weight of the man and his armor in her diminutive form. She grabbed the soldier's neck as he slumped, twisting it in the crook of her elbow. In swift, calculated movements she removed his armor, snapped the joints at his shoulders, elbows, and knees, and stuffed him into the hollow recess of the tree. His limbs curled horribly around his broken frame, his neck wrapped around his knee.

A veteran killer, Alaric stood stunned at Kate's ruthless efficiency, so at odds with his memory of her.

She slammed the dead man's helmet on Alaric's head, followed by the chest plate.

"Do his rounds," she whispered, pulling the needle from the soldier's sleeve.

"The guards know about her, Mehmnet *doesn't*," he insisted.

"I doubt Mehmnet tells his guards anything. I want to be sure."

"Is it silly to say be careful?" he asked.

"Yes," she answered with a straight face, and darted for the gate. Gaining access, she avoided the door and instead scaled the wall, slipping into a darkened room.

Four rotations passed. Alaric could not discern any movement within Mehmnet's abode. All was quiet. The inner rooms were obscured, save for one window that he recognized as the master bedroom from its excessive decoration. The view was heavily shaded, allowing only a sliver of candlelight to escape through the thick greenery blocking the open passage. Halfway through his sixth pass in the courtyard, the hooded waif he had come to know as Haydee entered the plaza. Her silk slippers made a faint scratching noise against the mosaic glass of the courtyard. Their beaded embellishments' dainty chiming blended into the shushing of the fountain as it spurted onto metal surfaces set at odd angles to produce a delicate, whimsical melody. He turned his face from her. It seemed a useless gesture as she passed, for she covered her own face.

"Good evening," she murmured, as if the only thing more humiliating would have been to say nothing as she traversed the open pass to Mehmnet's rooms. Alaric remained diligent at his post for close to an hour. His skin tingled, and his muscles ached. His masculine frame yearned to be free of its petite restraints, unused to the extended bondage of wearing the masque through the night. As the discomfort grew to a persistent distraction, he eyed the main window. There was certainly movement within—a rhythm whose source he dared not contemplate. He turned on his heels to complete the circuit, and almost tripped into Kate as she gripped his arm. She leaned a little too heavily, and drew in deep breaths of the hazy night air. Her eyes were firmly closed.

"What happened?" he asked. She cowered under the shadow of his outstretched arm. Her breath came in fits and starts.

"Give me a minute," she said, trembling.

"Open your eyes, let's get the hell out of here."

"I can't. The whole world is spinning," she said, her voice in a panic. She stifled a moan. Her visage was deathly pale.

"Come on," he whispered. He supported her under the elbows as she clung to him. They walked in tandem to the crevice where they had hidden earlier. Getting ready for the next leg of the journey back to Darien's house, Alaric was surprised when she pushed him away from her and slunk into the crack, bracing her forehead and palms against the unpolished stone wall.

"Finish your shift," she said.

"Are you out of your mind? I'm not leaving you like this!"

"*You* want to explain the dead guard up a tree?" she hissed. "Go."

"You're insane," he snorted, backing away from her. Alaric stomped through the courtyard for the next three hours. He stayed just long enough to see the next man exit the gate before ducking back into his room, dragging Kate behind him. Her condition had not improved.

Alaric barged through his own door, lifted her onto the bed and poured her a glass of water. He guided her fingers to it, her eyes still being closed.

"What the hell was that?" he demanded.

A long gulp of the cold water gave Kate more relief than she had felt all throughout Alaric's watch. She held out the cup, and he readily refilled it several times as she gorged on the cool water. Finally, she felt well enough to open her eyes. Alaric's skin jumped as she raised her eyelids. He crouched before her, staring.

"They're...they're empty, aren't they?" she asked, her voice as hollow as her gaze.

He nodded, unable to avert his gaze from her nearly colorless irises. "Tell me what to do, Kate. How do I help?"

"It'll pass," she answered, not even convincing enough for her. "It'll pass." She scratched at her neck as the masque dissolved.

Brows knit together, Alaric ran his fingers through her hair, tucking a loose strand behind her ear. She pulled back, and he returned his hand to his lap.

Kate closed her eyes, and took a deep breath. The eyes she saw behind her closed lids burned a brilliant crimson. She drew close to him, but Luca's mind was in chaos—he was having a nightmare. About another woman. His absolute fright at the thought of anyone but her was oddly soothing. She opened her eyes again, and knew from the relief that washed over Alaric's own face that they were the correct color. He implored her.

"Talk to me, *please*."

"I've never encountered anything like that before."

"Like *what?*"

"I was positioned near enough to Mehmnet's room to overhear him. When *she* walked in the door—"

"Haydee?"

She nodded. "Everything went black, *everything*. The whole world was a shadow. And that smell—"

She put her hand to her mouth even at the memory. "It was enough to make me vomit. I stayed long enough to get what I needed, but by the time I got to you…" She shook her head. "I couldn't take anymore."

Alaric looked perfectly helpless. "I don't understand any of this."

"I had a reaction to whatever kind of magic she's harnessed. I have a guess as to what it could be, but I can't be sure. Either way, it's bad news."

"You sensed her, is that what you're telling me?"

"Her magic, yes."

"Could she sense you?" Alaric asked.

"No, not without being precognitive."

"And…you are?"

"Only a little," Kate confessed.

"I didn't know that before."

"Neither did I. Not really. If she had sensed me, I'd have known it. Even so," she said, confused by the intensity of her own response, "I've never had that strong of a sensation before. My senses felt sharper than a hound dog's. I was at her wedding to Reza, and never felt a thing."

His face was still riddled with worry.

"I'm all right, Alaric."

"Is there anything you need?"

"I need to figure out what I'm up against. Do you know anything else about her?"

Alaric shrugged. "She's a quiet little slip of a girl, usually shrunk in the shadow of either Darien or Mehmnet."

"Poor kid."

"It's tough being a woman in Likhan."

Kate clucked her tongue. "*Darien.* You said he loves her." She paused, curling her fingers in front of her mouth in thought. Her eyes narrowed. "She was sleeping with Darien while married to Reza?"

"Yes. He may have lifted her out of a lower station, but he was much older. She was more a concubine than a wife, really. It makes sense that she would take a lover closer to her own age," Alaric reasoned.

"But why Mehmnet?" Kate pondered.

"She's hedging her bets."

Kate shook her head. "No, that isn't right. Chances are good she was sleeping with all three men before Reza's death. She already was the wife of the seht. What is she after?"

"How do you know she's after anything?"

"She's not toting around that kind of power for nothing," Kate said evenly.

"You're a woman," Alaric huffed. "Why would you be playing three sides?"

"Me? To get rid of them all." She sighed. "I need to know more."

"Darien trusts me. Getting him to talk about the woman he loves should be fairly easy."

"I'll try to get placed in her house tomorrow," Kate offered.

Alaric's eyebrows shot back to his hairline. "You just had a total breakdown after being in the same vicinity as her!"

"She surprised me. Tomorrow, I'll be prepared."

"Kate," he asked, his voice uncertain, "is your magic a match for hers? I mean...look what she did to you, without even trying."

She glared at him. "*More* than a match. But, I made a promise not to use it."

"A promise...to a man sucking the life out of you?" he asked in a gruff voice. He pulled at her collar and exposed Luca's bite marks, healing in his absence.

Her instinct was to pull away, but she kept her bold face.

Alaric stared at the wounds he had first glimpsed peering down through her clothes as he'd supported her on their walk back, so deep they had shown through the masque. "You let him do that to you?"

"I *beg* him to do that to me," she sneered, indignant.

Alaric didn't know what to say. He relinquished his hold on her shirt.

"It's not safe for me to use my magic. Not without him."

"Let me guess. He's also a sorcerer?" Alaric asked.

"No. Something much more terrible."

"What is it that makes him so godsdamnned special? Even *he* can be killed," Alaric said.

"*No*, he can't be. Luca is immortal, with a power of his own that I've only begun to fathom."

Alaric had no ready comeback for her confession.

"Nothing can destroy him, except..." Her eyes burned. "Except what he faces now. What he chose to face without me." She buried her face in her hands.

When Alaric reached out to grab her hunched shoulders, frostbite set into his fingers almost immediately. He shrunk back, but then, he chose to brave the cold. He embraced her, pressing her icy forehead to his chest.

His heart was ripped open as she sobbed against him. He was sensitive to her pain, pain at the prospect of losing someone who meant as much to her as she meant to him. Words of comfort stuck in his throat. But then, he never could bear to see her sad.

"Come now. You know he won't let anyone or anything stop him from holding you in his arms again."

She looked up at him, grateful.

"I know I wouldn't," he smiled. He bit his lip, and rubbed his thumb across her tears.

"Alaric..."

"Shh. Enough already. You love him, alright, who else could want you like that? You're hopeless."

Her smile widened. She stood up and stretched. "What I wouldn't give for a shower."

Alaric gestured behind her, to the back corner of the room. "There's a stall right there."

"What?" she said, surprised.

"I told you, Darien admires all things Icaryan. He had them built as curiosities."

"There are only communal baths in the servants' quarters," she said. "You're sure it's alright, if I—?"

He laughed, amused that his supreme leader was honestly asking his permission. "What's mine is yours, My Queen."

The light burgeoning through the cloudy sky was sufficient to illuminate the alabaster shower tucked into the darkest corner of the room. She stepped into the recessed space, hanging her clothes over the protruding wall that reached just below her shoulder. The cool water that came rushing over her head took her breath away on first contact, but once fully immersed, was incredibly restorative. It reset her equilibrium, and readied her to confront the magical assault she knew was imminent. Eyes closed, she inhaled the calm.

Alaric began to sweat. He ripped his outer layers off, stripping down to pants woven in a fine thin linen. He pulled at his own hair, trying to think of something, anything other than the naked siren mere feet from him. He admired her bare shoulders from a distance, knocking his head against the wall in an effort to shake the dreamy look off his face. She turned, flashing her smooth back in his direction before leaning on the tile and letting the flood pour down her face. The water raced down her frame in a perfect curve. Her mouth hung open, hydrating her lips. His eyes sparkled as he observed her swallow deep breaths, her full breasts rising almost into view. If only he were a little closer. He licked his lips.

"Bad idea," he mumbled to himself, drawing helplessly nearer to the shower. She ran her fingers through her hair, arresting his steps as his burning erection threatened to ruin the singular garment he still wore.

"Alaric…" she beckoned.

His heart thrummed in his ears. "Yes?" he croaked.

"It'll be the last thing you do."

"I hate you."

Her shrill laughter echoed through the room. Alaric buried himself under the bedcovers, shutting out the world for the next hour.

CONFIDENT SHE WOULD NOT BE INTERRUPTED, SHE LET THE WATER sliding off her flesh unwind her muscles and became still as a desperate plea rang between her ears.

Kate. I need you.

The corners of her lips curled upward. She craned her neck, feeling Luca's warm presence in the shower. She perched her drenched lips on a drifting impression of his shoulder and inched closer, enveloping him in her mind's embrace.

Hey there, tiger.

7

LUCA AMBLED INTO THE TAVERN AT SUNRISE. HE SANK LOW ONTO A BENCH just moments after the owner had moved it from its inverted resting place on the wooden tabletop. The thick grain was knotted and warped, perpetually saturated with ale and sweet seawater. Luca rested his forehead on the fragrant surface with supreme gratitude. His fine clothes were soaked through. The chill that had started at his feet had crept up to his aching knees. Many months had passed since he had foregone sleep in pursuit of a vampire. Every limb and muscle screamed. The smallest fraction of his old endurance now felt like obscene abuse. But even vampires had to sleep. His hunt postponed for another day, Luca could afford a few hours of rest. He could scarce afford not to.

The innkeeper, a burly round fellow with a respectable dark beard threaded with silver, struck up a conversation as he wiped the counter with a rag nearly as old as he was.

"You look awful. What are you doing out in the rain anyway?"

Luca looked up, bleary-eyed. He caught himself before divulging his true motives, but was too tired to come up with a suitable alternative. He switched gears instead.

"Have you seen anything unusual lately? Or anyone?"

"Well," the innkeeper said, placing a steaming bowl of fish broth in front of Luca, "I suppose the death of the herbalist's daughter counts as unusual."

Luca thanked him for the soup, inhaling its pungent aroma before letting it slide down his throat. It eased the biting numbness in his fingertips and toes. The steam opened his airways, and he filled his lungs slowly, the first deep intake after a long night of bone-chilling rain and sharp shallow breaths.

"When was this?" Luca asked.

"A few weeks ago. Horrible thing—she was as dry as a burnt-out plank of wood. The snapping of her bones as we moved her was enough to turn your stomach."

"Anything like it since?"

"No, no. I don't think Cathair could've handled more like that. The people around here are not used to losing their young, and certainly not like that. Not like that." The innkeeper sat next to Luca and shook his head, trying to shrug off the image. "We buried what was left of her in the cemetery."

Great. I'll bet she's hungry.

"Where's the cemetery?" Luca asked.

"At the east end of the docks, up the hill a ways. It's nice that you want to pay your respects. Her father will like that. He hasn't been himself since she died. I mean, I know finding her like that must have been terrible, but this is...this is something else." The man looked down at his oversized, calloused hands.

Luca eyed him with curiosity.

"Are you Icaryan by birth?" the innkeeper asked. His voice sounded far away, his mind elsewhere.

"No," Luca answered.

"Me neither. I'm from the same world as our queen. Different time and place, but same world. I've been here for a long time though, since before our queen was our queen. And these people," he said, gesturing to the town, "they barely remember what it was like to hide from things that went bump in the night. And even then, it was only ever the king's soldiers. The population being what it is, they've never feared...what's the word...monsters. I may be just an aging, superstitious fool, but, mark me, it was a monster what killed that girl."

Luca nodded, his expression grave.

"So," the innkeeper continued, "now that you know where I stand, do you want to tell me what you were doing walking around all night?"

Luca deliberated. As a hunter, he'd always been guarded about his thoughts, and for good reason. But things were so very different here. He was grateful for the open conversation, one he could never have hoped to hold with a human in his own time. Over the course of a day, he'd allowed himself to slide into old habits, habits that had kept him miserable for ages. Habits that, if he wasn't careful, could cost him everything.

Did I do the right thing, sending you away?

His query was met with a chill silence. As he felt the pang of Kate's absence, he answered:

"Looking for monsters."

"Mm. What will you do?"

"Visit the herbalist." Luca began to rise from his seat, but the innkeeper's meaty hand stayed his shoulder.

"How long will you be here?" the innkeeper inquired.

"As long as it takes."

The innkeeper nodded. "This job'll finish you if you don't take care of yourself." He placed a small brass key on the table. "There's an empty room upstairs, with a working shower. Rest up, then start fresh."

Luca accepted the man's advice, and the key. "What do I owe you, —?"

"Cyril." He shook his head, pointing to the golden crest hanging from Luca's belt strap. "I would never charge *her*, and I'll never charge you."

"My name is Luca. And thank you." He met the man's hearty handshake.

"Alright then," Cyril said as Luca ascended the creaking stairway behind the bar. The key opened a small, clean room in the middle of the hallway.

Luca slept in fits and starts. When he set out for the herbalist's shop several hours later, the fogbank had grown to an omnipresent pall, casting all of Cathair in a freezing gloom. The door to the herbalist's shop was open. Luca absorbed his surroundings, scanning the goods for sale. He was relieved to see nothing on the shelves that was remotely familiar to Kate's craft. He rapped his knuckles on the wooden counter.

"Hello?"

The ascending stairway that faced the outer door groaned under the herbalist's weight as he entered his shop. As the grieving father brought his gaze to Luca's face, his eyes widened in a manic fear. He gibbered incoherently as he attempted to clamber past Luca and out the door. Luca grabbed him by the shoulders.

"Hold on! What's the matter?" he cried.

"Please, let me go! I didn't tell anyone I swear! You've taken everything from me, please go! *Go!*"

The man's reaction to Luca was all the confirmation he needed. He hated to do it, especially after what he'd already suffered, but Luca looked the herbalist square in the eyes, holding his gaze until the man's frame ceased to shudder. He spoke in a low, soothing voice.

"It's not me you're thinking of. Someone else took your daughter. I can't bring her back, but I can avenge her death, and help her find peace. Will you help me do that?"

The man's breathing had slowed to a standstill.

"Yes." His thick voice was languid.

Luca took his time bringing him out of his trance. "Don't panic."

The man's body wavered. Luca reached behind the counter and offered the herbalist his stool. The man stressed the legs of the seat as Luca released his grip. The herbalist groaned, leaning his head in his left hand.

"Are you all right?" Luca asked.

"I think so. It's just…when you came in here, for a moment I didn't remember where I was. Or rather, *when*. You're the spitting image of—"

"Yes, I know. I'm sorry I frightened you."

The man's cheeks turned a bright red. It was the first time anyone had expressed remorse for responding to Luca that way.

"I'm so sorry. I didn't mean to—"

"It's all right," Luca assured him.

"Um, so why are you here?"

"To help you. Can you tell me what happened?" Luca asked.

The man squinted, trying to pin down the blurry images flashing in his head and bring them into focus.

"I remember a man came into the shop, just as my daughter came home." His eyes watered. "I only discovered her later. I couldn't recall anything at the time. Only seeing your face now makes me remember."

"I'm sorry for your loss."

"I was here," the man protested. "Right here. She was screaming, and I...I didn't do anything. Oh god, I can still hear her in my head!" The man wiped his face and sobbed. He knew he would continue to hear his daughter's last moments until his own.

"There was nothing you *could* do. Even then, you'd have been dead too."

"I should be, for what that devil did to her right over my head. But not yet." The man sniffed. "You said something about avenging her?"

Luca nodded. "What was the man doing here? Do you know what he wanted?"

"He had something he wanted me to look at, a magic container. Wanted to know how they work."

"How they work?"

"Yeah. Wanted to know how to use something he'd found. I told him he was out of luck, it was empty." The man paused, remembering. "I got the impression he didn't believe me."

"What did this container look like?"

"A remarkable thing, that I do remember. Hand-crafted. It was a little sphere, about this big." He gestured with his fingers. "Made of some kind of crystal."

Ohhh shit.

"All right," Luca said, his back stiff. "Where's your daughter buried?"

Luca paid careful attention to the herbalist's directions, thanked him, then turned to leave.

"Wait a minute," the man protested, "you haven't told me your name."

"Luca."

"I'm Nestor. Luca? My daughter was my life." The man wiped his face again, channeling his grief into rage. "Get this bastard."

Luca nodded, then departed.

FROM THE HERBALIST'S SHOP, LUCA HEADED TO THE DOCKS. THE *DEMETER* rocked steadily in her place. The hunter asked a passerby for the Harbor Master, and was directed toward a well-appointed building full of potted greenery. A slender young male with flaccid skin colored a silvery green was supervising the placement of the plants. As Luca approached, he observed the ribbed fin flaring out from behind the man's ears, tinted a pale gold by the overhead candelabra. His jacket was cut low to allow air to flow freely through the gills trailing down his neck. The dark navy garment was for decorum only—it hung unbuttoned, revealing a long, serpentine body that ended in a prehensile tail.

"No, no, there's no such thing as too much," he said in a tinny voice. "We're trying to brighten the place up, make it cheerful."

"Excuse me," Luca interrupted. He was put off as the creature turned to him. His wide, milky eyes seemed dead, not focusing on Luca as he spoke.

"Yes, how can I be of service?"

"Could you tell me where the *Demeter* was engaged last?"

"Yes sir, let me just take a look at our logs." The serpent slid to the back of the room, then returned with a thick tome in his hand. He licked his long knobby finger and opened to the pertinent pages, fanning out the webbing in his hands as he did so. His gills flared as he searched, prompting Luca to avert his eyes.

"Yes, here we are," the sea wyrm answered, drawing his sharp nail down the page. "It disembarked for Gilbraith, and returned ten days behind schedule. That was nearly two full seasons ago. Apparently, I've yet to receive the captain's log. Hmm. That's unlike him," the creature commented.

"Has it gone anywhere else since?" Luca asked.

"No sir, it's been moored since then."

"Does it have any upcoming engagements?"

The wyrm closed the book, handing it to a passing assistant. "No, that would require Rene's consent, and no one's seen him since he came to port. Off with that pretty wife of his, I imagine." His gills flared again. "I'm sorry, I didn't catch your name before?"

"Luca. I'm here on the queen's business." He flashed Kate's crest.

"Oh, forgive me." The Harbor Master settled himself down again, temporarily ruffled by his own loose lips. "Is there anything else I can do for you?"

"Do you mind if I take a look at it?"

"What for—mmph," the wyrm caught himself, and clicked his tongue in an odd fashion. "Never mind. The queen's business is the queen's business. Just a moment." He left Luca studying the aquatic motif set into the marble floor of the entryway as he scrawled a few lines on a slip of parchment.

"Show this to the ship's guard."

"Thank you."

The wyrm bowed. "If there's anything else you require, please don't hesitate."

Luca walked north along the docks until he stood before the *Demeter* once more. He handed his letter to the guard, and climbed the plank leading to the main deck. He stepped into the captain's quarters. Something glimmered on the floor near the doorway. Luca knelt to pick up a rosy-hued glass pendant, nicked where it had collided with the floor. That, and the small pile of glass shards crunched into a shimmery powder were the only remnants of Rene's struggle. Pocketing the necklace, Luca turned his head in the direction of the bed tucked against the right corner of the cabin. He sat on the crisp linens, remembering the night he had taken Kate into his arms for the first time.

She'd loved all of him on that day, not once showing hesitation or fear in the face of his dark power. The scent of her hair lingered on the pillow. He pressed his eyelids together, forcing back the dread that crouched deep in his soul that she might never look at him the same way, might never forgive him.

His thoughts loomed over him longer than he realized. To distract himself from the very real possibility that he might never know Kate's love again, Luca descended into the belly of the ship. The hull was sparsely loaded—the cargo that had been onboard during Luca's voyage had reached its destination, and the floor had been wiped clean of dust. In one shadowy corner, Luca's keen eyes spotted a few errant grains of dirt. He pressed the pad of his index finger to the floor and brought the soil to his nose. He couldn't place it, but it smelled oddly familiar. Just rubbing those few particles between his fingers sent a wave of calm into him. He scanned the rest of the hold. There were no visible signs of dirt anywhere else. He stood and pried the sides of each crate open just enough to confirm that they were filled with provisions standard to a ship and nothing more.

He disembarked and stopped to talk to the man posted on the dock.

"Anyone odd coming or going?" Luca asked.

"Not on my watch. I share a shift with two others, though. We're responsible for these," he said, pointing behind him at a row of a half dozen ships. "I haven't seen anything out of the ordinary here."

"Are you on guard tonight?"

"Nah, I'm through in a few hours. Hershel covers the night shift," he said, pointing him out of the flock of loons circling lazily overhead.

Luca looked through the dark skies at the sun's sinking position. The heavens were still shrouded in dense gray. He slipped back into the herbalist's shop just as he was closing up for the evening. Luca's unexpected appearance made the herbalist jump at first. But once he recognized his visitor, Nestor breathed easy.

"Luca. What can I do for you?"

"Do you put any garlic in your mixes?" he asked.

"Sometimes, as a curative. Why?"

"Can you concentrate it in some way?"

"Something like this?" the herbalist asked, pulling a huge jar of golden yellow powder from a shelf underneath the counter. He twisted the corkscrew lid off the jar. "How's that for potent?"

Luca turned his face away, covering his nose and mouth with the corner of his coat as he coughed violently.

"It's perfect. Close it, please," he requested.

"That's pure Icaryan garlic and salt from the Northern Mountains."

"Can you combine that with some kind of oil, something neutral, and put it in a small vial?"

"Sure I could. How many do you want?"

Luca pointed at the jar, and sniffed. "How many of these do you have?"

"Aside from this one? Three."

"Use it all. In something like this," he said, grabbing a handheld bottle from the counter's edge.

Nestor whistled.

"How quickly can you do it?"

The man shrugged. "If I work all night, maybe, three days?"

"Make it one. Hire someone to help you." Luca dug into his pocket for money.

"Is this going to help us catch my little girl's killer?" Nestor asked.

"Yes."

The man held up his hand. "Keep your money."

"Can I have just one now?"

"Certainly," the herbalist answered, taking his inventory into the back room built underneath the stairway. He returned in a moment with two full vials. "You know, it's strange," Nestor started, "sometimes when I look at you, you're just the same, you and him. But other times…" The man tilted his head, musing. "You couldn't be more different."

A warm smile spread across Luca's lips, the first in days.

"I'll see you tomorrow," he said.

The tavern was bursting at the seams with patrons when Luca returned. Ale glistened on the tabletops and the floors, reflecting the flickering light from the wrought-iron candelabras swinging from the rafters. Luca walked up to the counter.

"Any luck?" Cyril asked, sliding a full jar foaming with a sparkling amber fluid between Luca's hands.

"Some," he answered, downing the ale in a single draught.

"There's a good lad," Cyril said, passing him another.

Luca graciously refused. "Cyril, how hard would it be to gather the whole town up?"

"Considering that more than half the town is already in here, I'd say not hard at all. What are you thinking?"

"I want to talk to everyone. Not to scare them, just arm them. Put them on guard."

The innkeeper nodded. "That can be managed. Tomorrow night soon enough?"

"Just what I was thinking."

"Good. Now find a seat, if you can. Dinner will be out in a minute."

Luca squeezed himself onto the edge of a long bench, taking a mug of sweet water with him. He picked at the bread and oil spread on the table in long, wooden bowls until a slender young woman served him a bowl of slow-braised venison over boiled potatoes. Though he had been the last to sit, she served him first.

"Here you are," she said, batting her eyes at him.

"Thank you." He didn't bother to look up. She lingered at his side, waiting for acknowledgement. When it finally came in the form of a dismissive glance, she scurried away, heartbroken.

Luca thought of Kate. She felt distant. He sensed deep longing, masked by ire. She was aware of him, beckoning at her mind's door, and he knew it. But she didn't extend a focused word or thought. Luca pursed his lips, and buried his sorrow in his dinner. As he ate, he was overwhelmed with her regret.

He pushed it back at her, along with a tender yearning. *You didn't do anything wrong. I did. Forgive me my love.*

～

IN THE WEE HOURS OF THE NIGHT, LUCA CREPT OUT OF HIS ROOM AND turned his feet in the direction of the cemetery. The whole town was silent, save for the soft whisper of the fog rolling off the shore. Breaking into the caretaker's hut had been easy enough. Luca slung a broad-handled spade over his shoulder.

"I hate this job," he huffed aloud, seeing his breath form white puffs in the air as he climbed the hill to the graveyard.

The dark miasma was thick here, blanketing the ground. Only the tops of the gravestones peered out over the town and toward the sea. Luca quickened his steps. It was imperative that he reach the girl's resting place before she rose, or he'd have twice as much trouble on his hands. And the town would have ten times as much heartache.

He followed Nestor's directions to the summit, then surveyed the area. He was alone. He looked down at the newly placed grave dirt and dropped the spade. His irises glowed in the moonlight, spying a subtle depression in the center of the grave, pulling soil into itself like slowly churning quicksand. The prisoner underneath was nearly free. He knelt down, and unsheathed his sword. Laying it within easy reach, Luca put a cautious hand to the opening.

In less than ten minutes, his burrowing fingers collided with others not his own, scrambling furiously from the opposite side. They clawed at him as he picked up his weapon. Leveling it at her throat, he yanked on the revenant's arm, pulling her out of the ground.

She was as the innkeeper had described her—completely massacred. One of her breasts had been gnawed off, leaving her burial gown loose and unkempt on the left side. Her face fared no better. Her bottom lip was missing, and the roots of her exposed teeth gleamed under the moon's haze. Her canines strained above her row of teeth. When she set her eyes on her rescuer, she leapt at him in jubilation, tearing at his neck and pulling him closer to her mangled lips, soaked in the fetor of decay.

"My Lord!" she cried. "I thought you'd never come! I waited and waited! Oh, how I've missed you!"

Luca shoved her back into her hole.

She was crestfallen. "But...you promised." She squinted at him then, her glassy eyes turning a faint red. "Who are you?!" she snapped.

"I'm not the one you seek," Luca answered in a gruff voice. "*He* left you here to rot."

"Liar!" she hissed.

"I'm the only one coming for you," Luca said, lowering his voice as he lunged at her. Struggling was futile. She couldn't shake his determined weight off her, screaming as a wooden spear pierced her breast.

"I really am sorry," Luca whispered, rising off her as her grip on him loosened.

"Don't be," she replied in a plaintive tone. The suffering in her voice was enough to drive men mad. "He didn't come. What's the point? Can you...?"

Luca met her questioning gaze.

"Can you tell my dad I'm sorry? I never meant to leave him."

He nodded, and shoved the body of the stake through her torso and into the dirt behind her. He lifted her head up by the hair and cut it away from her neck, shoved it between her legs, and doused the ruined flesh with the garlic elixir, burying his face inside his jacket. He held his breath as he covered her again with dirt and gave the entire site a final unholy christening with what remained in the vial. He walked to a nearby tree, blooming a brilliant red. He plucked a thickly flowered branch and laid it at her grave. It occurred to him that he didn't know the girl's name. When he sought an answer from her headstone, his heart stopped. He read the sentiment chiseled in stone:

KATELYN – BELOVED QUEEN

. . .

HE JUMPED BACK, FORCING HIS EYELIDS TOGETHER AND SHUTTING OUT THE thought. "No no, no! This isn't right!" He opened his eyes again, seeing only what he should have:

CARLA—LOVED BY ALL. BEST BY HER FATHER.

LUCA'S BREATH CAME IN SHARP PULLS. HE WRAPPED HIS ARMS AROUND himself to block out a sudden chill. He quit the hill in a hurry, returned the spade to the gravedigger's shed, and put the door back on its hinges before trudging back to the inn. His heart was heavy as lead.

He fell into a deep slumber. As the morning sun's rays knocked at his window, he rolled over, and felt a warm body under his arm. He sprang out of bed, waking the barmaid he'd shunned at dinner.

"How did you get in here?" Luca roared.

She stretched, turning on her back and baring her breasts.

"You let me in, remember? I know *I'll* never forget," she smiled.

Luca's whole body shook.

What did I do? What did I do!?

His mind was crazed. He remembered nothing except returning to the inn from the cemetery and heading straight to bed. He grabbed a sheet from the bed and wrapped it around his waist.

"Don't be ashamed, baby," the girl purred. "You were an animal. The queen's a fool for leaving you here all alone."

He grabbed the girl's arm and dragged her onto the cold, hard floor.

"Ow! Not so rough!" she protested.

"Get out!" he screamed. He rushed into the bathroom and slammed the door. He splashed water on his face, and stared at his reflection in the mirror.

I don't know how this happened. Kate, please believe me.

"Oh, she'll never believe you again. It's just as well," the girl crooned in a haughty voice from the next room. "We're not meant for monogamy, you and I."

Everything stopped. There was a sinister quality in the girl's voice that sounded… familiar. Luca's gaze slid to the left, toward the door. His skin pricked. When he opened it, the nude girl sat at the edge of the bed, staring at him. The corner of her mouth was upturned, opening into a wide grin. Fangs bared. The rims of her eyes burned red.

Luca lunged, throttling the girl. As they landed on the bed, the room dissolved, leaving Luca falling through open air. Every muscle in his body tensed for the impact. It shocked him awake. Kate lay beside him, his back facing her. He exhaled in relief.

"I just had the worst—"

Luca's mind spiraled in confusion. He was in his bed at the tavern. Kate was not in Cathair with him, and yet here she lay. His fingertips shuddered at her cold, hard flesh.

"Kate?" he pulled on her shoulder. Kate fell onto her back, eyes milky, jaw wired open in fear. Her lifeblood soaked the sheets, flowing without end from two circular wounds sunk bone deep. Luca screamed, covering himself in her blood as he tried—and failed—to revive her.

"This is your fault."

A low voice reverberated throughout the room, tolling between Luca's ears like a death knell.

Helpless, Luca cradled Kate in his arms, burying his face in her gore. When he took his next breath, Kate was gone. The world was naught but blackness. A figure darker than the night itself stood in the distance. Luca's face was expressionless as he laid eyes upon his father for the first time. It was like looking in a mirror. The only difference was the age reflected in his visage.

"Giving her your life, my life, will be your ultimate misery. Your lust for fresh, young blood will turn her to your worst enemy. She must die, one way or another. At your hand."

Luca said nothing.

"This is your birthright. *Embrace* it."

Luca felt a blast of cold air in his face, pulling him awake. The vapor filling the room was impenetrable. Luca stumbled to his feet and made his way blindly for the coat hook just inside the door. He groped in his pocket for the spare vial of garlic oil. He popped the lid and tossed it headlong into the malignant fog. It rolled underneath the open windowsill, out of which the cloud beat a hasty retreat. Luca chased the last swirls of mist out and slammed the window shut.

He wiped his sweat-covered brow and leaned heavily on the window's frame. The portentous cloud shrunk, recoiling itself into a tight mass and settling far off the coast. Luca pulled the window shade closed, and stepped into the shower stall. He let the hot water roll off his back, and ran his fingers through his silken hair. He pressed his palms to the cool slate tiles, closed his eyes, and simply breathed. His soul's cry was so loud that the name in his head rode the air escaping his lips.

"Kate. I need you." He pressed his forehead to the back of his hand, and wept.

A wave of heat more comforting than the steam enveloped him. Kate's phantom presence in the shower was palpable as she wrapped her arm around his chest, and pressed her lips to his shoulder. Luca put his hand to his sprawling muscles, yearning to touch the hand he could almost feel if he concentrated. Her voice soaked into his brain.

Hey there, tiger.

He sobbed again, the tears falling from his face mingling with the water as it poured over him.

"I've missed you so much," he cried, his voice raw.

Mmhmm. And whose fault is that?

Kate felt his guilt and sorrow overwhelming him, and relented. *I've missed you too.*

I'm so sorry, he thought.

You did what you felt you had to. I was hurt, but I understand. He felt her smile. *It's kind of romantic.*

"I shouldn't have pushed you away," he said aloud. Not like that. Not ever like that.

Her voice was a whisper drifting in the steam. *You've held my soul in your hands for a long time.*

I need you with me, always. He came to me, made me think I'd betrayed you, that I'd killed you, that I—" Luca's voice broke off, still shaken by his father's psychic attack. "It was horrible."

Kate squeezed him tighter. *I know. Luca, I've been with you the whole time. I never left. And I never will.*

He felt her lips press against his shoulder, and hung his head lower. He was unworthy.

Are you going to be all right? Kate asked.

He nodded. "I will be when we're together again."

I'll be there soon. Kate assured him.

Just, stay with me a while, please?

I'm right here.

9

ALARIC SAT ON THE BED WITH HIS FACE TO THE WALL AS KATE EMERGED
from the shower. Braiding her hair, she sat in the wide-thatched chair
opposite. Alaric had never looked more sour.

"Thank you," she said.

He shrugged. "I've never touched a girl against her will." He turned
toward her, but kept his face down. "I haven't…have I?"

She craned her neck to meet his sad eyes, clasping the fisted hand on
his lap. "No," she assured him. "No."

Alaric blinked, nodding his head ever so slightly. He stroked the
hand he held folded in his own.

Kate pulled away from him and reached behind his back for the
satchel she had stashed under his bed the night before. From it she
pulled a large measure of coarsely woven fibers of shockingly vibrant
blues, purples, and reds among the mass of thick dull grays. With a small
sharp knife, she cut three equal amounts from the source. The frayed
ends of the cut pieces quickly unfurled, revealing a dense nexus of
differing fibers strung together. Kate worked to repair it before it
unraveled completely, her deft fingers moving in a mysterious fashion
to restore the weave to the exact configuration as before.

Alaric observed with keen interest, listening to the complex, upbeat melody she whistled in time with her fingers, trying to decipher its structure.

"What is that, some ancient incantation?"

She smiled. "No, just 'A Little Night Music.'"

He pursed his lips in puzzlement.

"Mozart. Helps me concentrate."

He remained at a loss.

"Never mind." When she was finished, each severed line had been woven into a continuous hoop, devoid of knots. Alaric examined it carefully. It bent and stretched at the slightest command of his fingertips.

"It will only do that for you. Put it around your neck, and don't let anyone see it." He did as he was told, accepting the second hoop in her hand. "This is Darien's," she said, donning her own. "It's the best protection I can give you right now. Darien is the only person we treat as an ally. Give him the good news, and stay on him all day. But remember…"

"You're not here. I got it. You're not dealing with an amateur, you know."

"Alaric, I'm serious. I'm not ready to engage Haydee without better intelligence. We'll learn what we can today, but I need to do some digging elsewhere, and that will take time. Time I don't have."

"Why, where are you going?"

"I'll stay until tomorrow, then I'm going home."

"Home! The whole town is going to explode tomorrow! You think Mehmnet's cronies are going to take Darien's challenge lying down? You can't just—"

The look on her face silenced him.

"I'm needed somewhere else."

He held his tongue.

Kate could see he wasn't satisfied. "I'll be back, but right now, I have to leave. Besides, he won't be stranded. He has you."

"Kate."

"You've excelled here. And as you said, he trusts you. I think you know me well enough by now to make some decisions."

Alaric turned his head. "I haven't done a thing to earn your trust."

She tilted his chin up with the crook of her index finger, and forced him to stare straight at her. She'd never been more regal in his eyes.

"*Act* in my stead. Help Darien ascend the seat of power here, overcome his enemies, and achieve his goals for his people. Bring Likhan into the fold. As a free land."

"If I do all that, I will have earned the pardon you've granted for my transgressions."

"You did that the night you strangled me, so I might not kill myself." Kate's voice caught. She ignored the way Alaric's throat bobbed when she spoke. "You saved my nephew's life once. Now I'm asking you to save the other one."

"I will not fail, Your Highness."

A STRAINED SILENCE PREVAILED THROUGHOUT THE DAY IN THE SEHT'S palace, punctuated by the torrential downpour that split the skies late into the evening and cleared only after the sun had already retreated. The chill of twilight stiffened the backs of the household as servants from all quarters labored in preparation for the passage ceremony set on the morrow.

Darien leaned over his eastern balcony into the lavender glow of the evening, staring out of the complex and contemplating the multitude of smaller lights below, each warming a family whose fate rested on his shoulders. Or, more aptly, the shoulders of the young woman standing next to him.

"You're sure about this?" Darien asked, turning to look at Alaric, hidden behind the masque of Christine. He scratched at the woolly rope around his neck.

"For the thousandth time, yes, and stop fussing with that," Alaric answered in a voice several octaves higher than his own. "I really thought you would be relieved by this. You're more nervous than ever."

Darien sighed in reluctant acknowledgement.

"The queen wishes for your success. She's eager to forge a new alliance, with you at the helm."

"Nothing would please me more. This is what I've been working toward for a long time. We could learn from your many successes. Now that the moment has come...I have done little to warrant your help. Or hers." Darien spun around, leaning his back against the railing carved from smooth, ivory-colored marble with only the faintest thread of gold veining.

"The woman barely knows my face, yet she is willing to risk the life of a dear protégé for my sake. Why? What have I done to deserve your aid?'

"It's what you *will* do: the promise of a future without slavery for both our peoples. Isn't that enough?"

"If you lose your life tomorrow..."

"I won't. Pardon my bluntness, but rest assured—you need not fear on that account."

"If you did," Darien insisted, "I could never again look myself in the face. It should be me in that arena. *I'm* the one who wants to lead them. How can I do that if I can't protect them?"

"You are protecting them. You're using every weapon you have at your disposal, without regard for your personal honor. That's bravery if ever I saw it."

"Maybe," Darien answered. He turned his face back to the city. "I thought he would come," he mused to himself.

"Who would come?"

Darien turned back to face Alaric. "No one. Never mind."

Alaric narrowed his eyes, but didn't press him. Instead, he presented Darien with a dagger, affixed to a hilt carved from bone. The blade was hewn into a thin column, ending in a menacing point. It was long enough to go through a man's skull and come out the other side, but light enough to ferret into a sleeping robe's lining without being detected.

"What's this?"

"A good start. Carry it around for a while," Alaric said, extending Darien's arm and tucking it in place inside his sleeve. "Familiarize yourself with the weight. In a few days, I'll show you how to hold it without ever losing your grip."

"A few days?" Darien repeated, with hope shining in his eyes.

"That is, if you still want me around then. I'm at your service, Darien, for as long as you require."

"Does your queen know about this?"

"It is her command."

Darien smiled. "In a few days, then. Goodnight, Christine. Thank you."

"My pleasure. And Darien…" Alaric lowered his voice before he took his leave. "Wear it to bed."

Darien knit his brow in confusion.

Alaric left the would-be seht to ponder his warning and passed through the courtyard back to his chamber. He searched for a glimpse of Kate performing her duties as a servant but could find her nowhere. He slipped into his room and out of Christine's confining wardrobe just as the sun stole its last breath and gave way to the glow of the twin moons. Lighting the oil lamp by his bedside, he noticed that his bedcovers were more disheveled than he'd left them.

They breathed. Rising and falling steadily, the bed harbored the queen in her own form, fast asleep. He tugged on her leg. She moaned as she rolled over to face him.

"Glad to see you hard at work," he said.

"Shut up, Alaric."

"You all right?"

"Fine. Just tired. I didn't think you'd mind." She sat up and rubbed her eyes. The thick night air made her hair swell. She ran her hands through the tangle of red, adding to the mess. She looked like a madwoman.

"Oh that's pretty."

She giggled as she stood and straightened the sheets. Alaric rushed to stop her.

"You don't have to do that."

"What's the difference? I'll be done in two seconds," she replied.

"No, really, I didn't even make it myself," he said. He tried to grab the airy white linens from her, but she wouldn't let him.

"*Really*, Alaric."

He stamped his foot. "You're my queen. You're supposed to have people doing that for you."

"It isn't difficult."

"Hardly the point," he growled.

She picked up the pillow and fluffed it.

"You're intolerable." The only remedy to his seething fury would have been to send her crashing into the mattress, dispelling his wrath in an outpouring of lust and obliterating the condition of the bed beyond repair. But his darling Kate wouldn't allow that.

She threw the pillow at his face. He grabbed it, crushed it in his hands, and slammed it back into place behind her.

"Would you rather I never left my bed, and kept a small bell at my side for anything my lazy little heart desired? Is that more worthy of a crown?"

He growled, having no reply.

She pushed him aside with her fingers, reaching behind him to tend to the mangled pillow.

"Thank you," he murmured.

"You're welcome," she said. "I don't deserve that pedestal, Alaric. I was born just another poor girl." She shrugged. "For whatever reason, I'm here now, and I'm just doing the best I can to deserve the honor you've all entrusted me with."

"You've more than earned your place."

She dipped her chin in appreciation.

"And yes, you do deserve to be content, and out of harm's way."

Her eyes pitched downward and welled with sadness. "That's all he wanted," she mumbled. "To keep me from harm."

"Does he know you're here?"

She shook her head.

"Tsk, tsk, tsk."

"He has enough to worry about," she said. "He was right. I am a distraction."

"A welcome one, I'm sure. He makes you happy?"

She pressed her eyelids closed, pushing the tears that pooled there down her face where they stained her cheeks. She nodded.

"Then *let* him."

She smiled. "You're a good friend, Alaric."

Alaric backed away. "*Friend*. What a filthy word."

"What else should I call you?"

He smirked. "Missed opportunity?"

She smirked back. "How does *kindred spirit* suit you?"

"That's just fine," he answered, humbled.

There was a faint tapping on the sill facing east. They turned in that direction and saw the hawk that had accompanied Alaric with a small parchment clutched in his claw.

"Forgive the intrusion, Your Majesty," the hawk started.

"No intrusion at all. Is everything all right?" she asked.

"Oh yes, quite. I bear a message from Prince Kaspar. He was quite anxious to deliver it quickly. Being privy to your whereabouts, I was only too happy to oblige."

She received the scroll with uncharacteristic caution and suspected its contents. What she read sunk her heart like a stone.

AUNT KATE, I'VE BEEN WORKING REALLY HARD ON THE MAP YOU GAVE ME, AND *I think I almost found the secret wishing room. It should only be another week or two. Please come home, so we can make a wish together.*

Love, Kaspar

SHE THANKED THE WINGED MESSENGER AND SENT HIM HOME WITH A return message saying she would be at Castelmor within a fortnight, and to please fetch Hercules and bring him to the castle to meet her at all costs. Off the bird soared into the indigo night.

Kate cursed under her breath. "Goddammit, goddammit."

Alaric was tactful enough not to pry as she crumpled the letter in her fist and fed it into the freestanding oil lamp to her right. She stood staring at the flame long enough for it to sting her eyes.

Alaric tried to divert her attention.

"Once his position is secure, Darien plans to make Haydee his wife."

No response.

"According to him, her hometown was raided for slaves. As a child, she was one of the first taken. When her parents resisted, naturally they were slaughtered. Recognizing her budding beauty, Reza took mercy and pulled her from the auction block to serve him at his table. She was grateful. Being whore to one beats being whore to hundreds, I suppose."

Kate remained still, the glow from the lamp dancing in her eyes.

"After a time he became seriously ill, and she tended to him. He attributed his miraculous recovery to her care. When Darien described the symptoms, I couldn't help but suspect Haydee was both the cause *and* the cure."

A flicker of intrigue flashed across Kate's irises, but still she said nothing.

"To reward her, Reza elevated her to the status of wife. Mind you, she and young Darien had been affectionate playmates, and their 'romance,' as he sees it, blossomed in time. Her marriage to Reza was quite the blow, but they buried their feelings and deferred to Reza's whim. You can see how well that's worked out. His impulse for freedom derives a great deal from his perception of her suffering. And hers is a story told a million times over, so Darien was not at all surprised as he grew to manhood to discover the majority of the Likhanni were ready to shrug off the yoke of slavery, save for a few stalwart families whose entire livelihood rests on the backs of others. These families are the ones backing Mehmnet, but the majority are praying that the rumor of Darien's challenge, fanned by his closest friends in the Hi'dinn, are true. *They're* the ones that pushed for the postponement of tomorrow's ceremony, drawing on the people's superstitious nature to buy him the precious time he needed to acquire a powerful ally. You. And that's where we find ourselves, kitten."

"Don't call me that," she said sharply.

He grinned. "I knew you were listening."

"Plucked from her family, eh? So sad." She faced him at last. Her eyes glimmered. "That's not what I heard."

"Oh?" he played along, one eyebrow raised. "Do tell." He fell forward onto the bed, propping his head on his fists like an inquisitive schoolgirl.

"She's one of Seth's," Kate said.

Alaric pushed up on his elbows almost immediately.

"What?? Seth's girls are the most expensive, most specialized entertainment known to man. And she's been here so long. She would have been little more than a baby!"

Kate gave a pained, knowing look.

He grunted in pure disgust. "That's…just…"

"Her parents."

Alaric ran a shaky hand through his dark hair, sweeping it over his shoulder.

"Apparently, she became his protégé. Before he died."

"Seth's not dead," Alaric interrupted.

"Oh yes, he is. She handed me a letter intended for the puppet she has running the place. She assumed I couldn't read."

Alaric was speechless.

"She's not that bright. And for a waif, she's rather violent. Unlucky workers have a habit of disappearing. Her servants are terrified of her. After she threw a plate at me, they feared for my safety, so they sent me back here."

"She threw a plate at you?! That stupid bitch," he spat.

"I ducked."

"*No one* treats the queen of Icarya that way."

"Damn right. But a wretched servant girl got railed at all day, all because of Darien's alliance with said queen."

That stopped Alaric from steaming. "Excuse me?"

"She doesn't want to be *wife* to the seht. She wants to *be* the seht. Then she's coming for me."

"What's her plan?"

"I don't know. But there'll be more than one battle tomorrow. That's as far as I can tell."

10

ALARIC WAS ROUSED BY THE AROMA OF SALTY MEAT, BUTTERY FRIED potatoes, and deliciously spiced eggs. He stretched his overgrown limbs and nearly fell out of the double chair configuration that served as his bed.

Giving a quick twist to his lumbar muscles, he inhaled the scent of sizzling fat greedily as it wafted his way from the bed. He opened his eyes to find Kate fully dressed, platter in hand.

"Oh, honey, you didn't have to go through all that trouble."

"No one else is awake yet. And it's no trouble at all," she replied.

He came eager to the feast. Kate's appetite for bread soaked and cooked in eggs was just as healthy.

"You like a big meal before a fight too, I gather," he observed between bites.

"I do," she answered with enthusiasm.

"Coffee?"

"Nn-hn. Never acquired a taste for it. Tea, if you please."

Plates cleared and hunger sated, Alaric reclined his head on the dark leather upholstery adorning the bedframe.

"This was nice."

"You're quite welcome," Kate said. "It's not close to what you deserve in payment. Just a small token of my appreciation."

"Not just breakfast. We got along all right. Sure, it was all work and no play," he said, eyes sparkling, "but, still."

Kate nodded. "I guess we did. And I don't mind saying, that I wouldn't mind doing it again sometime."

"That would be all the reward I need."

That she had no answer for.

"Kate."

"Mm?"

"If it turns out you're right, if Haydee should make a move today, I think Luca would forgive a broken promise if it kept you alive."

She stared out the window, her voice hazy. "Yes, I remember. You've been telling me how to stay alive since the first time we met."

"That wasn't the first time."

She turned to look at him, uncertain.

A boyish smile brightened his face. "I was a young man, just old enough to apply for the royal guard protecting our very new, very young queen."

Kate blushed.

"We were given a tour through the common rooms at Castelmor, and I caught a glimpse of you, sitting at the edge of a window, reading. Something must have distracted you, because you looked up and caught me staring at you. You smiled with those deep brown eyes, looking right through me, and I remember thinking, that you were the most beautiful girl I had ever seen."

Kate's heart fluttered. "Oh my god," she whispered. "I remember you."

He shrugged. "I didn't get the job. Falling all over myself in the queen's presence didn't exactly inspire confidence."

"When I asked after the dashing new soldier, no one would tell me who you were. Everyone was so busy bowing and rushing around me, but no one actually paid me any attention. You were the first person to look at me. Really look at me."

"I love you, Katelyn. I always have."

"Alaric." Her expression was pained.

He swallowed hard, and grabbed the back of her neck, pressing their foreheads together. They stayed that way for a long time, until the sudden interruption of a knock broke the heavy silence.

"Christine?"

Darien's voice beckoned from beyond the door.

The pair stared at each other, frantic. Alaric couldn't respond in his own voice, and couldn't effect the transformation fast enough to answer Darien's call. Kate was forced to stand in, modulating her voice.

"Just a minute, please," she begged as they scrambled to hide their breakfast under the bed and Alaric transformed and dressed in a flurry. Kate slunk behind the door just as Christine opened it.

Darien was paler than usual, the shadows pronounced under his eyes.

"It's time," he said.

"Did you get *any* sleep?" Alaric asked.

"How could I, after your little suggestion? Don't worry, in an hour I'll have rejoined the living."

"I'll be ready," Alaric replied firmly.

Kate whispered in his ear. "So will I."

11

By mid-afternoon, Luca descended the stairway leading to the main hall. People had already started to gather, and the barmaid was wiping off extra tables in the back to make more space.

Luca couldn't bring himself to look at her.

"Rough night?" Cyril asked, restocking his ale.

Luca rubbed his face. "Yeah. I'm okay now."

"Listen, Luca," Cyril said, setting his work aside. "The queen won't stay sore forever."

Luca tilted his head. "How did you know?"

The innkeeper gestured out the window. He had had a prime spot for viewing Luca's heartbreak as he had pushed Kate away into the moonlight.

"You did it because you love her," Cyril continued. "She knows that, she's just not used to it. She's been taking care of everyone else for so long, she's forgotten what it's like to have someone make hard decisions to protect her." He patted Luca's shoulder. "If she didn't love you back, she wouldn't care."

"Thanks," Luca smiled. "Is everything all set?"

Cyril shrugged. "What else is there to do?"

"Hi-yo, Luca!"

Just then, Nestor arrived with two dockworkers in tow, carrying crates of individual vials of garlic serum.

"Perfect, that's perfect," Luca said. Cyril made space on the bar for them to set the crates down.

"What's all this?" the innkeeper asked.

"For protection," Luca answered. "This should keep everyone safe. Now I just need to figure out how not to start a riot."

Luca paced and fidgeted for the next half hour as the population of Cathair packed themselves into the tavern.

"Almost ready?" Cyril asked.

Luca snapped his head in his direction, as if he'd been pulled away from an invisible distraction.

"Yes. It'll be fine. I'll be fine. I just…"

Cyril's grin widened. "Nervous?"

"Her Highness usually makes the speeches," he answered noncommittally.

"Relax, son. You're saving them from a monster. What could go wrong?"

Everything.

"Do you mind?" Luca asked, gesturing to an empty glass on the counter.

Cyril chuckled. "Whatever it takes," he said, and filled the glass to the brim with frothy amber. Luca downed it hurriedly, hoping to calm his frazzled nerves.

Once he got started, he felt more in control of himself. The countless eyes staring at him were open and inquisitive. Not full of suspicion and hatred.

It's different here, he reminded himself. *It'll be different.*

Things were bound to go a whole lot more smoothly for him when the people he was trying to protect were cooperative.

"Thank you for coming on short notice," Luca said. "In the coming days, you need to be on your guard. The man who killed Carla is no man. He's a vampire, and he may strike again."

A voice rose up from the back. "What's a vampire?"

"A blood drinker."

"Don't other animals do that?" another asked. The faces staring back at Luca were confused.

"No. Yes…" Luca scrunched his face as he fumbled over his words. "A vampire is a predator. They're more dangerous than anything that you can think of."

"What's it look like?"

"They look…human."

The crowd hummed with murmurs and gasps, but Luca seized control of the room.

"Please, please everyone, don't panic. Your queen sent me here to protect you, and I won't rest until Carla's murderer is found. But there are things you can do to protect yourselves. The most important is this…"

He gestured to the herbalist, who started passing out the vials.

"I know it smells awful, but just a couple of drops on your skin will act as a repellant. Make sure you hit these points," he said, pressing the pulse on his own neck. "Stay clear of areas with thick fog, and don't go into the forest unless you have to."

As the congregation applied the serum, Luca's eyes started to water. He turned his face away from the crowd to sneeze. Cyril, standing behind him, narrowed his eyes. He offered Luca a handkerchief to cover his nose.

"Thank you," he said, sniffing and clearing his throat to address the crowd again. "The vampire I'm after looks exactly like me. If you see him—come and find me right away. If you can help it, *don't* look him straight in the eye. I think that's it, for now. Any questions?"

"He looks just like you?"

"That's right."

"So how do we tell you apart?"

"With this," Luca answered, taking Kate's crest off his belt loop and hanging it around his neck. "I'll be wearing it like this from now on. If you see me *not* wearing this, run."

"Do *all* vampires look alike?" a little boy asked.

"No."

Cyril cast him a sideways glance. Luca pretended not to notice.

"Where's the safest place to hide?"

"In broad daylight. Or in the water. If you can live underwater for long periods, that is the best course."

"Can he be killed?"

"Yes, but do not under *any* circumstances try to force a confrontation. If you see him, you run and find me. He is fast, and cunning, and a seasoned killer. Keeping *him* away from you is how you survive."

The room was silent.

"There's one more thing, before you leave." Luca's voice became somber. "Carla was not the only victim. He's taken Rene as well."

The shock reverberated throughout the room.

"I understand this is difficult, and your queen shares in your grief. He was a beloved friend. Once the danger has passed, we will honor him properly. When his family returns, they will need help building a new home, and a new life. That's all."

Luca was finally able to take a breath as the town cleared out. Cyril came to stand next to him.

Please, no.

The man's presence made Luca's heart beat faster.

"You know, in my homeland, we had a word for people like you."

Luca lowered his eyes. "Did you?" He waited for him to say it. To utter that terrible word, "dhampir," that had marked him for eternity before Kate. He dreaded the return of that word, feeling its weight like an axe perched at the base of his skull.

Cyril nodded. "Friend."

Luca's eyes teared.

"You are a good friend, Luca. The queen has chosen well."

Finally, Luca looked up. "Thank you."

Cyril squeezed Luca in his burly arms, patting his back. "Rene too? I didn't think it could get worse. How about another drink? To Rene."

Luca assented.

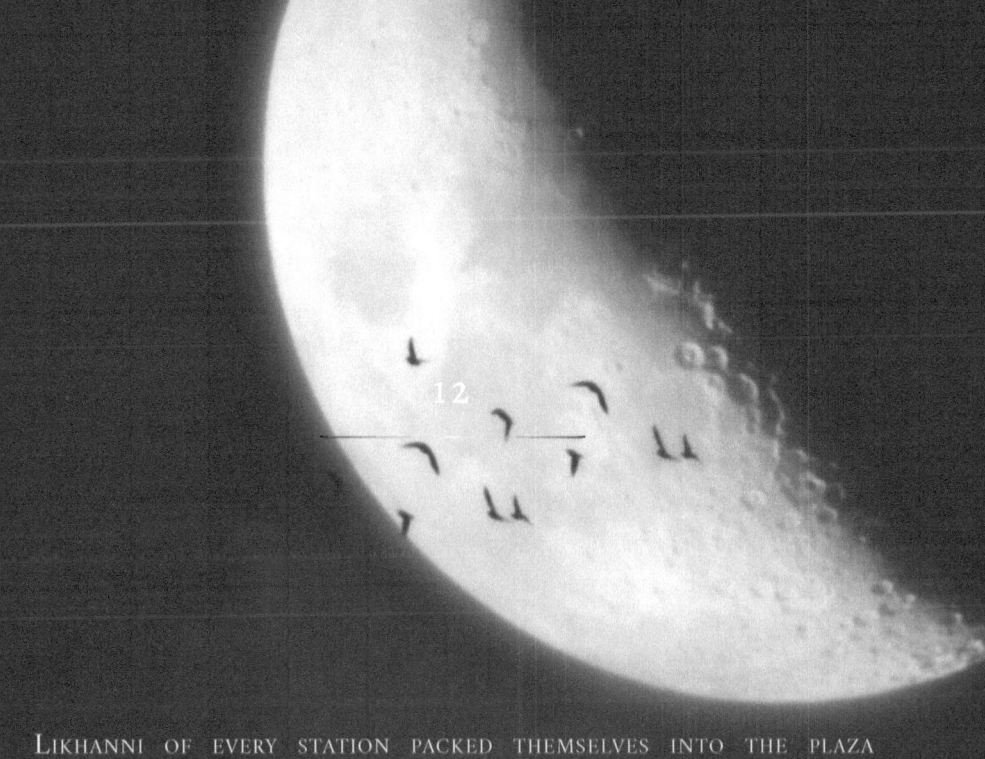

12

LIKHANNI OF EVERY STATION PACKED THEMSELVES INTO THE PLAZA preceding the rooms where Reza's Hi'dinn convened. The wide-open space felt liked an overstuffed broom closet. Gargantuan marble columns encircling the enormous space groaned from the pressure of hundreds of onlookers eager for a decent view of the impending ceremony. They filled the wide, sloping stairways leading away from the plaza, all the way up to the rest of the city. The opposite side backed into the sea.

A raised platform had been erected where the descending stairs converged into the plaza, facing out into the crowd. Throngs of people moved even closer together as the central area was cleared, exposing the meticulously designed mural of a scorpion with an exaggerated stinger that circumscribed the entire body twice over in shards of obsidian, surrounded by clean, smooth shades of ivory. Crowds made way for those beating drums, plucking strings, and whistling through wind instruments, along with dozens of costumed dancers.

Mehmnet emerged from the Hi'dinn's council chamber in all his finery, with the distinct exception that his neck was bare. He stood at the center of the platform and oversaw the passing ritual. Nothing could have wiped the smug satisfaction off his face in that moment.

Darien followed close behind. Alaric walked in his shadow, hands folded in his hooded robe, fingers curled around the hilt of a dagger. Strapped to his back was a broadsword nearly matching him in height.

A gesture from Mehmnet commenced the ceremony. Deep, rhythmic percussion resounded throughout the space, reverberating off the columns to signal the Likhanni in mourning for their seht. The movement was repeated and followed by a softer, lighter melody, to appease Reza's untimely separated spirit, trapped in his ashes, and to carry him on the winds of the tune down to the depths of the sea, where the world was made over. Not a soul moved as the last notes graced the cool morning breeze. The morning tide lapped against the base of the arena, swallowing up the discarded remains before rolling out again into open water.

Darien kept his head in a reverential bow, and bade his uncle a final, silent farewell.

Several silent beats punctuated the moment, followed by the jubilant harmony of winds and strings in time with frenzied jumping from the dancers. Out of the lead's costume of shimmering reds, oranges, and violets, bedecked with gems and crystals, she revealed a thick chain of gold. More than a dozen bands were woven together, each strand once presented to a long line of sehts. Each measure was distinctive in its sheen. Together, they dazzled brilliantly. The dancer and her coterie worked to braid a new length into the chain, fashioned in a pure pale yellow. The new addition was added to the full weight of those that came before. It was this piece that Darien stepped forward to receive. He turned back to face Mehmnet, who joined him in the center of the mosaic. They stood on the tiles representing the scorpion's heart. Grinning widely, Mehmnet lowered his shiny, sandy-brown head.

Darien clenched the chain in his sweaty palms. Tension gripped the entire city in an oppressive silence.

Alaric shifted his eyes as far to either side of his head as he could. He could not spy one sign of Kate, nor her servile counterpart. His heart pounded. The longer Darien held the necklace of the new seht, the greater the crowd's anticipation waxed.

Uncurling his trembling fingers, Darien let the chain rest effortlessly in his palm, as if to ask the crowd's favor. The cheering response was deafening, giving way to the clear chanting of Darien's name. Their upraised voices gathered his courage, and he slipped the heavy chain around his own neck.

The joyful outcry of the Likhanni refused to be contained. Mehmnet stood erect, hiding his rage behind a chagrin.

"You would dare to challenge my rule, dear nephew?" he asked.

"As you've reminded me many times, Mehmnet, I am not your nephew." Darien spoke with determination. "I am more fit to lead the Likhanni into the future than you."

"What future is that? One of submission, to a wildling who lives in a tree?"

"One of their own choosing."

Mehmnet laughed. "Very well, I'll play your little game. I know you're not my combatant, you're much too dainty for that."

Darien's eyes narrowed at the insult.

"Who shall it be, then?" Mehmnet bellowed louder. "Who dares to stand in the place of the bastard-seht?"

ALARIC TENSED AS HE TOOK A STEP FORWARD. A FIRM HAND ON HIS shoulder kept him in place.

"Oh, no."

Red hair flapping in the coarse breeze, Katelyn brushed past him and revealed herself to the crowd as she descended into the arena. Her military garb consisted of a sapphire dress overlaid with a silver breastplate that split into a leather strap skirt. Her leather boots nearly reached her thighs. The plaid scarf she wore constantly was splayed across her chest, adorning the front of her attire and fastened at the hip, the way it was intended.

The multitude paused in its cheering, stunned at the Icaryan queen's sudden appearance, only to rejoin in their cacophony all the louder. Many heads went so far as to bow. Mehmnet took a small step back, imperceptible to all but Kate and the man whose right hand she now approached. Darien's eyes were wide with disbelief, but Kate played it off, bursting with bravado.

"I dare."

"Good morning, Kate," Mehmnet said in a chilly tone.

"You will *not* address me so informal. You have not earned that honor," she said.

"I must confess I'm surprised. Such boldness outside your own boundaries is hardly your style," Mehmnet replied.

"More proof that you know me not at all. I am all too pleased to act as Darien's champion," Kate answered.

"Godsdamn son of a bitch." Alaric gritted between his teeth as he shoved his way to the front line of spectators. "If she lives, I'm going to kill that woman."

Mehmnet hesitated. He knew the threat he faced more than he cared to admit. He cleared his throat.

"Traditionally, only a man of Likhanni blood is deemed capable of rising to champion."

"It's a new day, Mehmnet," Darien argued.

One of Mehmnet's own cohorts goaded him on from the rim of onlookers closest to them.

"What's the matter, Mehment, afraid of a woman less than half your age?" they cried.

The crowd heartily assented.

The Icaryan queen flashed a sinister grin. "There's no way out."

Mehmnet took a deep breath. "The challenge is accepted then!"

The crowd rejoiced at getting an even better show than they had bargained for. The plaza was cleared, with the combatants retreating to opposite corners to be stripped of superfluous weapons.

The would-be seht was fraught with nerves. He spewed forth a string of protests and unsolicited advice as he and Kate reached the edge of the plaza where Alaric, in the guise of Christine, stood waiting. Kate appeared indifferent, straightening her clothes.

"I really was only hoping for help from a representative of yours...no offense, Christine," he said.

"None taken," Alaric replied. To Kate, he said, "You can't be serious."

She gave both men a placid look as she smoothed the chainmail underneath her wrist guards, pulling it taut.

"This was always my reason for coming here," she said coolly. "You required a champion, Darien. I'm it."

"Y-yes," Darien answered awkwardly. He had heard so much about her, had studied everything she had ever done in her capacity as queen. The stories men told of her skills on the battlefield filled him with awe. But he'd never seen her this close before. She was larger than life. She was entering a fight to the death for him, a total stranger, with the most respected swordsman in Likhan. She hadn't even blinked an eye.

"I never suspected you would carry that burden yourself. It should be me."

There. He'd said it.

"I don't want anyone risking their life for me. Least of all you."

The queen remained unmoved. "You wanted to make a statement about our relationship," she said. "A bold gesture. So do I."

Darien looked with desperation to Christine, but she was equally flustered.

Alaric gave it his best shot. "I can think of at least one person who'll kill me if I don't stop you right now."

Kate ceased fussing with herself, and finally looked at them. Darien saw her eyelids flutter just a fraction. He had the distinct feeling that she was trying to stop herself from rolling her eyes.

"Close your eyes. Count to ten."

Darien laughed. So she was as crazy as people said. "Your Majesty, I'm well aware of your reputation, but it is dangerously foolhardy to—"

"What is my reputation, then?"

Her voice was as blunt and forceful as a cudgel. Darien sputtered a moment. But he was afraid of what might happen if he hedged. So he answered frankly.

"That you can kill twenty men before breakfast, you can smell an ambush from a week away, that you have directly or indirectly led every army from here to the edge of the world in defense of your own country, that you've traveled back in time to revive an ancient god with necromancy. That you are the reincarnation of the forest gods, and the blood-heir to the Icaryan throne. That you breathe fire."

In all the time that Darien was talking, not a single muscle in her face had moved.

After a moment, she said, "I am all that, and much, much worse."

Alaric begged. "*Don't.*"

Deaf to his plea, Kate turned to take her place in the arena, unarmed. Alaric offered her the broadsword at his back, but she batted him away.

Darien called meekly after her. He might never get the chance otherwise.

"Good luck, Aunt."

She froze where she stood on the last step leading down into the tiled pit, and cast a burning glance at him.

He flinched at her brutal stare. But he pushed his luck. "You *are* my aunt, aren't you?"

Head down, Katelyn pointed her feet back again toward the theater of impending war. She grimaced, clenching her fists, then turned on her heels. She stomped over to Darien, grabbed him by the back of the neck, and pressed his forehead to her lips, the way one might do to a child.

It was the confirmation he'd sought all his life.

"Count to ten." She released him before he could react and descended onto the mosaic floor where Mehmnet was waiting.

MEHMNET HELD A THICK, FLAT BLADE IN HIS HAND, WICKEDLY CURVED with a double-pointed tip like the forked tongue of a serpent.

"Choose your weapon, *princess*," he said.

With an arrogant grin plastered on her face, Kate presented her open palms.

Mehmnet chuckled. "You're too brazen, even despite your youth. Today it will be your death sentence."

Kate continued to smile.

"If this doesn't go well, we'll both be dead," Alaric said, thinking of what Luca would do if Kate were butchered here in full sight of him.

"That makes three of us," Darien said, his own voice trailing off as all eyes fell to the heart of the city.

To stave off the blood from freezing in his veins, Alaric kept silent count as Mehmnet twirled his wrist, improving his grip on his weapon. Kate stood like a statue, arms and legs slightly apart, with naught to defend herself but her wired muscles and sharpened wit.

One.

Mehmnet took a cautious step to the side, and stopped again when it did not elicit a reaction. Kate's feet were planted to the ground.

Two.

Angered by her stubborn stance, Mehmnet bent his knees and leaned forward, menacing. Kate was unimpressed.

Three.

Mehmnet barreled at her, charging past as she swiveled her hips backward at the last moment and dodged his stabbing blow. She pinched his wrist as he passed, dislocating his thumb and relieving him of his weapon.

Four.

Nearly crashing into the column nearest him and Darien, Mehmnet howled in rage. He rubbed the skin covering several small bones Kate had crushed in her grip. The congregation burst with derisive laughter at the arrogant swordsman so easily bested. Kate, still standing in the center of the plaza, examined the blade she now held in her hand with feigned curiosity.

Five.

Without wasting a breath, Mehmnet pulled a dagger from beneath his robe. Kate still stood with her back to him. The crowd, hunched all around the steps of the Hi'dinn's council house, inched closer.

Six.

Mehmnet charged again, as Kate ignored him.

Seven.

With impressive speed, Kate knelt down on one knee to dodge Mehment's blow and slid the blade through the thin gap between her arm and torso. Mehmnet was run through his own sword. A collective gasp echoed as the serpentine point came out the other side of him, and he spat dark blood into Kate's hair.

"Holy…" Darien covered his mouth in shock.

Eight.

Kate rotated the blade, twisting it sideways and goring Mehmnet in his death throes. But beneath the din, Alaric heard the rapid chiming of slippered feet as they scampered back into the council house. Haydee. He did not follow.

Nine.

Shifting her grip on the hilt, Kate spun to her feet, pulling Mehmnet's sword out of his chest and slicing off his head in a clean, hefty stroke.

Ten. I'll be godsdamned.

Alaric and Darien finally breathed again as Likhan erupted in jubilation at Kate's triumph.

She dropped the sword onto the mangled corpse at her feet, caught Darien and Alaric's wide-eyed stares from a distance of twenty feet, and winked.

~

"Witch!"

An angry voice boomed from Kate's right.

Kate turned her head in the direction of the shout, where Mehmnet's loyal friends were fuming.

"Mehmnet could never be so easily taken! The she-demon has murdered him!" another cried.

She smiled fiendishly in their direction, opening her arms wide. "Come on, then."

Alaric rushed to assist her, but she pointed directly at him and screamed. "Hold!"

The hostility in her voice turned his feet to stone. He could only watch as an army of nine rushed at Kate, swords drawn.

Mehmnet's discarded weapon lay tilted across his unbreathing back, sloping toward the floor. Kate stomped on the handle with her right foot, sending it into the air before her. She caught the hilt and spun in a quick, tight circle that sent the blade hurtling straight through the chest of the nearest of her enemies, drawing closer. The blow knocked the dead man backward several feet.

The second pointed his sword at Kate's heart. With both hands she took hold of his forearm and drove his sword in between the ribs of the man furthest to her right as the small legion bowed in an arc before her. She kicked out with her left foot, sending a third man crashing to the ground as she overpowered the man who had attacked her head on, slashing the blade still in his grip at a downward angle and spilling the contents of his belly. She took proper possession of the blade in time to swing it over her head, deflecting blows from two men to her rear. She turned to face them, cleaving them from one man's neck through to the right hip of the enemy standing next to him. Their halved bodies pitched forward.

Another to her left jabbed at her with a spear. Kate dropped the sword in her hand and stepped into the attack, ensnaring the shaft in her armpit. She thrust upward, striking the man with the weapon he still held, but loosely, in his hand. Another hit to his lungs and the spear was hers. She spun it deftly in the air and snapped the man's neck. The spear had become a natural extension of her arm, obeying the slightest twitch in her wrist with deadly efficiency.

She sent the blunt end sailing to her right, into the cracked sternum of the man she had kicked just as he got to his feet again. Sending the spear upward and breaking his nose, Kate knocked him to the ground once more. She thrust the spearhead downward and tore open his throat. As she pulled the tip free, she was kicked from behind. Running forward into the fall, she raced up the column facing her, flipping in the air and landing behind her two remaining attackers. They spun around in confusion as she held the spear horizontally in front of her chest and shoved them into the column. A quick thrust upward dislocated their jaws, blackening their vision as Kate split the spear over her knee and impaled both men by their throats.

She was empty-handed once more as they slumped to the ground, completing the circle of destruction at her feet. She stood facing Likhan's newly orphaned sons. They quivered in their place and looked frantically at each other, shaky hands poised on the pommels of their swords.

Kate opened her palms out to either side of her and lifted her nose to the wind. Surprised screams pierced the crowd as her stretched fingers curled around a pair of swords that had lain at her feet rose into the air, coming into her outstretched palms by silent command. She coiled into an aggressive stance, a force of chaos waiting to be unleashed. She smiled like the devil.

"Gentleman," she asked with an eerie calm, "do I look tired?"

They were frightened. At a small gesture of her fingers, they laid down their weapons.

The contest was over. Darien was seht. The crowd was satisfied.

At Alaric's insistence, Darien ascended the platform's summit where Mehmnet had commenced the ceremony a mere hour before. The ritual concluded without regard for the lifeless bodies at the center of the square. The entire city again chanted Darien's name, for the most significant part of the ceremony was now upon them.

"As is custom, I am prepared to issue my first order." Darien stepped off the podium and approached Kate, still surrounded by death. She retrieved Mehmnet's impressively carved blade from the trunk of a nobleman's corpse and held it out to him.

Darien took the bloody sword from her and walked to a string of new slaves penned in the harbor, not yet sold, and bound together in irons. They outstretched their wrists in hopeful anticipation as he approached, smiling, with determined steps. The guards stood aside as Darien raised the sword over his head and cleaved through their rusted, blood-stained fetters.

~

KATE TURNED HER HEAD TO THE LEFT, AWAY FROM THE DEAFENING SHOUTS of the city as they were muted in her ear. A dull crackling sound, just a whisper at first, was getting louder. Her attention darted on instinct to the column northwest of her position. More specifically, to the shadows at the base. They were growing, filling in the thin grooves between the tiles. She backed away when the burgeoning shadow gathered itself, forming a dense cloud that crept up the column, absorbing the rays of the sun opposite it in the distance. Never losing track of her target, she dashed across the plaza, splashing blood on her boots as she rushed to Darien and pushed him deeper into the crowd.

"Get back!" she ordered, coming again to the center where an enlarged form was now very visibly taking shape. Cheers devolved into shrieking chaos. Many fled, seething through the impenetrable crowds, while others were petrified in full view of the horror blotting out the daylight. Those immediately surrounding Darien secreted him away.

The shadowy obscenity clawed at the tiles, pulverizing them under its weight as it labored to pull its shambling form out of the dark corner from which it had sprung.

Alaric seized the long spear of the guard nearest him and hurled it in the shadow beast's direction. Kate took possession of it as it sailed over her head, barely grazing the shaft with her palms and guiding its momentum into the dense fiber of its outstretched claw. The spear had no effect other than to set the horror's pale, sickly blue eyes on its diminutive assailant, marking her for death. Its muffled, guttural roar shook the ground under Kate's feet. The edges of its form billowed and shifted, an undefinable monstrosity. She jumped back, dodging the elongated snout snapping its massive jaw and mashing its bone-crunching teeth. Kate was not entirely clear of the horror when it thrashed its murky neck in her direction. She was propelled backward and slid on her hands and feet across tiles splashed with darkening blood. A river of crimson ran down her face from the skin above her left eye.

With a maddening shriek, the beast was free from the blurred edges and angles that bore its unholy existence. At full height on four legs, it towered fifteen feet above the queen. It snatched her up in its knobby claws. Darien and Alaric screamed her name from opposing borders of the ruined mural as the shadowy abomination swung its arm in a wide arc, Kate tight in its grip. It was intent on dashing her brains against the stone column.

Their hearts stopped at the crucial moment—Kate had vanished into thin air. The indefinite beast vented its rage. It toppled over the column and flung it far out into the sea. The upper lintel, now bereft of its support, hurtled to the ground, falling through the monster's head and down to the ground without causing it to so much as flinch. Its eyes flashed a manic glow in search of its prey, but neither it nor the human spectators cowering in fear could discern where the queen had spirited herself away to. Its eerie orbs locked finally on her form, crouching atop the still upright edge of the broken lintel, her fingers working furiously

Alaric's vision darted from her to the demon and back again. Her fingers worked frantically, weaving a small web of black thread extending from her index finger to her thumb. All the while she soaked it with the blood pouring out of the deep cut in her eyebrow.

"Come on, come on," she mumbled to herself. Every second she was visible was a risk. But she had to stay materialized for long enough to complete her task. Losing concentration meant death, but she couldn't help but let one thought slip. She was breaking a promise, and the consequences could be catastrophic.

Forgive me. I have no choice.

The shadow's ability to make contact with the physical world was a matter of timing. She could not afford to miss when it lashed out at her again.

It had finally noticed her. She was out of time. But it was just enough.

The beast slammed its paws into the remaining lintel and sent the stalwart remnants of the structure crashing to the ground.

Kate kicked off into the air, her fingers poised at the edges of her miniature web, holding the net taut.

She extended her arms as she plummeted to the broken ground, stretching the center of her work over the thing's muzzle, pulling the corners tight around its inky mass. The beast shrunk, contained in Kate's net as she descended. The extended links of her blood-soaked cage held the monster fast as it thrashed wildly. It oozed a pale blue ichor as the ropes drew tight like razors and cut through the shadow. It roared—not in rage, but in pain.

Kate closed the net at its furling edges as she touched down, sealing the opening in her palm and tossing it upward. It strung the weeping shadow up to the corner of a toppled column, ensnared like a spider's victim. The shadowy prisoner emitted soul-splitting wails, wallowing in its own blood as the web continued to contract.

BEHIND HIS BACK, ALARIC HEARD THE COUPLING OF THE BEAST'S CRIES with Haydee's. Her flesh scorched and scarred in the same gridlock pattern. She crumpled onto the floor, immobilized. Alaric kept his distance. He'd never been so aware of his mortal limitations.

KATE STOOD AT THE FOOT OF HER SUSPENDED PREY, HER CHEST HEAVING. She closed her eyes, and raised a clenched fist in front of her. Flames leapt from her palm as she opened it.

"Oh gods," Darien murmured, watching as the people surrounding him huddled closer.

Kate seethed with anger. She blew hard across her hand, engulfing the creature in unquenchable flames.

~

HAYDEE CAUGHT ON FIRE. IN DESPERATION, SHE SCURRIED AWAY. ALARIC
stared wide-eyed as she slipped into a minute shadow cast by a potted
plant positioned against the wall.

~

NOT A SINGLE GRAIN OF ASH FELL FROM THE NET KATE HAD WOVEN. BUT
she was not yet finished. She felt a sudden surge of power rising in her
blood. At her feet, a thick fog of freezing mist was forming. She had to
dispel it, or *she* would be the one responsible for destroying the city. She
pressed her open palms to the alabaster rubble. Ice filled the fractures of
the remaining pieces within the span of a breath, forcing its way
through the masonry's veins. The stones shattered. All that was left was
a thick layer of crystalline powder that lined the ruined mosaic floor.
The gigantic tree stump that formed the base of the plaza lay exposed
under pulverized tiles.

The sun showed its face from behind a white billowy cloud. It
melted the frozen debris. Stones, bodies, blood, all of it ran over the
brink of the demolished plaza and dripped into the sea.

Kate looked down at her hands, turning them over and over again.
She had sensed her pent-up magic and directed it. Discharged it.
Successfully. She stood dumbstruck. In that same moment, she became
aware of a force more powerful than gravity pulling her downward. It
drew her to her knees.

~

THE DENIZENS OF LIKHAN LIFTED THEIR HEADS AT THE QUIET CALM. THE
Icaryan queen's victory over the indescribable shadow was met not by
roaring cheers, but by an awesome silence. She rolled onto her back,
spreading her limbs over the deadened wood, getting as close as
possible, staring at the sky. She licked the blood streaming down her
face.

Alaric was the first to reach her. "Kate, Kate! Are you all right?"
"Fine," she answered. "Just tired."

∿

HER LIDS GREW HEAVY, HER MIND EMPTIED. THE SKY SEEMED TO STRETCH away from her, swallowing up the world. She was euphoric.

∿

DARIEN FELL TO HIS KNEES AT HER SIDE. WHEN ATTEMPTING TO CLASP HER hand in his, he found the tips of her fingers sunken into the grain of the stump. Her skin was stiff. Wooden. Her body was melding itself to the tree. Darien shrunk back, looking to Alaric for recourse.

"Kate," Alaric whispered nervously as her pupils dilated and her irises lightened in hue, reflecting a dazzling emerald green.

"Just, let me rest a moment," she murmured, barely moving her lips.

∿

WITH HER PRISMATIC GAZE FIXED ON THE HEAVENS, KATE'S PSYCHE ascended a state of purity. She had no fear, no hope, no pain, no joy—no breath. She simply existed. The rings of the dead tree beneath the grief-stricken men emitted a pale green phosphorescence. The dried surface on which they knelt grew tacky. A blanket of moss bloomed. Growth radiated outward from Kate, stretching all the way to the end of the obliterated plaza. Vines crawled down into the water in a thick veil over the city's stark shore carved in stone. A feathery layer of grass coated the ground, nurturing blossoms in vibrant blues, purples, and reds. Kate's eyelids closed.

"Come back to us, Kate," Alaric pleaded.

∿

Cool, clean air filled her lungs, and the Eden that flowed breathed, thrumming silently in tandem with her heartbeat.

"I'm still here."

The lush verdure released her, and her torso rose from the mossy down, blinking as her eyes resumed their rich brown. She drank in the sight of her creation. She smiled.

Darien bowed his head.

"You really *are* the goddess of the forest come back to us," he whispered, awestruck.

"You know," she said, looking at her hands, "I think maybe I am."

The trio rose to their feet.

"I don't really know how this happened," she said in apology.

Darien's words reassured her. "Whatever it was, it's beautiful. Add a few footpaths," he mused, "and it would make an excellent public garden."

She winked, the sting in her left eye finally returning. She raised a hand to her blood-smeared face. Alaric caught her wrist.

"Don't. It's a nasty cut."

Kate licked at the blood that was just now slowing to a trickle. "Despite the circumstances, I feel better than ever."

Alaric hugged her, reaching up to grasp the back of her blood-matted hair. She hugged him back. Kate's touch was strangely more comforting to him in his present state, where Kate was the taller of the two.

"Come with me," Darien offered. "I'd like to tend to that wound."

"Thank you for the offer, but you have other responsibilities now." She gestured behind him to the citizens of Likhan. They had grown confident enough to quit their hiding places and stand in wonder at what Kate had wrought, venturing into its dense center with caution, giving way to delight.

"That is true. But what kind of leader would I be if I did not administer to my own champion? They are saved. Thanks to you. I will spend the rest of my lifetime expressing my gratitude."

Kate smiled. "Your friendship is all the thanks I need."

The two men escorted Kate back to Darien's private parlor, where

Darien cleaned the searing gash above her eyebrow. He looked at the supplies laid out before him, his eyes darting from one ingredient to the next. His cheeks flushed red.

"The dark berries, at the edge," Kate said, absently aware of the contents and position of every substance in the healer's kit presented to Darien by his manservant. "Crush them."

Embarrassed, Darien complied, crunching the dried fruits under the weight of a stone pestle.

"The fennen leaves. No, the long, thin ones," she corrected, seeing him reach for the wrong plant without really looking at him. "A pinch of the first four, second row. Twice as much of the fifth."

Her plain tone in the face of Darien's ignorance humbled him. He did his utmost to absorb the lesson, grinding everything together with a small measure of oil. Kate dipped her finger in the mortar, rubbing the mixture together in her hands.

"Good."

When Darien applied the salve, Kate ground her teeth, and stomped her foot on the floor.

"Sorry, I'm sorry!" Darien cried.

"No, no, it's right. More," she growled.

Flustered, Darien packed as much as he could into the tear. "It's thin, but deep," he observed, poring over the wound as he threaded a needle. "I don't think it will scar."

"I *know* it won't," she replied, swatting his hand away. "That's more trouble than it's worth."

"So it's true, then? Your…uh…"

Kate's mind traveled back to a day that felt ages away. "Lover," Kate smirked. "His name is Luca."

"Right," Darien said, blushing again. "He has the power to heal?"

"He does," Kate answered, sitting still as Darien set the needle and thread down and covered the wound in thick bandages.

Alaric had waited long enough, and was ready to burst. "What the fuck was that thing?"

"Shadow magic," Kate answered, "just as I feared."

"Haydee was controlling it. You knocked her on her ass, but she escaped. I'm sorry I did not give chase, My Queen."

"Don't be ridiculous. You were right to stay away."

Darien bent his head, and wiped at his eyes with a grimy fist. Kate pressed on his shoulder.

"I'm sorry you had to find out like this," she said.

"It's better than never finding out," Darien retorted. "You've saved me in more ways than one. Both of you." He shook his head. "I just can't believe that, all this time, I've shared my bed with a necromancer." Darien blanched at the thought, assaulted with a wave of nausea.

"Not a necromancer," Kate corrected. "*I'm* a necromancer. It's how I bound the beast."

The confusion in both sets of eyes confronting her prompted an explanation.

"Necromancy is blood-magic. Power from life, even over death. It's not inherently good or evil, but it requires a terrible price. *Shadow* magic calls forth the dark and unnatural from the void."

"But your magic prevailed. You killed the creature," Darien said, fearful of the gravity in Kate's voice.

"But not its master."

"You dealt with her pretty handily, in my estimation," Alaric said. "She was running for her life."

"That's a relief," Kate answered. "But I would like a better guarantee."

"You're going to go after her?" Darien asked.

"Yes, but not alone. And not blind. Shadow practitioners are very rare, and very insular. I know very little about my enemy and what else she might be able to throw at us. You're both still wearing the binds I gave you?"

Both men demonstrated that they were.

"Good. I'll treat the house, so you don't have to spend every moment looking over your shoulder. But I do have to be on my way."

"You just got here—you're leaving?" Darien objected. "I was hoping to get to know you better," he confessed. "That you'd help me rebuild."

Kate smiled. "You need to find your own feet. But, I think I know someone who'd be eager to help."

Darien's face lit up.

"This was all *his* idea anyway."

Darien's eyes rimmed with tears.

She turned to Alaric, who was smiling softly at her.

"You did good today," he said. "You made me proud."

The corners of her lips upturned in satisfaction. "Before I leave, I'd like to clear the air. Darien, I leave you here with a trusted comrade, but you should know his name is not Christine."

"*His* name?"

Kate tapped Alaric on the chest with her index finger, returning him to his true form. He quickly drew closed his hooded cape to conceal the garments of a woman, burst open and hanging limply from his thick limbs.

"Alaric, at your service."

The young seht's jaw dropped in disbelief.

"The deception was for Mehmnet's benefit, not yours," Kate assured him.

"Fair enough," he answered, shaking Alaric's hand. "I'm sorry I flirted with you. That, too, was for Mehmnet's benefit, I'm afraid."

Alaric chuckled. "All is forgiven."

"Excuse me, my lord." Darien's manservant poked his head into the room. "Forgive the interruption, but you are needed outside."

"I suppose I am," Darien answered, rising to his feet. Kate followed suit.

"I'll be back soon," she said, hugging her nephew.

"I look forward to it." With that, Darien exited the room to cater to his hard-earned duty.

"Thank you," Alaric said. "That masque was getting to be a real pain."

"You wore it longer than anyone else. I'm not surprised you're fatigued. Take care of yourself—and keep me updated."

"I will, My Queen."

"Oh, and Alaric—no more love letters."

His lips twisted into a wry grin. "Don't tell me what to do."

13

A WEEK PASSED WITHOUT INCIDENT. LUCA'S FRUSTRATION GREW AS THE threatening vapor billowed and bulged, drifting to the southern shore. There had been no new developments, save for the cloud's glacial movement. Luca dreaded the dual possibilities that his father had escaped beyond his reach, or that their chase would be indefinitely protracted. He had heard little from Kate since their psychic reunion in the shower, save for a desperate apology from her—for what, he could not decipher. He sensed in her the urgency of battle, and had not dared to flood her brain with distraction. To the confusion of those he had passed on the street, he had stood immobile, eyes closed, until the restoration of her calm washed over him in an awesome wave. His separation from Kate grated on his soul, and he wanted nothing more than to be restored to her side with his father's menace definitively extinguished.

During his rounds on the docks, nothing seemed out of the ordinary. On this particular day, Luca allowed himself to wander further south down the beach, past the harbor to a series of jagged cliffs abutting the sea. The incoming tide crashed noisily on the boulders, sending up sand and a sweet spray. The waves had been long at work, eating away at the foot of the cliffs and creating a string of caverns. Luca traversed the uninviting terrain, seeing the mist concentrate in thicker and darker patches. The shrill cry of a gull overhead distracted him. Eyes still bent skyward, a sudden dread overcame him. Every hair on his body bristled. On instinct, he cast his gaze downward. Peering into the darkness of a gaping aperture, Luca saw a pair of eyes glowing a brilliant, malicious red.

The mist was dissipating, its edges only visible as the sun's beams bounced off its soft, wet curves. The cave was shrouded in complete darkness, the fog grew blacker than night, then was no more.

Luca drew his sword and rushed to the opening. His best hope was that the cave was a dead end. He stood at the threshold, glowering into the space. It was devoid of walkways or tunnels, being one large, open space with high ceilings of pitted rock and mud water for a floor. It was empty. Or so it might have seemed, to anyone but Luca.

His heart pounded in his chest. Every synapse fired at top speed, every muscle tensed, ready to fly into murderous action. Luca closed his eyes, and whispered into the obsidian silence.

"I know you're here."

If he made the first move, it would be over before it even began. If he took one step, he'd give Dracula the opportunity to flee behind him. Luca could not allow that. Neither of them was leaving until one of them was destroyed. He had to seal the entrance.

Luca dug the tip of his blade into the dirt. Gritting his teeth, he drew a long, vertical line at his feet. An instinct that ran through his soul forbade him from completing his task. He shuddered, struggling to retain his grip. His limbs became heavy as lead, the sword in his hand impossible to wield. Sweat dripped from his temples, and his very existence quaked. But he could sense he was not alone in his suffering, that the effect produced by his mere intention was acute in his enemy. So he waged his battle.

The blade squeaked as the tip scoured the rock on the ground, moving it from the southern end of the line he had drawn to a point directly west, halfway up.

"Luca?"

THE HUNTER'S BREATH DIED IN HIS THROAT AS KATE APPROACHED HIM. She stood directly behind him, wondering why he seemed immobile. His left arm lashed out, forcing her to grab his waist to retain her balance. He gripped her with every ounce of strength he had, keeping her closer to him than his own shadow. Kate was bombarded with cosmic doses of agitation, a killing lust, and a terror beyond anything she could conceive of. The intensity of Luca's consciousness nauseated her. She knew well enough not to so much as blink.

Her eyes traveled the length of the sword, and saw its position. Suddenly, she understood. Swallowing her sudden bout of vertigo, Kate moved her right hand slowly down Luca's arm, stretching her fingers over his. She took control of the sword under Luca's grip, and guided the blade across the stone to the right, completing the cross. Luca groaned at the sight of it. She pried Luca's stiffened fingers off the hilt, and directed the weapon upward, ever ready for the darkness to fly out at her. She repeated the pattern on the ceiling.

A howl like a lion stabbed through the heart echoed throughout the cavern, piercing their very souls. Kate continued in her work, covering the rim of the cave in crosses of all sizes. Words she could barely remember rang in her head, imposing upon her lips until she pronounced them.

"In nomine Dei, et non transibunt." *By God, you shall not pass.*

The menace breathing down their necks retreated, cowering in the furthest corner from the view of the opening. Dracula's wrath was palpable. They had succeeded in trapping him.

LUCA RECLAIMED HIS SWORD AND LIFTED HIS FOOT OUT OF THE MUD where he had planted it. He backed away from the cave's mouth with clutching him from behind. They moved as a unit. Only when they were some distance away did Luca spin around and cup Kate's cheeks in his palms.

"Are you okay? You sure?" His breathless voice bordered on panic. Once she had assured him enough, he took her in his arms and didn't let go. For the first time in weeks, his fingers tangled themselves in her brilliant red hair, his lips tasted her sweetness. The tide rushed at their ankles as they embraced on the shore, bringing with it all the passion he had yearned for in her absence. The memories of the months they spent in their island heaven, making love every day in the sand, and memories of Kate, the sun-kissed siren, flooded him. Kate's plaintive melodies when brewing streamed into his ears. Fresh fish and summer stew filled his nostrils and warmed his aching muscles. Kate's skin, her invigorating blood, coated his tongue. He felt whole once more.

His consciousness crept at the edge of her mind, humbled, afraid to enter unbidden after his violation of a bond he held sacred. His eyes implored her.

I don't deserve this.

Kate melted into her lover, opening her psyche unconditionally. She did more than forgive his transgression. She accepted it, and offered up her soul.

Moved to tears, he touched his cheek to Kate's and made a silent vow to never again abuse her trust. Their embrace tightened.

For the first time, Luca noticed the bandages pressed over her left eyebrow. He peeled back the layers to reveal a ghastly tear. In the absence of a threaded closure, it was healing poorly. Luca furrowed his brow and brushed his thumb over the wound, restoring her broken skin. He pressed his lips to the site as he spoke.

"They'll pay for that."

"They already have."

His fingers smoothed her wind-whipped hair as she relayed without speech what had transpired in Likhan. He ached at the loneliness she'd felt as she forged through the events that had forced her actions. He cursed himself for a fool.

"I should have been there," he protested. "I sent you into even more danger, all on your own." He felt their overwhelming need to always be near each other, a desperation that plagued them even now, knowing that they had both been where they needed to be, and that it had kept them apart. And might one day again.

Her soul begged forgiveness for not divulging her activity. Though she spoke no words, he raised his fingers to her sea-kissed lips to silence them.

The fault is mine, for leaving you to bear the burden of your duties alone.

He stiffened his neck to gaze into her eyes, his own blazing with a deep crimson jealousy. For he had beheld every word exchanged with Alaric, every unwelcome advance, every stolen touch. He spoke with an air of command that turned her speechless.

"If he ever touches you again, I will kill him."

Bringing Kate close to him, his passionate possession shook her to her core. She would never cease to hold his favor. He didn't begrudge her her compassion for Alaric, knowing with a soulful certainty that's all it was. Sweeping her into his arms, Luca quickened his steps for the tavern.

Kate's gaze was glued to the cavern. "Is it safe to leave him like that?" she asked. "Shouldn't you—"

"Let him rot. He's not going anywhere." He nuzzled her nose. Kate smiled, and her face flushed. His sparkling eyes, straight nose, and chiseled chin still frazzled her heart as if she were seeing them for the first time. Her heart ached as the wind blew through his dark, wild hair.

He carried Kate past the docks, into the village, and through the doors of the tavern. Cyril greeted them with a smile.

"Luca, what—"

"Not now. I haven't made love to this woman in far too long." He bounced up the stairs, a blushing Kate in his arms. Cyril chuckled and went about his work.

Luca set her down just inside the door, pressing her into the corner. His slender fingers traveled from her vibrant red waves to her smooth pale neck. They slipped under her collar, and pushed her violet traveling dress past the graceful curve of her shoulder.

Her lips ravished him. She tugged firmly, and bit his lower lip. The chink in his armor stung. She sought him out, her open mouth aching for a taste of him. He withdrew with a sharp movement, furrowing his brow at her. She stroked his face, and their eyes locked. Her deep brown irises gazed intently at him, licking the slim crack on his lip. His dreamy mind acquiesced, and he offered his mouth to her. His lust swelled as she drew from his eternal font. The gateway to his existence had lain open for scant seconds, but they would both remember the moment forever. They danced on a line that Luca had sworn he would not cross. And it felt right.

His caresses migrated to her throat. She laid her cheek in his loving hands as he sucked, summoning her blood just below the skin's surface and raking his fangs across her flesh. His right hand trailed down her body, grabbing her thigh and wrapping her leg around his waist, letting her feel the full weight of his excitement as he pushed her into the wall. Hopping into his arms, impatience overtook her. Luca spun around, and she landed on the mattress on her back, her mouth crashing hungrily into his.

In a single stroke they bared their bodies. Luca crouched between her legs, his broad shoulders rising and falling like a stalking panther. He lapped at her long-gone flesh just enough for her to cry out. Freeing himself from her desperate grasp on his hair, he rose, driving his burning erection through her. Their warm bodies reunited, and for just a moment, that was enough.

"I love you," he whispered, pressing his lips to her forehead as she buried her face in the familiar crook of his arm and dug her fingers in his back. He gripped her hip, and pushed himself deeper, senseless to all but the woman surrounding him.

THE TAVERN PATRONS BELOW THEM ERUPTED IN LAUGHTER AS DUST drifted down lazily from the ceiling, shaken from its mooring. It crescendoed when a beam buckled from the strain of the reunited couple's passions and snapped. A long table broke the fall, and both the beam and table lay together in a crumpled heap with crowded benches on either side. The guests cheered, clinking their drinks above the rubble and toasting to their queen in love.

"Ah, once again the world is as it should be," Cyril sighed.

LUCA GLISTENED WITH SWEAT, SHUDDERING WITH DIVINE EXERTION. Straining to catch her breath, Kate pulled on his neck, and drew him to her.

"Don't ever leave me again."

Luca rolled off her, spent. He shook his head, still lost to confusion.

"I don't know what's right anymore. Acting on my own was wrong. But you are in danger."

"I'm always in danger of something. But I won't risk losing you. Losing us."

"Your life is paramount. I will not allow him to take from me the only thing I've ever loved."

He felt a thread of anxiety slip through her. She inched closer to him between the sheets.

"Put me beyond his reach."

Luca's eyes watered as he stroked her face. "How can I make you something I hate? Something to be hunted?"

"Luca. How old are you?"

"Nearly eight thousand. And it all meant nothing compared to this past year. Nothing at all."

Kate ran her fingers through his silken tresses.

"Then let it go, and live with me, now."

HIS FEAR CHILLED HER. FEAR THAT IT WOULD CHANGE THEM IRREPARABLY. That she would regret it, and come to resent him. That she would blame him from pulling her away from her family. That his father's words, implanted in his brain, were but a confirmation of his suspicion.

"IF YOU LET YOUR FEAR COME BETWEEN US, THEN HE'S ALREADY WON. I will always want this. I will always want you," she pressed.

Luca considered, clinging to his love for her, and pushed his father's poison out of his mind. He let the burning desire she'd ignited with her bite be his only truth. "Even if I said yes, it wouldn't decrease the threat. He could still destroy you, still make you suffer. I don't want him to be the reason one way or the other."

She bit her lip. Luca's skin tingled.

"There's something else, isn't there?" he asked.

Kate spoke through her nerves. "I have to go to Veruna Lake. Do what you must here, but, if you're able, I need you to come with me."

"Why? What's in Veruna Lake?" Luca sensed she was being evasive.

"I heard from my nephew while I was away. He's nearly solved the puzzle I gave him."

"So?"

She sighed. "It's time."

His eyes narrowed.

"Time for me to grant his wish, and give him back his mother."

"Excuse me?"

"The Resurrection. It's time for me to cast it. I wasn't ready until now."

"That's why you came," he realized. The blood in his veins turned sour.

"It was a reason. But *don't* pretend it was the only one."

He blinked. "No."

"Luca, things were set in motion before I met you." Her calm façade cracked with her voice.

"I don't care," Luca insisted. "You started it, you can stop it."

She cast her eyes downward.

"But you *won't*, will you?"

Kate propped herself up on one elbow. "He's my brother. Before you, he was the only person who ever cared about me. He was my whole life. And I took everything from him," she sobbed.

"What was that you said, about letting it go?" he growled. Their bodies were no longer touching. He felt impossibly cold.

"I can't follow you and leave him alone. I can't."

Her happiness hinged on what he said next, and he knew it.

"I'll go alone if I have to," she said, "and you can do what you came here to do."

I don't want to go alone.

Luca exhaled. "Why Veruna Lake?"

"Because it's very far north, and it's already a snowy, icy place. The lake is near the top of the mountains. If there are side effects, which I suspect there will be, it won't affect the environment."

"Is there blood involved?"

"Not blood. This spell requires…it's my life. A set amount of my life."

Luca sat up, leaning his back against the wall as he pinched the top of his nose, trying to process what she'd just said. His heart screamed at him to forbid her. She didn't begrudge him the instinct, but he chose pragmatism. He was drowning in her guilt as he asked, "How much time?"

"Three hundred years."

He threw his arms around her waist. "Three hundred years! Kate, no! I've been living in hell here! I don't want to be without you another minute!"

Tears streamed down her face. "You think I want to cut three hundred years off my life, when I could be spending it with you? When I set my mind to this, I didn't think my life was worth what I was getting in return. And now it's tearing me apart." Her head fell onto his shoulder. He squeezed her.

"I'm begging you. Don't do this. I don't want to be alone anymore." He wept openly.

"Please, please think about this. About changing me. Then what I'm about to do won't mean anything to us."

"You can't promise that," he moaned, chest heaving.

Kate held her tongue, and let her own tears mingle with his.

As the sun drifted into slumber, the vampire lord stirred. Hanging from a hidden crevice in the ceiling, he stared upside down at the cave opening. The threshold had been made impenetrable, but he refused to let it debilitate him. Acting in the presence of the seal was somewhat like learning to breathe with a knife sticking out of his throat. He outstretched his leathery black wings, and let the orb he kept clutched to his stilled heart drop to the ground. He followed, unclenching his minute claws and landing upright. His boots pushed the mud surrounding the sphere into a mound, where the orb's weight settled into place. Undisturbed, Dracula opened his vein and drenched the orb in gore, his eyes gleaming a pure hot white as he watched it expand.

VERUNA LAKE WAS BEAUTIFUL. THE AIR WAS COLD AND CRISP, AND everything gave off an iridescent glow. It had snowed on the mountain that morning, covering the area in a light dusting of pure white powder.

The lake and the surrounding mountain peaks were populated by naiads, who were half-fish, half-men, the water nymphs, and the merfolk. They preferred the icy waters to warmer climates. Kate and Luca were welcomed into the village. Philip had dropped them off before flying back to Castelmor to attend to Cara, who was very near the end of her pregnancy, and still feeling the worse for it. Both Luca and Kate wore tired expressions, exhausted from the arguing and crying that had kept them up all night, and which had brought no resolution other than the one Kate reluctantly made for them both. Luca had left Dracula to suffer while hoping he still had time to deter Kate.

"Welcome, My Queen," said Glaucus, a naiad, who led the fatigued pair to their quarters. Glaucus was generously adorned with jewelry made from a variety of corals and shells that reflected prismatic colors off his shiny, pale blue scales. His long, white hair was partially braided, and embellished with bright colorful beads. Luca found the naiads fascinating. Or, he would have, if his mind were not fixated on more serious matters.

"Everything is as you requested," Glaucus said as he opened the door to her mountaintop abode. It was carved out of a recessed wall behind a waterfall, and appointed very sparsely. Kate did not come here often. The bed was wider than the one in the cottage, and was covered in thick blankets to keep out the cold misty air.

"Everyone's been cleared out of the northeastern corridor. No one will go in or out of the pass until you give the word," Glaucus said.

Kate thanked Glaucus as he left the couple alone in their silence. She laid on top of the bed on her back, and tried to close her eyes. Luca stood at the foot of the bed.

"We can still turn back, you know. Just turn around and go home," Luca pleaded, standing at the foot of the bed.

Kate breathed deeply, but said nothing. Luca sat down, feeling defeated, helpless to stop Kate from doing what he dreaded.

"I wish I could do this for you. Those kinds of magical costs wouldn't affect me the same way."

Kate's eyes snapped open, clear and sharp. She sat up quickly.

"You can't do it for me. But you can do it with me." Her brain's synapses were firing at lightning speed, hatching a plan that just might be suitable to both of them.

"What do you mean?" Luca asked. The pace of her heartrate was enough to choke him.

"When that purple mist invaded me back in the cave, you knocked it out. Negated its effects. Could you do that again?"

"Of course I could. What are you getting at?"

"If you cast the spell with me, and focus your regenerative energy on me, it could minimize the amount of life that's taken."

Luca perked at the prospect of being able to save her from making a huge sacrifice. "By how much?"

Kate shrugged. "I don't know if I'd ever be able to figure that out. But it might be worth a try."

He touched his knuckles to her cheek. "If it only gave us one more second, it would be worth it. I'll do my very best."

Finally, they had come to an agreement, and Kate's restless heart was grateful.

"Thank you."

Their lips met for the first time in several hours. It was a sweet reunion.

Kate told Luca everything. What she was planning, how the spell worked, what she needed to do, and what he could do to assist.

While he didn't like the choice he was given, Luca respected her decision and was glad that she was allowing him to participate. They spent the rest of the afternoon catching up on some much-needed sleep.

Luca had never been so cold. Naked under the thick skin of a stag, his muscles shook with exertion. Profuse sweat was wicked away into the coarse hairs dancing wildly in a bitter wind. The frosty air bit at the exposed tips of his ears. The heavy cotton wrapped around the lower half of his face was damp with his own labored breath. He dug his feet into the mountainside, the tightly packed snow nearly reaching his knee. His limbs felt languid and rubbery as he followed Kate up the side of a rock ridge stretching fifty feet high. Sliding down the smooth back of the crest, their momentum slowed as they arrived at a low-lying plateau, broad enough for a small camp before rising into the next ridge. Kate stood, shaking the loose snow from her legs before pulling away the layer of cloth covering her mouth. Her breath released thick, white puffs into the frigid, still air. She pointed at the sky.

"The peaks will carry the wind above us," she panted. "We'll be warm here."

The eyes peering out of Luca's face covering were vicious.

"Well, *warmer.*"

A barren tree sprawled to the heavens at the edge of the flatland. Luca snapped a few long branches from the top, breaking them in half and setting them in a pile, while Kate flung a heavy leather skin on a thicker protruding limb, and tucked the corners of the tent under heavy pack-snow. She unrolled the furs strapped to her back and laid them out under the skin's protection. Luca was still working on getting a fire started as she sat in the white powder beside him.

"Shit," he muttered, his bare fingers turned clumsy as they numbed to the cold. Kate picked up a wet twig by her leg and tossed it. By the time it hit the pile, the whole collection of wood was blazing.

"Come on," Luca said, his voice gruff. "Just because we're doing this doesn't mean you can be careless. Conserve your energy."

"Sorry." Her face glowed, highlighting the debilitating sorrow that suffocated her spirit. Luca put his arm around her. He reached with his free hand for the crest she had lent him, but she waved it away, refusing its return.

"It's yours now. Wherever you go, all that is mine will be yours. I just haven't quite sorted out your title yet. I don't suppose you have a preference?"

Kate's offer was an unexpected one. One word *did* come to mind, but he obscured it from her mind. He knew that her gesture was more than that—it was a step forward, a commitment that blended her person and her position. But he didn't want a response to tip his hand.

His own thoughts were distracted by Kate's mounting nerves. She answered a question he never asked.

"I don't know what to expect. Ever since my fight with that shadow, I've felt so...balanced. My senses are sharper—*all* of them. It was the first time in my life, I think, that I used my ability with good reason, and felt *good* afterward. Better than good. It was perfect." She pursed her lips. "I'm afraid I may never feel that clean again. Last time I cast this spell was...unbearable."

"*Last* time??"

Kate stared at the cloudless sky, turning from a bleak gray to absolute black. "I did this once before. For Corbin."

He turned to face her.

"Before he could talk, he was just one more rat flooding the streets of London, keeping one twelve-year-old girl company," she said, pointing at herself. "He was my only friend, especially when Allistair was away. I was on my way home, and a bunch of older boys were harassing me. Corbin was hiding in my coat sleeve, so when one of them tried to twist my arm, Corbin bit him. He got tossed into the street, and a passing coach split him in half. I cried my eyes out. Much later, when I first approached Drigory about this spell, he explained that I could only cast it once for a single being, whether I succeeded or not. He suggested trying an animal for a test run. Corbin was the first thing that popped into my head."

She huddled closer to him, increasing his sense of her anxiety. "He meant to scare me off it. He seemed perfectly shocked when I actually did it. But reliving Corbin's death hurt just as much as it did the first time. And I noticed things. Differences. Maybe they were insignificant, but...I'm afraid I'll get stuck when I'm looking for Cyrene. That I won't be able to find my way back to you."

"I'll be with you the whole way." He pressed his lips to her hair, damp with snow. Her mouth searched for his, her fingers tugged on his neck, pulling him onto her. They pressed their bare forms together, blocking out the biting cold. Sweat dripped from Luca's brow as he pushed into her. The heat radiating from the furs and their lovemaking turned the air stifling.

When he collapsed on top of her, he felt the moisture of tears chill his shoulder. She wrapped her arms around him, gripping him.

"Don't let go." Her voice shook, barely above a whisper. "When I'm gone, you'll love someone else, won't you? Then another, and another. One day you'll decide to keep another woman with you, and you'll forget I ever existed," she sobbed.

Her question tortured Luca's soul, and formed a knot in his own stomach. Her vulnerability in that moment broke his heart.

No, my love. My heart will always belong to you. Only you.

He cradled her head in the crook of his neck, never breaking their embrace as he rolled off her and pulled the furs over their shoulders as they settled into sleep.

16

THE STARK GLARE OF THE SUN ROUSED THEM EARLY. LUCA TENDED TO THE fire after consuming cured meat and a heavy bread for breakfast. Kate set to work forming long narrow mounds in the snow, embedding a small bundle at the head of each mound. When she was finished, their camp resembled an arctic graveyard. There were four full-length mounds, and an equal number only half the length of a man.

"Do you need all those?" Luca asked.

Kate licked her lips. "I do if I'm going to fetch Hercules's family."

He stared in disbelief. He opened his mouth to protest, then closed it just as quickly. The look in his lover's eyes was earnest. For as close a friend as Hercules was, he understood why she would want this. He stepped nearer to her, stroking her windblown hair.

"Always thinking of somebody else," he said.

"I won't if you don't want me to," she answered. "That's why the price is so high. The jerk had to go and have *four* kids," she chuckled grimly, her breath a series of small white clouds puffing in quick time.

Luca remained silent.

"I do think of other people," she answered, "but none more than you. Your call."

He sighed, warming Kate's heart as he gushed at her gesture. "If we're going to do this," he shrugged, "we should do it right."

They waited until the sun dipped below the horizon. Luca drank from her neck to ensure his powers were at their height before they walked to the two leftmost mounds in their snow-capped cemetery, and laid themselves in the cold. Their bodies sank into the graves, their fingers folded together. Kate stared up at the stars, concentrating on the wind howling in her ears until it was deafening, and its source seemed internal. The powder surrounding them drifted upward into the northern airstream, blinding Kate, and sealing her into her frozen tomb as her mind slid backward, unraveling the fabric of her life.

LUCA TOOK UP RESIDENCE IN KATE'S MIND AS TIME UNWOUND. LIGHT began to fill the edges of all-consuming darkness. Kate heard dead grass crunch under her boots. Conversation had slowed. The band she led was tired, and hungry, and moody. Luca sensed Kate was ill at ease. He was aware of a deep sadness—lonely and undeserving. He knew that feeling well. Falling behind, Kate's skin tingled, warning of the presence behind her. She looked over her shoulder and saw the familiar, long-absent face of the last reigning queen.

"Meryn?"

The woman was gone before Kate could blink. Kate spun around, looking for any sign of her. In the distance, the hill rose into a line of trees. Kate spied Meryn's shadow pacing, eyes trained on her. She was waiting.

Kate walked uphill at a brisk pace. Shielding her eyes from the sun, Kate noticed a trail of dried blood in the grass, leading to where she was headed. She walked even faster.

Meryn's face came into view. But when Kate reached the hill's summit, Meryn was gone. The soil was disturbed, bloody. Two feet ahead of her, a hat lay in the dirt, seemingly worn by a shadow. Kate took a cautious step forward. The dark figure under the hat moaned softly as she neared. She crouched down, and lifted the brim. There was the most beautiful face she had ever seen. He seemed restless, delirious. He licked his lips. The man was trapped in the dirt. She woke him gently. When his gaze settled on her, she entirely forgot entirely the reason she'd come up there.

KATE PULLED HERSELF AWAY FROM THE MEMORY. A DULL CRACKLING TOOK root in her ear as she forged a path further back.

"YOU LIED TO ME. YOU SAID THERE WASN'T A SPELL THAT COULD BRING her back!" Kate cried.

"Some things are set in stone, My Queen," Drigory answered.

"No. It's in here, I saw it," she said, flipping through the tome she had slammed on the desk. "The Resurrection. What is that?"

Drigory shook his head. "No."

"No, what? No it doesn't work or no you won't help me?"

"That goes *beyond* magic, Katelyn. Even yours."

"What is it then?" she cried.

"*Necromancy!*"

"I don't care what you call it. He's my brother, you understand? My flesh and blood! I can't...I can't..." she gripped a nearby chair, and sobbed. Drigory was moved. "He's dead without her. *I'm dead* without him," she murmured.

The troll grimaced. "You won't succeed like this," he replied. "You have to calm yourself. You'll only get one shot, and it may cost you your life."

"I'll pay the price."

"First, try something with lower stakes. An old pet, maybe?"

KATE CAUGHT HERSELF BEFORE FALLING AGAIN INTO THE DAY CORBIN HAD died, swallowing her pain and leaving the memories untouched as she sought the one she needed. The crackling in her ears increased as her mind shifted again.

KATE WAS INTANGIBLE. HER FORM WAS DISPERSED IN THE AIR, CARRIED BY the wind. It made Luca's head swim. The only sharp thing he could bring into focus was Kate's sense of longing, her homesickness. The skyline was one Luca had never seen.

Kate was eavesdropping on a conversation between two men dressed in finery.

"She's become unmanageable. If she won't sell us land, we'll just take it."

"You'll provoke a war," the other countered.

"A war with farmers is no war at all," the first man chuckled. "Tell the men to gear up. The wealth of the world is waiting for them."

Drifting on a balmy breeze, Kate materialized at a street corner of the foreign city. Spires and domes plated in bronze poked at the heavens. Rows of white plaster homes were illuminated by countless oil lamps lining the streets, made of a mirror-like surface that reflected the night sky.

Her mind was an utter blank as she dipped her finger in the oil fountain. The blaze soared to the clouds. She let the blaze consume her. *Become* her. The bronze pedestal toppled over, unable to contain Kate's inferno and spilling it into the street. She focused her rage, finding the nearest open flame, then the next, and the next, until the screams of the entire city split the night's calm. When next Kate opened her eyes, she was back where she had started. The fire she'd left behind consumed everything in its path, and refused to be abated. She turned to leave.

"Wait!"

A little boy in rags ran up to her.

"Please help me! My house is on fire. My parents are inside! Please, you have to help me!"

She turned again to leave, but the boy was insistent. He raced after her and tugged on her leg.

"No, please don't—"

His voice was silenced in his throat. The moment his fingers touched her garments, he had frozen in place. Startled, Kate sprang back. They icy statue toppled to the ground and shattered into a million bloody pieces. She stood dumbstruck, staring at the icy mess, and listening to the city's wails.

Somewhere in her brain, a broken chain recoupled itself, her thoughts awakening as she stared into the chaos. The reflection in the street saw her eyes darken from an icy void to a familiar brown. She ducked into an alley and retched.

The snapping and hissing of fire in Kate's ear swelled as she pulled away again. Her sorrow was strong here. She would be trapped by it if she held the thought any longer.

～

KATE STARED AT HER FACE IN THE MIRROR. THOUGH THE BRUISES ON HER neck had long faded, she still felt their tenderness. Her legs ached, her head burned. She closed her eyes, wishing for a strong pair of hands around her throat.

Luca felt her flinch, and turn away quickly.

～

SHE WAS CORNERED IN A BARN. THE FIRST TWO SHE KILLED EASILY, BUT the third attacker sliced open her leg. She crumpled to the ground, bleeding into the straw. The fourth man dug his fist into her wound, forcing a scream.

"Treatment fit for a queen who pretends she's a warrior."

"No, no, this is where she belongs. In the dirt, on her back."

Kate heard the fourth man unbuckle his belt, but the sound of the cheap metal rasping against itself was drowned out by the buzzing in her ear. She closed her eyes, and gave in to the incessant hum. She felt her face getting hot.

"What the fuck?" the man screamed.

The dried straw beneath her burst into flames. The man's clothes caught fire first, then his flesh. Kate's eyes peeled open at the smell of searing meat, the inhuman screams. The other man turned on his heels, but Kate lunged at him. They crashed to the ground, just as the straw around them ignited. The man beneath her was reduced to ashes. She stood, and stared at her hands. They were on fire. The flames licked at her clothes and the tips of her hair. But they did not burn. She was surrounded by a heat thick with her rage. Something inside her mind came unhinged. She laughed.

THE MEMORY FAILED TO EVOKE A REACTION. LUCA FOUND IT UNSETTLING. It was simply acceptance, a cold reconciliation with reality. Neither frightened nor ashamed, Kate pulled away again, turning her attention again to the crackling in her ear. Her unease grew as she seemed to realize where her memory was settling next.

SHE WAS WALKING THROUGH A MEADOW AT NIGHT, TALKING TO HERSELF. Practicing.

"I'm sorry for how I acted. I still want to be with you. Nothing else matters. Ugh, that hurts so much when I say it out loud."

Her heart thumped harder as she approached a small cottage. The window was open, the sounds of the lovemaking couple inside escaping into the night air. Kate stopped dead in her tracks. She heard Lilla's lusty voice, exhausted.

"Still thinking about Kate?"

"Who?" Julian asked, his voice delirious.

Lilla laughed. "She couldn't love you like I do. You know that, right?"

"Her, *love*? Honestly, I don't think she's capable."

Kate had to remind herself to breathe as she shuffled homeward. But it was hard. Impossible, even as she collapsed in the grass and covered her face to silence her sobs. She pulled at the medallion around her neck. It felt hot and heavy, like it had just been plucked from the forge.

The center stone glowed brilliantly. She closed her eyes, surrendering all other senses to that incessant buzzing sound. The darkest part of her soul made a wish.

The stars winked out. The sky turned black. The breeze died, catching every blade of grass unawares as they bent toward the ground in an unnatural stillness. Kate felt a deep chill from the inside out, churning at her guts. Her forehead touched the stiffened grass at her feet, and she held her breath.

The world was no more.

Seconds passed into the void. Or millenniums. At last Kate breathed, giving the meadow life again. She looked up, spying the clouds wafting away from the moons, refusing to hide them any longer. The medallion hanging from her neck went dark. She got to her feet, and resumed walking.

KATE FELT THE HEAT OF FLAMES SNAPPING IN HER EAR AS SHE PUSHED further back still, not having found her destination. When she felt the next wave rising, she resisted. This one she wanted to pass over. But the memory drew her nearer—the spell demanded it, and she submitted.

KATE LAY STRETCHED OUT ON HER BED, PUSHED AGAINST THE WALL OF A shabbily lit room. The flickering of the light gave her a pounding headache as she strained to read. A toddler played on the floor, banging his wooden toy against the warped hardwood.

"Teddy, stop that!" she cried. He resumed rolling his little car along the floor as before, blowing raspberries as she settled back into a comfortable position. She extended her legs, which nearly reached the edge of her childhood bed now. But asking for a new one was useless, and might lead to nothing more than a sound lashing for ingratitude. She fixed her plain dress. Her breasts had already begun to swell, her hair flowing free between them as she rested her head once more on the pillow. She became engrossed again by the tale she was reading.

Luca could see the scene playing out as she imagined it, could feel Kate's exhilaration as the protagonist came ready for the first of three duels scheduled that day, only to see all three challengers appear at once. Her imagination was pulled back out of the book and toward the sound of someone entering their tiny apartment with lively steps. She sat up, resting the book on its face. Her elder brother appeared in the door, a knapsack slung over his shoulder.

"Al!" she shouted, jumping into his arms.

"Katie, Kate, I've missed you darling!" Allistair cried, swinging his sister around in his arms.

"I expected you hours ago. What kept you?" she asked.

"I missed my train," he explained, reaching into his bag. "Stopped to pick up this." He held a volume to his chest, the latest installment of a story both siblings were eager to see the conclusion of. Allistair's eyes were alight with intrigue.

"The boot returns!"

"No!" she cried. "How?"

"A simple deduction of the facts, my dear," Allistair replied, putting on airs.

She squeezed her brother around his middle. "I missed you, Ally."

He kissed the top of her head. "Missed you too, love. Class is so boring. The professors prattle on, and we all sit there like statues," Allistair said, resting himself on his bed on the opposite wall, "scribbling furiously not to miss a single word from those hallowed, decrepit lips. Hello Teddy! My, you are looking fatter than when I saw you last!"

The little boy crept up into Allistair's lap and bounced on his knee.

"That still beats playing housemaid around here," Kate complained. "What are you learning now?" she asked, rifling through his bag.

"Sing, O goddess, the rage of Achilles," he answered plaintively.

"It doesn't interest you?"

"It does. But what interests me more are the practical courses. I promised to get you out of here," he answered in a low voice. "That means I will." They exchanged somber glances, stifling their conversation as they heard the key in the lock.

"Where's my boy?!" a loud voice boomed through the small apartment.

"Here, Father!"

"Get up, let me look at ya!" A tall, wiry man entered the room. His gait was unsteady, and his breath already stank of ale. The stench had been a permanent fixture this past year.

"How's school, my boy?"

Allistair answered with reserve. "Fine, sir."

"Good, good!" their father said, patting Allistair hard on the shoulder. "Soon you'll be in charge of taking care of *me*."

"Yes, sir."

"Dinner ready yet, mum?" he turned to Kate.

"Nearly," she said.

He slapped her across the face. "You're charged with one thing around here so's I don't kick you out to fend fer yerself. And alls you can say is *nearly*?"

"It's more than one thing."

"Don't," Allistair whispered.

"Don't what?" their father cried. "Let the lady speak if she wants. Maybe one day her smart mouf will catch up wif her." He leaned toward Kate menacingly. His breath in her face was unbearable.

In the presence of her brother, she stood her ground.

"Your shirts are clean. The dishes are clean. The *floors* are clean. Your pants are mended. The food is bought. And then there's Theodore. He's become quite the handful."

"Has he now?"

"Yes."

"Well, I'll fix 'im then." He knocked the boy out of Allistair's arms, sending him crashing to the floor. The child screamed, holding his head. Kate scooped him up, enraged.

"He's a baby, you fool!"

"You want some more?"

"No, sir, please!" Allistair interjected.

The man their mother had married was counseled by the one source of pride in his life. He turned his back to Kate.

"You're lucky he loves ya," he sneered. "Can't imagine why. Get back to work." The ogre left the room and sat at the kitchen table, counting the minutes until supper was in his mouth. Kate held Ted close and hushed him.

"Are you all right?" Allistair asked, rubbing Kate's cheek.

"That's nothing," she replied.

"I know love, I know. I'm supposed to be meeting some friends for drinks tonight. Why don't you come with us?"

"I can't, Al."

"Why not?"

"What about Teddy?"

Allistair sighed. "Oh, come on. I've been showing your picture around school, you know. My mates, they want to meet you."

"I've asked you not to do that!" she protested. "I don't like being set up with strangers!"

"They're not strangers, they're my friends. I trust them. Kate, you're growing into your looks. You must know that."

She turned her head to the side, blushing. Allistair inched closer.

"It may be your salvation."

"What? To go from serving an old man to a young one?" she cried.

"Clive's not like that. He's a progressive thinker. Like you."

"Who's Clive?"

Allistair shrugged. "A friend. He asks about you more than the rest. He wants to be a surgeon."

"How nice for him," Kate replied.

At the corner of her mind, Luca couldn't help but smile.

Allistair sat on the bed next to his sister. "You know, this was his idea."

"What was?"

"He begged me to get you to come out. He was pretty pathetic, really."

Kate turned her face away from him, smiling in spite of herself. She was flattered. Allistair elbowed her.

"Come on, give the bloke the thrill of his life. He just wants to meet you, buy you a drink."

Kate tapped her foot. "Is he tall?"

"Yes," Allistair chuckled. "He's tall."

"Taller than me? I can't date a runt."

"Taller than you, yes, by at least a head. Tall, dark, and handsome, just the way you like them."

"Don't joke. Is he smart? Does he read?"

"Uh-huh. I caught him reading *The Man in the Iron Mask* just last week."

Kate turned to her abandoned adventure on the bed. "I'm not quite that far yet," she ruminated. She took a deep breath. "Alright, fine. But just a drink, I make no promises."

"Can I be the one to give you away?" he teased.

"Oh, come off it. Dinner's waiting."

"Waiting? But you said…"

"So I did."

KATE PREPARED TO GO OUT AFTER SUPPER, EXAMINING HER FACE IN A small dingy mirror set on a hook on the wall. The paint on the wall was peeling away, loosening the nail that held the hook in place. The mirror sat askance, and could not be righted for the world. Kate stared at herself in the glass, anxious, but hopeful. She left her glasses at home.

Allistair was right. Clive was tall, dark, and handsome. Kate liked him very much. They flirted the night away, one round after another, ignoring the rest of the table at the local pub. Clive spoke softly in her ear, away from the clanking, swearing din of the other patrons. Finally, Allistair called an end to the evening's festivities. Clive backed her into a corner to bid her farewell.

"I really enjoyed getting to know you," he said in a low voice. He leaned against the wall, and against Kate. Her heart pounded in her chest.

"Me too."

"Have lunch with me tomorrow?"

Kate hesitated. "I don't know," she grinned. The blood in her cheeks flashed hotter every time her eyes caught his.

She didn't recognize the jealousy flaring at the back of her mind. Luca could tell where this was leading.

Clive insisted.

"Say yes. Please. I'll die if I can't see you tomorrow."

She laughed. "Don't be so dramatic."

"Well?"

She clucked her tongue. "One o'clock?"

His eyes brightened. "It be twenty years 'til then."

She flushed again. This time, when his eyes sought hers, she was bold enough to hold his gaze. He wrapped his arm around her slender waist, and kissed her. Her heart raced as his tongue slid across her lips, and she grasped the back of his neck. He pulled her closer.

"Oh-kay, that's quite enough." Allistair pried his sister away.

"Goodnight," she whispered. She held onto Clive's fingers until the last moment.

She was creeping into her nightgown, with Ted curled asleep on Allistair's bed, when her stepfather stumbled into the room. Her dreamy expression soured.

"Allistair stepped out," she informed him. "He'll be back in a minute."

The man's eyes narrowed. "Yer not a little girl anymore, are ya?"

Kate brought her hands slowly to her side. A sinking feeling took hold of her stomach.

He lumbered toward her, his dead weight sending her falling backward onto her own bed.

"Get off me! I'm your daughter, you drunken sot!" She pushed back at him, but it was no use.

He looked her dead in the eyes. "I don't believe that. I don't think you do, either."

She sneered at him. He pushed back the skirt of her dress. Her legs shrunk away from him.

"Stop."

"I say, your skin's jus' as cold as yer attitude. 'Art of ice, you've got."

Kate became increasingly aware of a buzzing in her ear, like the crackle of a nascent fire. It swiftly overtook all her other senses.

"I said stop!"

They struggled, and she screamed. Ted woke up crying.

Allistair came home in the nick of time. He grabbed his father from behind, spun him round, and punched him squarely in the jaw. The man stumbled back, knocking the mirror off the wall and shattering it. Kate backed away from it all. She tucked up her knees and pressed her back against the wall.

Allistair was panting, his heart pounding in his chest. Their stepfather lay unconscious on the floor.

"Are you all right?" her brother asked, breathless. Kate leapt into his arms. He soothed her, holding her head in his hands. "Shh, shh, I'm here. I'll always protect you, Katelyn, no matter what, okay?"

"Okay."

"Get Teddy. We're leaving."

Kate grabbed what few small possessions she had. She wrapped her plaid blue scarf around her neck, the only clue she had to her true father.

Luca sensed hope fill Kate's heart as she donned it.

She hoisted Ted onto her hip. He rubbed the sleep out of his eyes.

"Where are we going?" he asked in a small voice.

"Somewhere safe, Teddy. Come on." She turned to Allistair, who had a strange look in his eyes. She'd never seen him like that before. It scared her.

"Al?" She noticed the mirror shard in his hand. He looked down at his stepfather. The man he thought was his father.

"I won't let him touch you again," Allistair said, his voice cold. "Never again." He looked up at Kate.

She didn't know what to say. She took Ted out of the room, and waited for her brother on the steps of their apartment. He came out wearing a different shirt under his coat. He put his arm around Kate, and pressed his siblings' heads to his own.

"It's just us now."

"I love you, Ally," she whispered.

"Love you too. Let's go."

She sighed, feeling her heart sink. Forgive me, Clive.

When they reached the train station, they stared at the long list of destinations spread across Britain.

"Where should we go?" Allistair asked. "Mother had some family in Manchester, didn't she? I can't remember."

Ted tugged on Kate's scarf. The buzzing in her ears was back. When it became too loud to bear, it ceased altogether, along with the chatter of the passengers, the screaming engines, and the clicking of the tickertape. The world went silent. Kate felt someone approach her from behind. A familiar brogue whispered in her ear.

"Time to come home, lass."

She looked up at the board. One location seemed brighter than the rest. As she stared, the sign fell away, leaving just that word flashing white. Her path was marked before her.

"Where to?" the man behind the ticket booth asked.

Kate turned her head in the direction of the booth. The world was as it should be. She looked over her shoulder, the way she did every time she had a sense of someone behind her. It was a frequent thing. But as usual, there was nothing, or rather no one, there.

"Well?" the teller asked again.

Kate reached into her brother's coat pocket and laid a wad of cash on the counter.

"Edinburgh."

Kate.

Kate heard her name being called, but couldn't tell if the sound came from inside her head or without.

Kate.

The echo grew fainter, then disappeared. The next sound, coupled with a strong nudge of her elbow, woke her with a shock.

"Katelyn? Wake up, darlin'."

Her whole body shook as she was dragged suddenly into consciousness. Her spinning vision settled on a wooden table. She was seated on a matching bench. She gripped the edge of the knotted wood to stop herself from falling into the grass. Gloomy clouds conspired overhead, and tiny droplets of rain stained the table's unpolished surface. She slammed her eyes shut.

There was something important at the edge of her memory. She knew it. But she couldn't recall it. Her mind was in chaos. Nothing she saw connected to what she was doing. What was she doing? What had she been thinking of?

A wave of nausea pulsed through her. She looked up at the freckled face of a middle-aged woman with bouncing red curls. She was totally unfamiliar. The woman held an oversized basket of laundry at her hips.

"Come now, yer brother'll have ma hide if I let you nod off in the rain."

The woman grabbed Kate's arm and pulled her to her feet. Kate touched her chest, reaching instinctively for she knew not what. Her fingers met only her plain, dampening dress.

Kate.

Her hair stood on end, and she spun around. She had been staring at the woman's face— When she'd heard her name, the woman's lips had not moved. But she was the only one around.

I'm right here.

"Where?" she asked aloud.

"What?" the woman looked as confused as Kate. "Where's what, darlin'? Come inside now, before ya catch yer death!"

Kate remained silent as she was shuffled up the stairs of a humble stone cottage and shown into a small but neat guestroom. It was modestly appointed, with fresh sheets and a homemade quilt on the narrow bed. Across from the foot of the bed was a worn burgundy rug, and a lattice window set into the slanting ceiling, overlooking a meadow that stretched into a thick treeline. In the left-hand corner of the room was an empty set of drawers, a wardrobe, and a free-standing mirror.

It's not safe for me in the sun.

The voice she heard was much deeper than the woman's. It was distinctively masculine. It was smooth, and melodic, and strangely familiar, more familiar than the woman guiding her. And seductive. Oh, so seductive.

"Are ya needin' anything, miss?" the lady of the house asked.

"No, thank you," Kate answered, ignoring the noise in her head for the moment.

"All right then, supper's at eight. I'm sure yer brother wull be back by then."

Kate nodded and managed a polite smile as the woman closed the door. She sat on the bed, her mind still reeling from being shocked awake. She couldn't grasp what had been running through her mind only seconds before, but she intuited its overwhelming importance. She'd been at the crux of...something, and she'd been interrupted.

Can you hear me?

"Oh, I hear you," she finally answered. "Who are you?"

17

WHO AM I? OH NO.

"Who are you and how did you get inside my head?" she insisted. Her voice trembled as she spoke. The interloper's voice belied a level of maturity that intimidated her.

You invited me. Don't be afraid.

"How can you say don't be afraid?" She spoke in hushed tones in the confines of her room. "I'm hallucinating."

I am not a hallucination.

"Says the voice in my head. That makes me feel so much better."

Luca remained silent, but he smirked.

"This is *not* funny," she said.

Her reply gave Luca pause. *How did you know I was smiling?*

"I don't know *how* I knew. I just did."

That's something.

Luca wanted to be considerate of Kate's tender age, but he had to push her. *Kate, you need to remember, fast.*

"Remember what?"

Who I am. Who you are.

Kate put her hand to her brow. This pseudo-telepathy was giving her an intolerable headache, and she struggled to understand.

"Does this have anything to do with what I was dreaming just now?" she asked on a lark.

It wasn't a dream.

"Kate, can I come in?"

Her brother was just outside the door. He rapped, but didn't wait for an answer before turning the knob. Luca spoke quickly before losing Kate's attention.

It wasn't a dream Kate, he repeated. This *is the dream. It isn't real. Wake up so you can come home. I need you.*

The desperation in the strange voice strained at her heart as her brother entered her room, with Clive at his side. Rainwater dripped from their coats. Clive blew past his friend and bounded toward Kate, arms wide open.

Kate took a cautious step back, but he outstripped her immediately, pulling her to his chest and cradling the back of her head.

"Thank God you're all right," he whispered in her ear.

Kate was nearly brought to her knees by the fire that raged inside her. She couldn't think, couldn't speak, as if the entire world had fallen on top of her. Suffocated with a furious yet tender passion, she didn't know if her immeasurable pain truly belonged to her. It made no difference. She shared in the suffering of the intangible voice, definable by a single word: heartbreak.

Kate moved to escape Clive's grasp. When he moved his mouth closer to hers, she turned away from him. As he withdrew, Kate caught a glimpse of devastation in his eyes. She was keenly aware that, only two days earlier, the man she pushed away had held a great attraction.

Clive was a true gentleman, and recovered from Kate's cold reception with a polite smile.

"I'm so sorry, I didn't mean to startle you, especially after what you've been through." He held his open palms defensively in front of him. "I'm just so glad you're safe." Clive cleared his throat.

Allistair attempted to diffuse the awkwardness. He held out a paper shopping bag. "Looks like you didn't escape the storm either," he said to his sister. "Here, some clean clothes. Compliments of Clive."

"Oh, it's nothing really," Clive said. He ran a hand through his hair. "They're nothing special, but they'll do in a pinch."

"Thank you," Kate said.

The chill in her voice washed over Luca like a salve.

"Mrs. MacLeay has a piping hot dinner downstairs. Join us when you're ready," Allistair said.

Kate stared queerly at her brother, cocking her head to one side.

"Are you all right?" she asked.

"Me? *You're* the one who's not yourself. MacLeay must've given you quite the fright, knocking you out of deep sleep like that."

"Yes, but..." She inched closer to her brother and peered at him through narrowed eyes. "You look...younger."

There was a faint sound of crackling in her ear, akin to the blistering of a log-fed fire. Barely audible, yet unmistakably present.

"Younger?" Allistair laughed. "We only get older as time goes on, darling. Change into something dry. We'll see you downstairs."

THE VOICE IN KATE'S HEAD HAD NOTHING TO SAY AT THE MOMENT. Though he seemed relieved that they were alone again. Kate didn't know what to do, other than accept her brother's invitation. She was hungry. And wet. She opened the bag her brother had left her, choosing not to rifle through it and instead selecting the clothes at the top of the small collection. She went to lift the shirt she was wearing over her head, then stopped. She remembered that she wasn't alone.

"Is it possible for you to look away? Close your eyes, or, something?" She felt stupid the moment the request left her lips, for she knew she had no way to tell if he'd honor it.

Yes...

She sensed her mind's visitor hesitate.

"But?" she asked.

I don't want to upset you.

Even the consideration, the gentle affection of the voice between her ears, attracted her to him, drawing her closer, even though her instincts told her to stop nurturing her newfound madness.

Luca wanted to say something, but he feared a misstep. He felt as if every word mattered, every utterance required careful choice.

Kate took a deep breath, and pretended to be brave. "What?"

Her query was met with silence. Then,

I know every curve. Every sweet, perfect inch.

Her skin bristled with a sense of arousal her young body did not know. After several deep breaths, she lifted her shirt over her head, with the full understanding that she was being watched.

Every muscle ached with longing as she faced the mirror, her upper body bare. Her skin was flawless porcelain. Her bosom heaved in time with her wildly beating heart. Breasts that had not yet reached their zenith swelled, attentive. An errant curl caressed her collarbone. She pressed her eyelids together, and let a gasp escape her dry lips as the sense of her unseen companion culminated behind her. She inhaled sharply at the feel of slender fingers grazing the skin below her navel, interlocking with her own hand. She could almost feel his warm breath on her neck. Her head craned backward. She imagined it was supported by a broad, inviting chest.

You are as irresistible now as ever.

"Kate, are you coming down?" her brother cried out from beyond the door, snapping her out of her haze.

"I'll be down when I'm goddamned ready!" she barked.

"O-*kay* okay! Excuse *me*," he retorted, and stamped back down the stairs.

Kate turned to the mirror again, pressing her palms to her cheeks to diffuse the flames blooming under her skin. Her eyes were wild.

"I'm absolutely insane," she chided.

18

KATE JOINED HER BROTHER AND HIS FRIEND AT A ROUND, LACE-COVERED table in a crowded dining hall. The wallpaper was peeled and yellowed, the floorboards reeked of liquor.

"Feeling better?" Clive asked, the hope in his voice painfully obvious.

Kate avoided his gaze. She felt only sympathy for him now, for her soul had been stirred by a powerful, intimate force. Even one without a face.

"I fear I am not quite myself," she said by way of apology.

That's an understatement.

Kate didn't offer a response, not even a silent one. Her heart still quaked from their exchange, and she tried to focus on people she could see.

"Here, eat something. It'll get your spirits back up," Allistair said, pushing a bowl in front of her. "Teddy's in my room. I'll take care of him tonight so you can rest easy."

"He's a grown man, he can take care of himself," Kate answered, distracted.

Allistair and Clive laughed nervously.

"What are you saying?" Allistair asked. "He's three, he's not a grown anything."

Kate looked up from her meal, confused. "I don't know. Nothing, never mind." She remained silent for the better part of supper. Her interloper was quiet. Present, observant, ever mindful of her sensitive disposition, but quiet. She appreciated the opportunity to collect her own thoughts as she only dimly listened to the conversation.

The stillness of her mind brought much-needed calm to her wearied nerves. Brooding set her mind unknowingly into familiar grooves.

The men exchanged glances, confounded by Kate's erratic behavior. Allistair attempted to steer the conversation toward Clive in a ploy to spark Kate's interest.

"How's your father getting on in his new position?" he asked.

"He's settling into it quite well. Being the queen's surgeon has freed up his time," Clive said. "Without having to see other patients, he's considering taking over a few lectures to fill his days. If he can hold down the fort long enough, I hope to fill the void when he's ready to retire."

"That would be a nice setup," Allistair replied, raising his voice.

Kate was unresponsive. She stared out the window against the far wall as she slowly but surely emptied the bowl in front of her. The blur of a woman with dark auburn hair stood at the summit of a distant ridge, hands on her hips. Impatient. She was too far away to be sure, but Kate had the distinct impression the woman was staring right back at her.

Allistair leaned his elbows on the table.

"I say, Kate, isn't that nice, the queen's surgeon?"

"Yes, I heard," Kate answered, impatient to return to her own devices. "If you want a surgeon, Allistair, get one. I made you king so you wouldn't have to run every little decision by me, yeah?"

Laughter rang inside her head, reverberating off her skull. That's my girl.

Allistair and Clive stared wide-eyed, their utensils and bits of rustic bread poised midair over their hunter's stew.

"What *are* you talking about?" Allistair shouted.

Kate stared at her brother, his confusion contagious. The room was suddenly too hot for her. Her head tingled and she pitched forward, almost crashing into the table before Allistair caught her in his arms.

"I've got you!" he cried.

For an instant, Kate felt a blast of cold tile against her bare back, as hissing steam rolled over her shoulders.

"I've got you." The voice belonged to the one who possessed her. He was real, tangible, and pressed against her. Inside her. Kate strained to look up, to see his face, but it was enrobed in deep shadow. As quickly as the vision came, it dissolved. The fervor of the moment was dizzying, set right only by the stalwart hands of her brother, bolting her to her seat.

"Here." He shoved a glass of water into her hands.

"I'm fine. I'm fine." She struggled to catch her breath.

"You really had some shock, didn't you?" Clive asked.

She looked at him for the first time that day, his eyes filled with worry. She caught herself wondering about the features of her unseen companion. The one who claimed an intimacy with her she could only catch glimpses of. She was quickly becoming obsessed. When she didn't hear his words pouring like velvet in her mind, she feared she would never hear him again. The thought of sinking into madness weighed on her soul. Yet she couldn't help but fall deeper into the fantasy, that the voice in her head was the only part of her world that was real.

"I think I need to lay down," she said. She excused herself from the table, wishing to be alone with her thoughts. But not quite.

"Yes, of course," Allistair conceded, ready to guide her upstairs.

"Wait," Clive intervened, grabbing a book from his valise. "Allistair told me you barely had time to pack, so I brought you one of my own. It might help you sleep, although I don't know what kind of dreams it may produce."

Kate read the title as he passed the tome to her. *Dracula*. The light reflected in her pupils dulled as she fixated on the cover. The crackling fire that had been a barely perceptible yet constant din between her ears roared. She heard the sound of a log, hissing and collapsing into the blaze. The edges of her world began to melt and crack.

"Al said you haven't read this."

"I haven't," she answered, as a pale creature climbing down a castle wall headfirst flitted in her mind's eye. "Thank you."

Clive nodded.

"And thank you for the clothes. You're very kind, and I'm not being fair to you. I'm sorry."

Clive smiled for the first time since his arrival from London. "It's quite all right. It's my pleasure." His expression took a serious turn. "I can give you more than that, if you'll let me."

Her eyes inquired as to his meaning, though she had a guess. Allistair became suddenly enthralled by an oil seascape in the next room. Clive took hold of Kate's hands. She could feel him trembling.

"I know that this may be sudden," he started, "especially coming after all that's happened, and it may not be something you or even I had yet hoped for, but I may be able to provide a remedy for your troubles, if only you would consider…"

Something stopped him. He swallowed hard. Gaining back his breath, he said, "There are some Celtic ruins a stone's throw from here. They're overgrown now, but I've heard it's a quiet spot, beautiful and possessed with an unusual verdure. Will you go with me, tomorrow?"

She had waded through her day as through honey. For a reason she could not fathom, Clive's invitation imbued her with an imperative urgency.

"Yes," she answered.

Clive beamed. "All right. Tomorrow then. Goodnight, Kate."

"Good night."

Still clasping her hands, Clive leaned forward, and left a light kiss upon her cheek. Kate blinked back tears, drowning in her interloper's sorrow. Or was it her own? She didn't know. It didn't really matter. Kate was astutely aware of the choice being deliberately thrust upon her. Her options were so vastly different, she felt incapable of forming a judgement in that moment. The only thing she knew for certain was that the anguish of her twin soul was unbearable.

Clive took his leave, and Allistair led Kate to her room. As they ascended the stairs, he cast an inquiring glance at Clive, who only responded with a shake of his head. Allistair followed her into the room, closing the door behind him.

"What happened?" he demanded in hushed tones.

"When?" Kate said apathetically.

"What did Clive say to you?"

"Nothing. He asked me to visit the ruins with him tomorrow."

Allistair was losing his patience with her. "What is wrong with you? You've got to shake this thing, and get your head on straight."

"I'm *trying*, Al," she said, her eyes burning with tears. "I really am. But nothing makes sense, I don't know what's real, or what's—" She took a deep breath, choosing her words. "Or what's just in my head."

"Clive is positively crestfallen," Allistair replied. "He's crazy about you. Tomorrow, he's going to ask you to marry him. You'll be very well taken care of."

Kate grunted in protest. "I can't do that, Al."

"Why the hell not?! You were very cozy a couple of days ago," he reasoned.

She shook her head.

"Is this about your dream?" he asked. "Whoever you thought you were, whatever you thought you were doing, it was just a dream. A beautiful dream, nothing more."

She blinked, flooding her eyelids with a vision of war, of hacking her way through a sea of enemies. The reflection of herself terrified her.

How many more would die, if you were not there to protect them? It was the voice she'd grown attached to, but quieter, from farther away. A memory.

〜

LUCA REALIZED THEN THAT THE SPELL HAD NOT MISFIRED. THIS *WAS* THE spell. She had to choose.

Come home, Kate. Come home to me.

〜

Allistair sat on the bed, his expression softening.

"The way that Clive looks at you," he began, "I'd give anything to have that look possess me. To have my soul rise and fall with someone's every breath."

Kate looked at him, stunned by his sudden sentimentality. Sorrow stained her cheek.

"I took that from you."

"No," he replied, brushing her cheek. "You couldn't take what I never had. You're the best thing in my life," he said, hugging her. She squeezed her brother.

"I've missed you so much," she sobbed.

"I've always been right here." Allistair dried her tears, and left Kate alone in her room.

She spoke into the still evening.

"Still there?"

Mmhmm.

"What do I do now?"

I don't know. Sleeping might help.

"I am tired." She bit her lip. "Will you be here when I wake up?"

I promise.

She changed into her nightclothes hastily, not quite ready to repeat their last encounter. She climbed under the bedcovers, curling up on herself to get warm. Her eyelids felt heavy as a warm current slipped into bed behind her. She reached for the book Clive had given her, to aid in her sleepiness.

Luca reveled in the vivid nature of her imagination as she soaked in the words on the page. The Transylvanian forest leading to Castle Dracula was teeming with nocturnal life. Each stone forming the castle had the texture of aged rock and the featheriness of cobwebs. The raiment of the titular character and his victim were imbued with rich color, movement, distinctive fabric and patterns—she had even conjured the moody clouds in the sky. He appreciated more than ever her attraction to works of fiction, as he stood in awe of the creative impulse, the germ of her identity that fostered the bold adventure that defined every day of her life.

The world she created faded to a dull beige as her lids pulled her into sleep, no longer able to recognize the print on the page. She dug her face deeper into the pillow, wishing instead it was a loving arm. Heat radiated up her thigh and settled around her waist. She breathed deep, safer than she'd ever felt before.

Goodnight, my love.

"Goodnight, Luca," she whispered dreamily as a cool breeze from the window carried her into slumber.

His heart fluttered at her pronouncement, sending a thrill through her body that upturned the corners of her mouth as she slept.

Kate dreamt fitfully, always with the distinct impression that she'd had this dream before, dooming her to wash a bucketload of shirts, ones that she cleaned with precision only for them to appear again in the washbasin, covered in mud. She washed the same shirt more times than her dreaming mind could count. The discomfort of the dryness of her hands was enough to wake her, prodding her to rise and tend to her cracked, long-soaked skin, but the weight of her sleep was oppressive, pinning her chest to the bed. Her lids did not open. Even in her dream, she was exhausted. But she had nowhere to stay, and was compelled to sleep on the floor of the washroom, shrouded by laundry. Spillage from the basin soaked the trousers on which she laid her cheek, as well as the heavy coat pulled up to her shoulders that provided no warmth. The sudsy liquid dripped slowly from the tip of the woolen collar onto her mouth, seeking entry past her lips. As she slipped deeper into sleep, the taste of soap turned to blood.

The coppery rawness gave her the urge to vomit. But she couldn't retch. She couldn't move or make a single sound, or she'd be as dead as the body on top of her, its life force draining into her throat. She had escaped this field with nothing but her life before, and had found a way out, transported to a mass grave where she climbed out of the pile of mangled soldiers and sprinted into the forest. Philip had hidden there, waiting. She remembered how to escape, so why could she not do it now? She was the only thing on the battlefield that moved. She tried to roll the corpse on top of her off to the side, but could not. It was still too stiff, too heavy in its unyielding death. The incessant dripping of blood when it should have slowed evoked a scream. She opened her mouth in primal horror, her throat scorched with supreme exertion, but she made no sound.

Without warning, her head turned upside down.

She was falling into an abyss, a gold, circular amulet inches from her face. The red stone in the center glowed like a burning ember. She stretched her arm toward it, wrapping her fingers around the intricately carved metal, only to have the amulet disappear. Kate opened her palm to see where it had gone. It floated away from her again.

It wasn't an amulet, but the outstretched fingers of a woman with dark, flowing hair and dark eyes. An invisible force pulled her downward, causing her to fall faster.

"Cyrene!" Kate dove after her, but was blocked by a solid wall of absolute blackness. Kate pounded on the obsidian surface until a pair of fiery red orbs filled her view.

The intensity of their piercing gaze woke her with a start. The veil of her night terror lifted, and at long last she succeeded in opening her eyes. She sat upright in bed, wiping sweat through her hair.

The room was completely dark. She fumbled toward the mirror. The absence of light passing through the glass gave it a transient quality. Bending her fingertips toward its surface, her reach extended beyond the mirror's edge, into the mirror. She retracted her hand on instinct. Her whole body tingled, every fiber on edge. The room's aspect had changed. All its angles converged on the curvature of the mirror. It was the only thing of consequence. The very walls inhaled expectantly, a latent space wishing itself into existence.

Kate felt along the wooden closet at her left for a candle. She searched the wardrobe for a box of matches. Her prize was found on the top shelf, and she sent a matchstick ripping across the striker. Feeding the tapered candle on the nightstand provided a weak halo of light. Her bleary eyes looked again at the mirror, and saw her mind's guest standing in her shadow. No. He was her shadow. His eyes glowed with a blood red light, outstripping the dim candle. His pale skin flickered in and out of existence as the candle winked out, leaving Kate shrouded in night.

~

SHE DID NOT DREAM THE SLENDER FINGERS LUCA CURLED AROUND HER neck, turning her to face him. She swooned, melting into his embrace as he marveled at Kate's youth. He closed his mouth over hers, and she blossomed in his kiss. Their eager lips parted as his fingers slipped under her nightgown, clawing at her thighs, her hips. The urge to ravish her enchanting young form was too great for him to resist. Her forehead rested on his chest as he lifted her dress higher. He pulled it over her head and nuzzled her, caressing her collarbone as she hid her face from him. She trembled in his arms. With a crooked finger to her chin, he lifted her eyes to his, and brushed her silken hair behind her shoulders. Smiling, her anxious hands gravitated to his hips, undoing his belt. She wrapped her arms around his neck as he hoisted her onto the mattress.

~

KATE DRANK IN THE SIGHT OF HIM IN WONDER AS HE STRIPPED, CLINGING to him as he climbed on top of her, afraid that at any moment she might wake to an empty bed.

She ran his fingers through his dark tresses as he suckled her breasts, desperate for the return of his mouth to hers. His hardened flesh heaved against her, beckoning at the door to her existence. Her whole body tensed, the hands carelessly flung over her head subconsciously clenched.

Luca smiled at her, uncurling her fingers with his own, tempting her with kisses and subtle thrusts at her thighs. Her body belied her consent, relaxing into the bed and opening to receive him. She sighed softly at the sensation of their union, his nose grazing her cheek as he dug deeper. He pumped into her with a fury that stole her breath.

Surrounded by him, she buried her nails in his sculpted shoulders to convince herself he was really there. He wrapped her leg around his waist, challenging her untested sex as he drove deeper, the hair between his legs bristling against hers. The fervor of their lovemaking was mindless, primal, fresh—and yet, familiar.

He pulled her upright, sprawled his hand across her back and flipped her over, maneuvering her into the dominant position. He released a guttural moan as she ground into him, exhilarated by the sight of her nakedness as she shrugged off her modesty in his arms. He dug his thumbs into her tight nipples. When her cries threatened to echo into the adjoining rooms, he reached up to silence her, caressing her chin and pressing his digits to her lips. She opened her mouth, letting the salt of his skin soak her tongue. He felt her tender muscles throb against him as she reached the pinnacle of her desire. Luca rolled her over again onto her back, driving deep, shuddering with satisfaction. He grinned widely, kissing her cheek as he rose off her, settling next to her on his stomach. Kate sought his lips, and snuggled into his side. She wanted to say something, but didn't know what. Her mind and body were reeling. He smiled at her, brushing her cheek with his knuckles.

Luca swooned after a long silence of simply gazing at her. "I'll always want you with me Kate. Always."

He turned his back to her, nuzzling into the bed to get comfortable. Kate reached under his arm, her fingers tracing over his chest as she pressed her lips to his back. He took hold of her fingers, kissing them and weaving them into his own, coming to rest over his heart. He smiled as she slung her leg over his hip in her familiar fashion. He pulled it closer around him as they nodded off to sleep.

KATE'S FRACTURED MIND SLIPPED SEAMLESSLY INTO PLACE. SHE KNEW WHO she was. Or, who she *had been*. She rolled over onto her stomach, reaching for her lover. He was gone as the sun peeked through the clouds and into her window. When she drew down the covers, she smiled. The condition of the sheets bore the proof of her midnight tryst.

She dressed, grabbing the plaid scarf she had folded neatly in the closet, and walked to the window, hoisting herself up the by elbows onto the tiny inset sill.

She pushed the window out of its thirty-year hibernation and dropped down into the grass below. Rising slowly to her feet, she surveyed the inn—all was quiet. She dashed down a disused dirt path, her steps guided to a ridge bearing its rock face to the south. She slid into a narrow crack, pressed against the wall for several minutes. Keeping her head turned to the side saved her from scratching her nose against the opposite wall. Dust and small rocks fell into her hair as she groped along the wall, anxious to reach the open space she knew was just ahead. Her hand passed through a silky film that adhered itself to her fingertips.

I swear, if there are spiders in my hair I'm going to scream like the little girl I am, she thought.

Luca's soft laughter in her head made her feel like she was prancing in an open meadow, completely devoid of arachnids. The mouth of the crevasse stretched before her, and she shook out her hair before rushing to the left. Grime riddled her hands as she searched for a soft spot, an opening in the wall that should have been there. The stone face was infuriatingly solid.

"No, no, no," she banged and clawed at the wall until her fingertips bled. But the cave was unyielding—if there had once been a gateway there, it was closed. She leaned her forehead against the impenetrable barrier and sobbed. Wiping her tears away only served to smear mud on her face. Her feet dragged as she headed back to the inn.

"I'm not giving up," she insisted as she neared the door.

I never said you were. By the way...last night was incredible.

She stopped in her tracks and smiled. The flush rising to her face coursed through her whole body, alert in ways that still felt new.

Hurry back. I want more.

Luca's throaty overtures lifted her spirit. Her spry footfalls bounced up the stairs, her thoughts drifting on a cloud as she nearly crashed into Allistair and Clive in the upper hallway.

"Mornin', gents," she said, unabashedly chipper.

"What in the hell happened to you?!" Allistair cried, shocked by his sister's appearance. Strands of hair flew wildly about her besmirched face, her hands and clothes were caked in mud and blood.

"Oh, um, everything," she replied with a girlish smile. The glint in her eyes flashed brighter at the sense of Luca's amusement. She descended from her rapture at the sight of Clive, completely at a loss.

"Are we still on for the ruins?" he asked, defeated.

"Yes," she said. "Give me ten minutes."

Just as she completed the task of brushing her hair and changing into clean clothes, she heard Clive clearing his throat on the opposite side of the door. The light tap of his knuckles on the door was fraught with hesitation.

Kate came to the door wearing an open, honest expression that gave Clive a false sense of ease.

"You're looking much better," he said.

"I'm feeling much better, thank you." Kate insisted on small niceties now. One of the few pleasant memories she had of her youth was of him. She had no intention of trampling upon it by abusing Clive's good nature. Real or not, performing this ritual with him would grant her the closure she had craved for many years after her sudden disappearance from his world.

They wended their way northward to the secluded grove where scant stone traces remained of a long-faded culture. Before ascending the final stretch of grass between them and their destination, Kate slowed her steps to a halt. Clive gained a short lead, then turned to face her.

"Is everything all right? Do you need to rest?"

Kate puffed up her chest, building up her courage. "This is as far as you go."

"Excuse me? I thought we were—"

She approached him, speaking slowly and taking hold of his hands. "Yes, I know. I know why you asked me here. I may have wanted that too, once."

He cocked his head, bewildered and embarrassed by her forwardness.

"I want you to know that you might have made what was an unbearable life bearable, even joyful. But that's not what happened," she said.

Clive was at a loss. "You haven't made one bit of sense since I got here, ever since you had that stupid dream." He stopped. "Is that what this is all about, your dream?"

"It wasn't a dream. It's my life, and it's waiting for me."

I love you, Kate.

I love you.

Kate released her hold on Clive's hands, and backed away toward the grove.

"This is madness!" he shouted.

"You're probably right. But I will go on dreaming of Icarya until I draw my last breath." She embraced him, and kissed his cheek. "Be happy," she whispered, then dashed out of sight.

19

PASSING THE FIRST STONE COLUMN THAT MARKED THE EDGE OF THE RUINS, Kate stopped running. She knew she entered a hallowed place. The wind blew slower as it passed overhead. Faint light filtered in from the tree cover, casting the scattered crumbling pillars and lush grass in a soft glow. The sounds of the forest came in hushed tones. Every flap of a bird's wing, every brush of a blade of grass against its neighbor was furtive and deliberate. The trees beyond swayed in a portentous dance. Kate drew the air into her lungs in long draughts. She was in the presence of deep magic. But it slumbered.

Her tentative steps turned her toward the first stone's inward face, weathered bare. Resting her scarf on its head, she examined the pillar. Invisible grooves effaced with time pulled her fingertips along their edges. She closed her eyes, and let her hands brush across the surface of the stone, the tallest ruin, standing mere inches higher than Kate herself. Eyes closed, she walked through the space, her feet directed from one stone to the next. The wind called to her in a secretive, intangible voice, using a name she had not heard in millennia. Her hand touched unseen surfaces where standing stones had once been, completing the abandoned circle. Magic collected on her skin as she traversed the space, building unleashed momentum on her fingertips as she returned to the primary stone. It absorbed the charge, sucking it from her like a cool flame. Pressing her forehead to the smoothed edge, she offered her soul's plea.

"Wake up. Carry me home." Silent tears fell from her eyes. When the stone face's chill became unbearable, she pulled her face away. Her tears had frozen onto her cheeks. She brushed at them, tearing away her skin. The stone was sheathed in solid ice. It exhaled a freezing mist, encircling the column like a glittering shroud. The aspect of the grove darkened, turning from solemn to menacing. Kate took a fearful step back. The frozen cloud expanded, racing along the path Kate had trodden. She was trapped.

She stood firm as the ground beneath her feet trembled, separating itself from its roots and hanging in suspension. The hollow melted away, leaving only darkness above, below, and all around her, made absolute by its stark contrast to the luminescence of the restored stones. A voice echoed behind her, cruel and haughty. Her own.

"You're a fool."

Kate spun around, and saw a hooded figure looming behind her, stepping on her heels. She gaped in fear at the absent blackness where a face should have been. Pale, bony fingers peeled back the hood, the fluidity of its movement ungraceful, unnatural, unnerving. Staring at her, through her, was a reflection of her older self. Her skin, hair, and even eyes shone in the grays and whites of winter. She approached, her expression going from vacant to vicious. It shrugged off its robe in a single jarring motion, revealing a muscular body beneath a steel breastplate, armed to the teeth.

Kate braced herself, ready for a fight. But before she could blink, the shadowy warrior clutched Kate's throat, lifting her off her feet and smashing her into the stone. As fingers crushed her vocal cords, Kate relived every battle she'd ever fought. Every beating, every heartbreak, over and over and over again.

The pain was shattered by the roar of a cheering crowd. Kate turned her mind's eye toward the source of the commotion and beheld the most beautiful girl she had ever seen. Wrapped in an exquisite dress in the deepest violet, Kate recognized in the girl her own slim nose, full lips, and large round eyes, shining a crystalline blue. Her creamy skin was framed by her father's dark, lustrous curls. On her head was a wreath of leaves woven in gold, a crown whose weight Kate knew all too well.

As the woman turned to face her mother, she smiled, amplifying the rapid heartbeat ringing in Kate's brain. She strained to hear the crowd's repetitive chant.

"Long live Queen Charlotte! Long live Queen Charlotte!"

Kate's captor realized her prey had seen something unintended, and tossed her to the floor.

The being wearing Kate's face snarled. Kate fought to regain her footing, breathless and feeling old wounds and bruises anew. She heard a dagger scraping out of its sheath. Torn muscles screamed as Kate rose to stand in enough time to block the blade aimed at her chest. She twisted her enemy's wrist, squeezing her flesh until it surrendered the weapon. Kate turned it back on its owner without a thought, driving it through her heart. They both staggered backward.

Kate surveyed her lethal blow, the blade plunged in up to the hilt. The wound refused to bleed. Kate felt a splash of cold on her ribs, and reached for her breast. Her fingers fell into a hole in her flesh. She looked down, and found herself standing in a puddle of blood. She stared at her enemy, who stood unharmed. She looked down again, and clasped the knife buried in her own chest. The bloodied metal echoed on the invisible floor as she pulled it free.

"Who did you come for?" the specter asked.

Kate blinked, her vision darkening. She felt Luca's hands grip her by the arms, stopping her from falling.

"Who did you come for?!" it repeated, the demand resounding in Kate's head.

"For Cyrene," Kate sputtered. "For Megara. For Therimachus. For Creontiades. For Mecaria. For Deicoon." With her last breath, Kate stood tall. She passed her hand over her chest, now whole.

The rage left the phantom's face. It bent at Kate's feet to retrieve the dagger, and handed it to her. It was her gold medallion. The center stone flared, summoning the energy from the surrounding pillars into itself.

Kate accepted the amulet, and looked into her mimic's face. Flesh tones replaced its icy void. Kate recognized the chocolatey-copper hair, dark eyes, and slightly altered features belonging to Meryn. The resemblance between the former queen and herself was striking. She wondered how she hadn't noticed it before. The phantom repeated the phrase Meryn had spoken to Kate upon their last meeting.

"It's yours anyway. One day, you'll need it."

A thousand questions gurgled in Kate's throat. Before she could ask them, Meryn shoved her hard on the shoulders. As Kate fell backward, a blanket of snow drifted up to meet her. She scrambled to dig her way out, refilling her lungs at last with the crisp air of Icarya's Northern Mountains. When she sat up, she pulled Luca with her, his hand frozen to hers.

Kate hurried over to the nearest mound, where snow had already begun to shift. She worked quickly, fending off frostbite as she unearthed her sister-in-law. Cyrene coughed back to life.

"What happened?" Cyrene asked. She shivered and rubbed her arms, senseless to the time that had passed since her fateful fall. "Am I dead?"

Kate grinned. "Not anymore." The women hugged, but Kate cut it short, assisting Luca in uncovering the wife and children of their friend. Kate gestured to Megara and herded everyone back to their tent, covering them with the extra clothes and furs they had carried with them through the pass. Kate stoked the fire, and distributed their extra food.

WITH EVERYONE SETTLING IN, LUCA LED KATE BY THE HAND AROUND TO the back of the tent, where the warmth of their tight embrace fended off the night air as wind howled around them. Beyond Kate's shoulder, something blue flapping against a tree limb caught Luca's eye. He reached for it, and held out the scarf she had left on the Scottish ruins. She turned to stare at the tree, studying its queer lines. Her fingers lingered on Luca's skin as she extended her hand to accept it, then clenched him suddenly as the ground beneath them quaked.

Luca pushed Kate against the tree, using his body to cage her. In moments, the world stood still again. As Kate caught her breath, Luca cursed. A low rumbling crept into his ear.

"We can't stay here," he said.

As he spoke, he saw Kate's expression go blank. She gaped upward and behind him, at an unfathomable mass of snow racing down the nearest peak.

"Kate, are you okay? What's—" Cyrene had exited the tent, her eyes drawn immediately to the avalanche crashing toward them.

"We can't outrun that," she muttered. Her expression shattered. "I want to see my son."

Kate snapped out of her shock, and returned her gaze to the tree. The sunlight glistened from its branches in well-worn treads through the bark, shooting down into the tangle of thick roots scoring the frozen dirt. The web of tree limbs bore small openings to the hollow deep in the heart of the tree. Kate watched unblinking as the sunbeams flowed straighter in their uncurling path, widening the hollow space. Kate grabbed Cyrene and shoved her into the opening. She and Luca pulled Hercules's family to safety before scurrying like rabbits into the tree's protection.

Their wooden sanctum was impossibly spacious. Behind them, the darkness of the bark seemed illuminated by a soft glow far in the distance. Kate could barely hear Cyrene's whispering query.

"What's that light? It's so green. Is that...a forest?" Cyrene stirred to get a better look, but Kate trapped her wrist, yanking her back into a crouch, eyes glued to the snow rushing past them.

"*Don't* move. Don't even look."

20

Away from the stinging glare of the crosses etched into the border of his cavernous prison, the prince of shadows sloshed in the mud. He trudged up to a relatively dry spot, covered in slick stones rather than seawater, where a large cocoon-like structure was taking shape. It was constructed mostly of flesh, skin, and blood, but was cold to the touch. It pulsated in gestation. The shape and structure were crystalline in nature, its contents obscured by a cloudy white substance that just barely hinted at the blue tint of the orb from which the cocoon had developed. Only the faintest shadow could be seen of the creature growing within. The cocoon buzzed horribly.

Dracula cursed, drawing the sword from the scabbard at his back. Drained, he had been forced to withhold his outpouring of blood. Still, the rate of growth had slowed well before he had closed his veins in exhaustion. He grabbed the blade by the hilt, a silver dragon coiling its tail around the base of the steel, and slid his palm down the length of the long, heavy blade. He smeared his hand across the cocoon before the wound closed. It was done in a matter of seconds.

A small hand with remarkably long fingers braced the wall of its icy shell. The streaks of red disappeared as the vampire's blood seeped into the structure, causing the stiff noise of expanding ice and crackling crystals to echo throughout the cavern.

Dracula watched and waited.

21

KATE'S PARTY CRAWLED OUT OF THEIR HOLE WITH THE SUNRISE AND headed down the mountain and back to the lakeside village of Veruna. Before descending the ridged entryway to their camp, Kate cast a final glance at the mysterious tree that had taken them in to safeguard their lives. It looked just at it had days before, when she'd laid eyes on it without much ado.

Heaps of freshly fallen snow barred the way, forcing the party to snake a treacherous path through the mountains. Five days of tumbling down and around what they had climbed in a few hours caused their bodies to give out when they reached the plateau marking the edge of the corridor. Luca collapsed. Kate's overexerted muscles twisted tighter, and she retched.

Their extra visitors were cleaned, rested, and secreted away to Castelmor. For Luca, the effects of their labors were mild and ephemeral. Kate caught the brunt of it. Cora, the water nymph who was part of Kate's mining crew, brought extra blankets and firewood to Kate's room and cooked a large bowl of clam chowder to help get her temperatures back up. Kate shuddered hard in bed, and Luca pulled her naked body as close to his as he could to stop her teeth from chattering. It was late in the night by the time her breathing became less labored, and Luca's fingertips sensed her blood pressure return to its normal pace.

He was shocked back into consciousness by an overwhelming choking sensation. His eyes shot open, assuming that it was a dream, and that he would breathe again once awake. He was frozen solid, with no oxygen. A thick layer of ice had formed over the bed.

He tried to turn his head to look at her, but couldn't. He couldn't hear her breathing. Couldn't feel her pulse racing against his skin. He panicked. He attempted to shake his body free, but made very little progress. Then, he felt Kate's body start to shudder from lack of air. He was running out of time. He screamed, putting all his strength into his arms as he blasted through the ice. Shards of it flew across the room in a crystalline explosion. He tapped Kate's face and shouted her name, but she still wasn't breathing. Her lips were blue. Luca put his hands over her lungs, his mind's eye racing to find lingering threads of ice and dispel them.

In what felt like an eternity, Kate jerked awake, gasping for air. She coughed so hard she bled. When she came to her senses, what she saw horrified her. She sobbed into Luca's chest. He did his best to comfort her, tell her that everything was all right, convince her that she hadn't almost killed them both.

"Everything's all right because you were here," she said, her face wet with tears.

"I'll always be here," he answered in a sweet voice.

KATE AND LUCA INTENDED TO STAY AT THE LAKE ANOTHER DAY OR TWO, so that Kate could regain her strength before moving on to Castelmor. Then, they would return to Cathair to finish what Luca had started. Then, on finally to Drigory, to arm themselves for a second encounter with Haydee. But today, they would rest. Along with a warm, hearty breakfast, Glaucus brought them a pair of coral ear cuffs—one to replace Kate's broken one and one made especially powerful for Luca, to overcome the last traces of his aversion to running water.

"You'll be able to swim like a fish now," Kate said. She huddled in several layers of blanket. Only her head was exposed, and sometimes a hand when she reached for her tea.

"You look like a turtle." Luca was comfortable in just a midnight-blue shirt and coat lined with ash-gray fur. The color complemented his crystalline eyes.

She pouted, and tucked her head into the covers. Luca smirked.

"Thanks, by the way. I assume this was made at your request?" he said as he donned the earpiece.

"Naturally." Her muffled voice came through the heavy blankets.

"I appreciate it. You're always looking out for me."

"It's no problem. That's what turtles do."

Luca laughed. The return of her good humor was a good sign. The spell was cast and the side effects dealt with, for now. It made every minute more precious.

Their peace was shattered when the griffon Gideon arrived at the top of the mountain in a state of nervous agitation.

"Kate, you must come, quickly," he blurted out as he barged in unannounced.

"What is it?" she said as she stood and threw off the bedclothes.

"It's Cara. Her labor's begun, but—"

"But what?"

"I don't know. Something is wrong, and she needs you. We don't know what to do."

Kate and Luca grabbed their belongings quickly. When she stumbled, Luca steadied her. He gave her a boost of energy while Gideon transported them as fast as he could to the southern border of the castle. He dove up the cliff that abutted the edge of the southern gardens, and dropped them off at the edge where Cara, a well-muscled but very rotund gray horse, had collapsed. She was attended by Philip, Gideon, and several female creatures who were practiced in midwifery, but who were stumped as to the nature of Cara's pain. Everyone had been too afraid to move her, so she'd been stuck there, groaning for several hours. When it appeared that something was awry, Gideon had been sent to retrieve Kate without delay.

Kate hopped off Gideon's back before he touched the ground and rushed over to Cara. The midwives had given up trying to account for the extraordinary pain and had resigned themselves to making Cara as comfortable as possible. They were failing even in that. They made way for Kate, with Luca fast on her heels. Kate stroked Cara's sleek nose.

"Hi, Cara, I'm here, honey. Tell me what's going on," Kate said.

"It's no good," interrupted one of the midwives, "something's not right with the foal. It's a bad match."

Philip stamped his feet on the ground.

"Shut up. I wasn't talking to you," Kate snapped. "What gives you the right to say such a thing to a new mother? You're scaring her, just go away." Kate dismissed all the midwives, and was left there with Philip, Luca, Gideon, and Cara. "Gideon, go get some blankets and some hot water. Fast."

Off he flew.

Cara groaned.

"Cara, I'm going to help you, but you have to talk to me. What do you feel?"

Luca petted her overextended flank, taking the edge off her pain by repairing some of the muscles that had torn.

"It's ready to be born, I know it is, but I can't push. Nothing's happening." She broke down in tears. "Something's wrong. Please save my baby."

"All right, all right, just calm down and breathe." Kate put her hands on the horse's abdomen, and closed her eyes. She grimaced.

"There's not enough room. It needs to come out. Now."

The horse whinnied. "What?"

"It's okay, Cara, this is going to be over soon. But you have to trust me, okay?" Kate pulled out one of her blades from her hip. Gideon gave her what she asked for, and she plunged the short sword into the hot water.

"What's that? What are you doing?" Cara screamed, while Luca held her head in his lap.

"I'm helping your baby find its way out. Be brave, and brace yourself."

Cara looked desperately at Luca, who put her in a light trance to stop her from panicking. One quick movement, and Kate's blade could cause a disaster. Cara needed to stay calm.

"Stay with her, Luca," Kate said as she slowly made an incision in Cara's stomach.

Kate's fear slipped into his mind.

I've never done this before.

She cut slowly, as delicate as possible.

Philip trotted back and forth, fluttering his wings nervously as he watched every move Kate made.

Finally, Kate dropped her blade and pulled at her incisions, peeling back Cara's wet flank with a slopping sound, until finally Kate's arms were in Cara's stomach up to her elbows. Kate closed her eyes to give her sense of touch the advantage, and reached for the fetus.

Cara twitched at the sensation of Kate's fingertips on muscles completely unused to the stimulation. It was like being disemboweled.

Eyes still closed, Kate smiled as she touched slick fur, and felt around the baby's edges.

"It's fine," she announced, "just a little backwards."

Cara and Philip both breathed a sigh of relief. Kate put her hands around the baby's head, and led it out to the surface. As the head emerged from Cara's stomach, Kate reached around with her right arm to lift out the legs.

"There you go, little one!" she said as it tried to gain its balance and stand up next to its mother.

"It's all right!" Cara exclaimed before plopping her head back in Luca's arms.

"It's a boy!" cried Philip, rearing up on his hind legs with pride.

"It's a perfectly healthy colt," Kate said.

"That's no horse," Luca retorted. "Look."

As the colt struggled to walk, its limbs wobbled, bringing it closer to the edge of the cliff. Just before it plummeted off the edge, the wind unfurled a pair of wings. But the young thing was inexperienced, and didn't catch the proper amount of speed. Philip dove after his son, correcting his path and guiding him high into the air.

Cara and Kate both cried in joy.

"It's a pegasus," said Kate, "and it's absolutely beautiful!" She smiled at Luca, who stopped to smile back at her as he patched up Cara's side. Cara was as good as new again.

"Oh, thank you, Luca. Thank you, Kate. We are so very grateful."

Luca put his arm around Kate and kissed her on the head.

"Luca, I'd like to hug you right now, but...I'm sort of covered in blood."

She was dripping up to her elbows. She used her leg muscles to bring herself to her feet.

"How did you know?" Luca asked.

"Know what?"

"That the baby was all right?"

"If two people love each other that much, then it's meant to be."

Her eyes shone at him. In the back of their minds, they remembered what they had seen in their own future.

Philip and the newest little Icaryan landed by Cara. She worked diligently to lick him clean before the pair dozed off. Her tongue revealed a magnificent dapple coat, gray speckled with white, a tribute to its parents.

Philip came over to Kate and licked her face. "You both have my eternal gratitude."

"Any time," said Luca. He was very happy at how the day was turning out so far. One family already mended. Two more to go.

Luca and Kate walked to the fountain at the center of the garden to clean themselves off. As they rinsed the blood from their hands and arms, Luca just stared at her with a dreamy smile on his face.

"Can I help you with something?" she asked, trying to decipher the reason for his smile.

"I'm just wondering."

"About?"

"If you have one human-magic parent and one human-vampire parent, what does that make the child?"

"Ours," she said, flicking water in his direction.

Luca couldn't stop grinning.

As they approached the castle entrance at the edge of the garden, they ran into Hercules.

"Hey, you two—heard we have a new pegasus," Hercules said.

"That we do," Kate answered.

"That's just wonderful. So, are you gonna tell me why you called me here?"

"Nope."

"Seriously?"

"You'll see," Kate said, happy to see her very good friend.

Kaspar came out screaming, "I found it! I found it!"

"Hey, Prince Kaspar!" shouted Hercules.

"Hey. Hercules! I found it!"

"Found what?" he asked.

"Aunt Kate gave me a treasure map, and it said the treasure was in a secret room, and whoever finds the room gets to have one wish granted, and I had to keep it a secret, but I finally found the secret room, and I'm ready to make my wish, and I want everybody to come and see, and you can come too!"

Kaspar blurted all this out without losing his breath, and ran off in the other direction, back into the castle. He was such a bundle of energy, he hadn't turned around to see if the trio was following him.

Hercules chuckled. It reminded him of his own sons' excitement when he had come home from a long journey, running around their room, picking up things left and right to show him what they had been up to in his absence.

"Is this your doing?" he asked Kate.

"*Our* doing," she said, taking Luca's hand.

"Let's not keep him waiting then," Hercules said.

"Yes. He's waited long enough," Kate replied.

They followed the trail that Kaspar had blazed through the castle doors to the throne room. Kate's brothers were already there.

Allistair moved to stand beside Kate, looking less than pleased.

"Hello," Kate greeted her brother.

"That was a rotten thing you did, telling him he could have any one wish granted. You know what he's thinking about. You could have at least explained that part to him," Allistair growled.

Kate ignored him.

Kaspar drew everyone's attention back to him. Now that everyone was gathered, he had no intention of waiting another minute.

He hovered around Kate's throne. "The final bit of the map said something about being at the southern root. At first, I scoured the southern gardens, digging the whole place up," Kaspar said.

"Yeah, thanks for that," Ted said to Kate.

Kate just shrugged. "Trial and error. Go on, Kaspar."

"Then I remembered. You all have titles. Daddy, what's your title?"

"King, of course."

"No, no. Your full title," Kaspar said.

"Allistair, King of the Northern Mountains, Lord of Castelmor."

"Uncle Ted?"

"Theodore, King of the Western Valleys, Master of the Great Sea."

Kaspar looked at Kate.

"I am Kate, Queen of the Southern Forests, Empress of the Far Islands."

Kaspar smiled. "Queen of the South. And a root lives underground, right?"

Kate gleamed. "Right."

Kaspar pushed back the thrones, and pulled up the red carpet lining the floor. Where Kate's chair had been, was the outline of a trap door.

"Hercules, can you help me?" the boy asked.

"I sure can," he said, stepping up to the door and pulling the metal handle. It pulled up a thick slab of marble, revealing a narrow opening with a ladder leading down.

Kaspar turned to look at Kate. "Can I make my wish now?" he asked, his tone tender.

Kate took Luca's hand. He squeezed back.

"Yes, Kaspar, make your wish," she said.

Kaspar closed his eyes, and remained silent, thinking of his mother. A small tear ran down his cheek.

ALLISTAIR THREW A HATEFUL STARE IN KATE'S DIRECTION, KNOWING THE disappointment she was leaving him to deal with when his wish wasn't granted. He closed his eyes too, in the pain of missing his wife.

WHILE FATHER AND SON BOTH HAD THEIR EYES CLOSED, A SLENDER WOMAN with dark, flowing hair ascended the ladder and snuck up behind Kaspar. She touched her hand to his shoulder, and his little heart skipped three beats. He spun around, and jumped for joy.

"*Mommy!*"

"Kaspar! Kaspar, my baby! I've missed you so much!" Cyrene scooped up her son in her arms, twirling him around and smothering him in kisses.

THE MINUTE ALLISTAIR HEARD HIS SON'S CRY, HIS EYES SHOT OPEN. HE became a statue as his brain processed what his eyes were seeing, then he collapsed to his knees, tears streaming down his face.

"Cyrene!"

KATE COULDN'T HOLD IT IN ANY LONGER. SHE SOBBED FOR JOY, AND leaned on Luca for support, who smiled widely at the reunion of the little boy and the mother who loved him dearly.

Allistair ran to them. Cyrene turned to face Allistair, still holding Kaspar in her arms. First he touched her face, cradling her head in his hands.

"Are you real?" he asked.

"I'm real, Allistair. I'm really back," she said.

"My god!" Allistair hugged his family so tight, he squeezed the air out of them. The little family stood there huddled together for the longest time, their faces covered in tears.

Allistair broke away and turned to look at Kate. She just stared at him, and said nothing as he approached.

"You did this?" he asked.

"What wouldn't I do," she said between sobs, "for my big brother?"

He hugged her close, and whispered, "Thank you. Thank you thank you thank you. I love you, Kate."

"Love you too, Ally."

WHEN THEY TURNED AROUND TO LEAVE, HERCULES WAS SHOCKED BY WHAT he saw. Standing before him were Megara and his children.

They shouted at him in unison, rushing to him and knocking him over.

He laughed as they wrestled, hugged, and kissed their long-gone father. He stood up, a child under each arm and two on his back. His wife ran over and kissed him, wrapping her arms around his thick waist. Hercules didn't know what to say. He looked back to where Kate and Luca were standing behind him.

"You didn't think we'd forget you, did you?" said Luca, smirking.

"THANK YOU FOR HELPING ME DO THIS. IT MEANS A GREAT DEAL TO ME," Kate said, leaning on Luca for support.

Luca hugged her back, and kissed the top of her head.

"Thank you for letting me in, and allowing me to help you. You've done something wonderful today. I'm honored to stand beside you."

She looked up at him and kissed him. "Likewise."

"CONFOUND THIS INFERNAL THING!"

In his fury, Dracula lashed murderously at his sanguine chrysalis, having reached the end of his eternal patience. The shell that housed a creature of great power, fueled with his own blood, refused to grow any larger. Stymied, Dracula trembled with a wrath he was forbidden to unleash. The chains binding him to this chill, mud-laden maw of rock howled between his ears. It shredded his customary reserve. The blood light seething from his eyes reflected his fettered ferocity.

The deep claw marks he had inflicted on the object of his obsession disappeared immediately, filled in with a mindless surety. A frustrated growl gurgled and died in the vampire's throat as the air of the cave thinned. All the moisture in the air blowing in from the evening tide coalesced on the surface of the crystalline cocoon as it hardened, becoming a thin, sharp casing of glass speckled with rounded drops of sweet dew.

Dracula's pupils flickered with delight as the seawater froze, surrounding the icy shell in a thin film of snow. The tiny ice crystals flitted away on the back of the outgoing breeze, ignored by the dark lord, whose eyes remained fixed on the razor-thin crack racing from the crown of the chrysalis down to its base.

THE EVENING PASSED QUIETLY. ALLISTAIR, CYRENE, AND KASPAR ATE AND spent the night in private, as did Hercules and his family. Kate and Luca dined with Ted, where Kate conveyed the news of Darien's ascension to power.

"He knew? All this time, he knew?" Ted asked, shocked to hear Kate tell of Darien's knowledge of his true lineage.

"He did," she said. "When I acknowledged him, told him that you had sent me there, he acted like it was the best news he'd ever heard."

Ted smiled, his eyes glassy. "Really?"

Kate nodded. "He wants to know you as much as you want to know him. But," Kate said sternly, "we have to let him find his own path. It won't do for you to be too involved."

"Of course," Ted answered readily, his mind already planted in the near future.

"*You* may both know, but I wouldn't recommend making that information public. His hold on Likhan is precarious, and we don't want to give his people the impression that he's our puppet."

"But he *is* our ally," Ted prompted.

"Yes, absolutely. And as if that major shift wasn't enough, he may still be in danger from Haydee." Ted made to speak, but was stilled by Kate's hand. "We'll ensure a safe and stable transition, but to do that, I need other things before we set out for Likhan again. And, there are other pressing matters to consider," Kate finished, looking to Luca.

He nodded almost imperceptibly. The battle that awaited him in the caverns of Cathair was no little thing.

"So much for the lazy days of summer," he lamented.

"Winter will be here soon," she said by way of acknowledgement, "but springtime will come again." She curled into his warm embrace, feeling every ounce of her exhaustion. Kate made her excuses, and she and Luca retired early.

She slept little. She tossed and turned for hours, and when she finally drifted off to sleep, her dreams disturbed her.

LUCA NOTICED KATE'S AGITATION AS SHE TWITCHED IN HIS ARMS. HER breathing was ragged, as if she were choking. He stroked her back and her hair, trying to calm her down. When her limbs became cold and rigid, he shook her awake. A shock ran through her as he did this, and she gasped for air.

"Are you all right?" Luca asked. "What's the matter?"

"I couldn't...breathe..." She clutched his arm. "I felt like I was suffocating. Everything was completely dark. Not even that. It was a void. I was about to be ripped inside out." She panted, and rested her head on his shoulder.

She felt a little better, now that she had spoken her dream aloud. The reality of it began to fade from her mind.

"It's just a nightmare, my love, you're safe. I'm right here." He rubbed her arms to reassure her.

"Is it?" she said. Her eyes took on a vacant tinge as she stared at the foot of the bed, her gaze focused on the pattern of her bedcover.

"Of course it is. What else could it be?"

"I don't know."

"You need some rest, Kate. We both do. We had a long day, and you're still not fully healed from Veruna Lake. There are plenty of hours left for us to sleep."

"I can't go back to sleep," she said, sitting up and rubbing her face.

"Why not?" he groaned, ready for sleep himself.

"I'm not tired anymore."

Luca smirked. "I can fix that."

Kate caught his meaning, and smirked back as he caressed her breasts.

"You're so kind, how thoughtful of you," she said as Luca sat up and swung her leg over his shoulder, kissing the inside of her knee.

"It's my pleasure," he said in a deep voice.

Another hour later they were both sound asleep, with no dreams to speak of.

KATE WOKE FEELING ENERGIZED. SHE STRETCHED, AND KISSED LUCA'S shoulder to let him know she was awake.

"Feeling better?" he asked.

"Much better, thank you. And you?"

"I feel great. But I wasn't the one shifting in bed all night."

"I'm sorry about that."

"Don't be," he said as he opened his eyes and caressed her face. "It worked out all right."

She smiled, then plunked her head back down on the pillow.

"I could stay here like this all day with you," Kate swooned.

"Fine by me. Let me just use the water closet. I'll be right back."

"Hurry," she said, as he sprang out of bed. She rolled onto her stomach, exposing her round ass and bending her legs in the air. "Or I might get started without you," she said.

"Don't even *think* about it."

He reached for the door to the water closet and caught a quick glimpse out the window from the corner of his eye. He paused in front of the door as his mind raced to catch up with his eyes. Instead of opening the door, he released the handle, took three steps backward, and turned his head to the left.

"Kate," he said without averting his gaze, "you'd better come and look at this."

At the tone of his voice, she promptly got up and stood beside him. She followed Luca's stare out the window.

"Oh, god."

"How much longer is autumn supposed to last?" he asked.

"Another month, at least. I've...I've never seen anything like this before."

They continued to stare out Kate's windows at the gardens and forest below. The world outside was covered in three feet of snow.

"HOW COULD THIS HAPPEN?" KATE ASKED AS SHE AND LUCA DRESSED. IT WAS late enough in the morning—they were sure the others had already noticed.

"A freak of nature? It must have been while we were sleeping," Luca suggested.

"That was only a few hours. Even in the dead of winter, you won't accumulate snow that fast!" Kate kept tying the front of her tunic wrong, and had to undo and redo it several times. She finally gave up with a grunt, putting her hand to her forehead as her shirt hung open.

"Calm down," Luca said, coming over to help her. "We'll go downstairs, talk to the others, and figure out what's going on."

She took a deep breath. "You know, before you came along, I could do all kinds of things by myself. Now I feel like a big ball of fluff. I depend on you, and I don't like going anywhere without you."

"Was it fluff that took Mehmnet's head clean off?" he quipped. There was pride in his voice at the thought of how Kate had handled her enemies. "It's the same with me. I spent thousands of years on my own, and now that feels completely unnatural. It was unbearable being without you in Cathair."

"I guess that's a good thing, in a way," she said.

"It is," he smiled, finishing the closure on Kate's shirt. "Now let's go."

Everyone was waiting for them in the enclosed sitting room adjoining the western garden. Hercules, his wife, and Cyrene were outside, playing with the children in the snow. Kate's brothers were seated, wearing several warm layers. Allistair poured Kate a cup of tea as she sat down.

"Luca?" he offered.

"Coffee for me, thanks."

"I've got that," said Ted. "Lovely weather we're having for this time of year, isn't it?" he said as he sipped from his own steaming cup. Kate grabbed a bowl of hot cereal with apples and cinnamon for she and Luca to share.

"How can you joke at a time like this?" Allistair asked.

"Aside from doing a sun dance," Ted retorted, "there's not much else I can do."

Kate looked out through the glass doors to those outside, having a snowball fight. "Are you sure that's safe?" she asked.

"I checked it before I let them outside," Allistair said. "It smells, feels, and tastes like snow."

"That's because it is snow, you blockhead!" Ted exclaimed.

"Ted!" Kate chided. "Take it down a notch."

"Sorry," her brother sighed. "We're all a little nervous. Any idea what could have caused this?"

"It was probably me," said Kate matter-of-factly.

"What do you mean, it was probably you? Don't you know?" asked Allistair.

"I can't be sure. If it was me, I can assure you it wasn't on purpose."

Kate's siblings stared at her, confused. "It could be a side effect," she explained.

"From what?" asked Ted.

"From bringing Cyrene and the others back."

"Oh," said Allistair. He paused a moment, as if in thought. "Does that mean it was an isolated incident? The snow will melt, and everything will go back to normal?" he finally asked.

"Let's hope so," said Luca, putting his arm around Kate. She looked frightened.

"But what if it's not?" Ted asked. "What if it's something else?"

Kate and Ted looked at each other. They shared the same concern.

"What else could it be?" Luca asked.

"I don't know. But we have to be ready," Kate replied.

"For what?" Allistair asked.

"Anything."

Luca noticed Kate's gaze shift down and to the left, looking at nothing in particular. Her eyes were unfocused, yet all her muscles were tense.

"Kate?" he asked.

She blinked, coming back to her senses. "Did you say something?"

Luca shook his head. "Are you all right?"

Kate furrowed her brow. "I don't know." Without explaining further, she stepped outside to greet Hercules good morning.

HERCULES TURNED TO HER, AND HIS YOUNGEST SON TOOK THE OPENING and launched a snowball square at his face.

Kate laughed.

"Is that how I taught you? To fight dirty?" Hercules asked in his native tongue, hands on his hips.

The little boy giggled. "It's not dirty, daddy, the snow is clean!"

"Oh, you think you're clever, huh? I'll show you clean, come over here!" Hercules chased off after his son, leaving Kate standing there without having said what she came out to say.

Megara had seen that look on other people's faces many times. She scooped her son up as he ducked behind her for cover.

"It looks like you're needed," she said, tilting her head in Kate's direction. The queen waited patiently, but Hercules could tell she had something on her mind. He grabbed his wife by the elbows, kissing her and then his son.

"Be right back!"

"Morning, Herc," Kate said as he approached, kicking the snow with her feet.

"Morning." He turned to look at his family, and then back at her. "You've given me the greatest gift, Kate. If there's anything I can do for you, you know you can always count on me."

She looked down. "It's funny you should say that. I need you to go someplace far, far away." She looked up at him, staring him straight in the eyes. "And I need you to leave now."

What she said stunned him. Kate kept her voice low, so no one but Hercules could hear her request.

FROM THE SITTING ROOM, LUCA OBSERVED HERCULES'S HEATED demeanor, gesticulating at Kate as she stood in front of him, her gaze glued to the ground. The glass obscured his hearing, but he made out snippets of Hercules's shouts.

"I just saw my family for the first time in over a thousand years, and you expect me to leave them now?!"

"How do you know that will even work?"

"Isn't there anybody else?"

"THERE'S NO ONE ELSE," KATE MURMURED. "NO ONE ELSE COULD DO IT, no one else would even know where to start. It has to be you." Her eyes were full of humility. "Please, Hercules."

HERCULES GLARED DOWN AT KATE, LET OUT A GROWL, AND STORMED OFF in his wife's direction. "Megara," he said, wearing the same look on his face that he had always worn when he had come to tell her he was leaving again. So much time had passed, and nothing had changed.

She simply said, "Go."

"What?"

"Go, Hercules. It's clear that she needs you. And after returning you to us, we can't deny her anything."

"But—"

"We'll be here when you get back. Katelyn will make sure of it. Go," she repeated herself, "make us proud."

He smiled at his wife, and her kind wisdom. "I love you," he said.

"We love you, Hercules."

"Yeah, we love you, Daddy," his children echoed. "When you come back," his little girl Mecaria asked, "can you teach me to be a hero like you?"

He beamed with pride, and his mind was set. "Yes, *koúkla*, I can." He said his goodbyes and walked off to the far edge of the garden, looking for Philip.

"I'll bet he'll be just as pleased as I am," Hercules muttered to himself.

KATE RECLAIMED HER SEAT BESIDE LUCA AND FINISHED HER BREAKFAST. She said nothing about her quarrel with Hercules.

Luca knew Kate well enough by now that she would tell him when she was ready, so he put it out of his mind, and joined Allistair outside to even the odds on the snowball fight.

Kate and Ted watched from the sidelines as the children wiped the floor with the grownups. Kate laughed at the scene, until she suddenly cried out in pain. She doubled over in her chair and grabbed her left side. Luca flew to her side, followed by Allistair. Ted started from his chair, but didn't know how to help her.

"What's wrong?" Luca asked, running his hand along her side to stop the pain. Her skin felt like a wall of ice, and Luca met resistance in attempting to heal her. Her mouth hung open in pain. She was left breathless, unable to answer. She fought to breathe, but the pain was so intense that she didn't know what to do with herself. She writhed in her chair.

As quickly as the pain came, it passed. Kate finally felt able to inhale, and the inside of her throat burned as she breathed deep and fast.

"Kate! Kate answer me—are you okay?" Luca cried.

"I'm okay...I'm okay. It's gone."

"What's gone?" asked Allistair. "What the hell just happened?'

"I don't know," she said as she leaned back in her chair. Ted offered her a glass of water, which she gulped down greedily.

"I was sitting here, watching you play outside," she said as Ted handed her a second glass. She sipped at it more slowly as she began to calm down. "And all of a sudden I felt this burning pain in my side, like my intestines were being ripped out."

She carefully stretched out the muscles that had contracted on their own and threatened to throttle her, afraid that a false move could cause a repeat of the scene.

"And now it's gone, just like that?" Allistair asked.

"Just like that," she said, in a voice so calm it bordered on the absurd. In reality, she was more terrified by the minute. In her mind, her restless night and the horrible dream, the snow on the ground, and this last episode were all related. These events in rapid succession hung portentously at the front of her mind, casting a look of unbridled terror on her face, hidden by a thin veil of sanity.

LUCA HAD NEVER SEEN KATE LOOK SO GLOOMY. THE DISTANT LOOK IN HER eyes worried him, as did the fact that he had been unable to banish her pain. That was his signal that something was very seriously wrong.

He walked her back to her chambers to lie down, not taking his hands off her for a minute. Halfway down the long corridor to her room she stumbled, and Luca stopped to pick her up and carry her the rest of the way.

"I'm okay, Luca, I just tripped."

"Then let your feet enjoy the break," he answered back. He was going to take care of her, whether she liked it or not. Kate rested her head on his chest as he walked the rest of the way without any change in his gait; it was as if he was carrying a feather.

He kicked open the solid doors to her chambers with little more than a nudge and laid her down on the bed.

"I'm fine, Luca, really. I wouldn't lie."

"I know you wouldn't. Is there anything you didn't want to tell your brothers? Anything you left out?"

"No. It really was just a sudden, incredibly intense pain. And it's gone. Why?"

Luca laid down next to her, kicking off his boots, and helping Kate out of hers. "Whatever you experienced was not physical in nature."

"What do you mean?"

"When I put my hand to your side, I tried to heal whatever was bothering you. I failed."

Kate voice dwindled to a whisper. "If it wasn't physical…"

"It must be magical. I think we should go see your friend the troll. He might have answers."

Kate nodded.

"Try to get some sleep, and we'll head out tonight. I don't want to waste any more time," he said. He drew the bed curtains closed to block out the sunlight, undressed, and slipped into bed next to Kate. While Kate slept, Luca kept silent watch over her.

24

Drigory stood at the window of his underwater study, watching a humpback whale swim by through the latticed glass. His silver spoon clinked against his porcelain teacup as he steeped a slice of lemon, flipping it over and over again in deep thought. He heard the bickering of his company, a mother and son, echo behind him.

"I still don't see how this is her fault," the son said. He was tall, with dusty-brown hair and dark eyes. He looked thinner and only slightly older than when he had reached out to Kate many years ago on a rainy autumn day.

"She broke a cardinal rule," his mother said. "She cannot cast a blood spell without paying its price. Now we all must suffer the consequences."

Kate's grandmother was dressed in plain clothing. She had begun to age gracefully, her flowing auburn hair only now starting to show threads of silver. She gripped the arms of a high-backed leather chair. Though it had been many years since she was recognized as queen, Meryn had retained her regal composure.

"She wouldn't have had the need or the opportunity to, had you not dragged him into the picture," her son, William, argued.

Meryn cast her son a knowing glance. "Dragged? Is that what I did?"

"What do you call that dream you fed him?"

"I merely suggested what his life might be like. He made all his own choices. I think they're well-suited," she said.

"He will take her life, eventually," Drigory chimed in.

"When he does, it will be entirely with her consent," Meryn countered.

"How bad is it? How much of the cost did he negate?" William asked.

Drigory pursed his lips. Mother and son went wide-eyed.

"The *whole* thing?!" William cried, astonished.

"She didn't lose a single second," Drigory stated. Luca was more powerful than any of them had imagined.

"But she doesn't know that," William said, defending his daughter's actions.

"She damn well knew the risk. She doesn't care. I told you, she is reckless. She has no discipline," Drigory said, agitated. "She is ruled by her emotions."

"And where should she have learned such discipline?!" her father protested. "She's had a hard life. All she's ever known was a father who rejected her and a mother who resented her. She didn't know us," he argued, indicating himself and his mother. "We were not there to help her understand her talent, to teach her how to control it!"

"You have two other children who don't know you either," his mother said in a soothing tone. "Why do you feel her absence more smartly?"

"The bond I share with her," he said, "is the same as the bond I share with you. Our gift binds us."

"And it is that gift that she has misused," Drigory said flatly.

"It was a hard choice, between the only two men who have ever meant anything to her," Meryn reasoned. "What's done is done," she said. "There's no use in us arguing about it. Does she know what's coming?"

"Oh, she knows," her father answered. "She had the same dream that brought us here. The question is whether or not she needs our help. I think she does."

"Much as I love you, William, she is my true heir. She will rise to the challenge in her own way," her grandmother said. "We must not intervene."

"What will he do?" William asked. He and his mother looked to Drigory.

"I cannot read every thought of a man I have not yet met," Drigory said, defending his ignorance. "They'll be here in two days. Then I'll know."

25

KATE AND LUCA WERE AWAKENED IN THE WEE HOURS OF THE MORNING BY an intensely cold sensation at their feet. They shifted in their sleep, and Kate moved to get up out of bed and close her window. But she couldn't. A thick sheet of ice covered the far end of the room, and was now creeping up her bed.

"Shit!" she cried, waking Luca up as she kicked at the ice with all her might. They broke the ice on top of them, and scrambled out of bed. They dressed in a matter of seconds. By the time they descended the stairs and entered the main hallway, the frost had reached the pillows.

Castle workers were spilling out of their bedrooms down the length of the hallway.

"What is going on?!" Allistair shouted, carrying Kaspar on his hip with one hand and holding his wife's hand in the other.

A confused murmur rose from every direction, everyone half-dressed and fleeing from rooms that were freezing over. Kate and her siblings crowded together, trying to figure out what to do. They barely had time to speak to each other before icy mists billowed from under the doors, and ice crept up the walls of the hallway like crystalline vines.

"Get everyone to the throne room!" Kate cried.

Ted ran to the end of the hallway, directing the throngs of visibly frightened people down the stairs to the great room. When Kate reached the foot of the stairs, the throne room was already half-filled with people. Citizens from all over Castelmor had flocked to the castle complex when their houses had been overtaken by ice and snow. Kate went straight to the trap door under her throne and flung it wide open.

"Everyone inside!" she shouted.

She and Luca supervised as the throngs of Icaryans filed down the ladder leading down from the trapdoor. Ted and the others herded everyone toward the throne room. They hurried, starting to slip on the ice forming along the floor.

"Come on, come on!" Kate cried as the frost threatened to overtake their escape route.

"That's the last," Ted said as he brought the final group from the hall near to the thrones. As far as the royal family knew, everyone except them was packed underneath the throne room. They climbed down the ladder and slammed the door shut as the sheet of ice filled the gap over the entryway.

"Won't the ice seep through?" Luca asked.

"There's a magical seal protecting the door," said Kate, sensing his apprehension. "Nothing gets in or out unless we want it to."

"If anyone is hungry, there's a larder to my right," Allistair announced, his voice echoing in the darkness, "and a room lined with beds for those who are sleepy."

"I doubt *anyone* is going back to sleep tonight," Ted commented.

"I know," said Allistair. "But we don't know how long we'll be down here, or how much danger we're in," he whispered.

"It would help if it wasn't so dark. I can't see my hand in front of my face," said Ted.

The tunnel that the entire population of Castelmor had just descended into led to a space cloaked in complete darkness. Kate pulled a small yellow bead from her pocket, and held it at arm's length. She snapped it between her fingers and dropped it, producing the sound of something falling into water. The bead ignited as it fell into a small channel of viscous fluid that lined the wall. The surface of the liquid caught fire. The flames raced along the channel, illuminating the room. It paralleled the grand dimensions of the throne room and adjoining rooms above. It was an armory, with shields, helmets, swords, axes, maces, catapults, and all manner of things necessary for waging war on a massive scale.

"Wow!" shouted Kaspar, his voice reverberating throughout the space.

Allistair took a look around while his son examined the weapons.

"I haven't been down here since we—"

"Mmhmm," Kate cut him off.

"These weapons are pretty impressive," Luca observed.

"Mmhmm."

Luca touched her elbow, and realized that she was rigid with tension. Her siblings looked exactly the same way, as if being there made them uncomfortable.

"Hmm. The design is odd. They don't look like Icaryan weapons to me," said Luca.

"That's because they're not," said Kate. "This armory was built by the previous rulers. We just inherited it."

"Daddy, what's that?" Kaspar pointed to copper etchings on the wall that spanned the entire space.

"It's a history of the world, Kaspar. From the very beginning…to the very end." He swallowed hard.

The etchings on the wall depicted the creation of the world from a bundle of stars, and a kingdom led by a series of women rulers. It portrayed a bloody battle, above which three crowns were etched. In the darkest corner of the room was an etching of a tall figure in flowing robes. The oversized carving lent it its forbidding air. The obscuration of the face by a darkened hood made it even more ominous.

"Who's that?" Kaspar asked.

"We don't know," his father answered.

"It's creepy."

"Don't look at it."

The three monarchs exchanged glances. Luca observed that not one of them looked at the final etching directly. They all turned their heads to the side or stared at the floor, as if they were afraid to look at it. This made him curious. But he decided to reserve his questions for later. Luca examined the sculpture. Something about it struck him as queer. His eyes trailed to the bottom of the figure's robes, underneath which was a line of strange characters marked in a sharp, crude script.

"What does it say?" he asked, his eyes fixed on the inscription.

Kate and her siblings answered simultaneously in a droning voice, making their words sound like a chant.

"When the Unnamed is named, Icarya meets its end. Then the Three shall cease to be."

Kate turned to Luca with a doleful expression. "It's our death knell."

Ted whispered to avoid being overheard by Kaspar. "When we were young, and new to Icarya, we accidentally got ourselves locked down here while we were playing. We banged and screamed for help, but no one heard us. We were stuck down here for hours. In the darkness. With the faint reflection of that thing staring down at us. We were frightened, and our minds started playing tricks on us. We would have sworn that we saw the robes moving, swaying. Kate—"

He looked at his sister, who stood close to Luca, focusing her gaze on some random place along the opposite wall. He continued.

"Kate went to touch the lettering, and—" Ted broke off, visibly shaken by the memory, and unable to finish the tale. He had been so young, and the experience still burned in his mind.

"The carving thundered at us," Allistair filled in. *"When the Unnamed is named, Icarya meets its end. Then the Three shall cease to be.* We nearly died of fright. Suddenly the door to the throne room opened. We climbed over each other to get out, and we slept together camped out in the gardens for weeks. We were scared."

The monarchs stood in a circle, trying to figure out what to do.

"We can't just hide out here forever," said Ted.

"Certainly not," agreed Allistair, "but we can't just open the door and let it in, either, whatever *it* is."

"What about the people outside of Castelmor? We have no idea how far the frost extends. Other Icaryans might need our help," added Ted.

"How can we help others when we're holed up down here?" asked Allistair.

"You might be able to send out a small scouting party. Is there another exit?" suggested Luca.

"We don't even know what we're up against," countered Allistair. "Sending people out there could be extremely dangerous and foolhardy."

"It would be even more foolhardy to sit here and wait for whatever's coming," Luca replied.

As Kate's family argued, she slowly raised her eyes to stare at the blank face of the sculpture, imagining the horrible visage lurking behind that metal façade. She moved closer to it without thinking. The conversation she had left behind was drowned out, now nothing more than a buzzing in her ear. She cocked her head to one side, and the fingers of her right hand reached out, hovering at the base of the sculpture's robes. She hesitated.

No one was paying attention to her.

After several moments of deliberation, she pressed her fingers to the base of the carving. The metal underneath her palm made a cracking sound, and ice stretched through the crevice, filling the shadowy lines of drapery on the copper robes. She let out a cry, and drew her hand back. But she couldn't. Her hand was frozen to the wall.

Screams erupted everywhere. At the sound of Kate's cry, Luca came rushing to her aid while all of Icarya scrambled to arm themselves with the weapons surrounding them. Luca grabbed onto Kate's wrist and pulled, freeing her from the wall.

They took several steps back, looking up to see the copper figure writhing to life. Its form was outlined in frost, and a deep crumbling sound emanated as it pulled itself free from the wall. The copper tone of the statue changed to a pale blue. The figure was covered in ice, and a freezing mist surrounded it, giving it an ephemeral appearance.

With lightning speed, Luca drew his sword, and bisected the figure from the left side of its neck to its right hip. His sword went clean through, meeting a strange kind of resistance. The enemy before him was not metal, but was also not entirely flesh and blood. Cutting through the misty aura was most difficult of all, like slicing through honey. The mark that Luca's blade left disappeared in an instant.

Kate tried her hand, igniting a handful of fire orbs before throwing them at the creature's hidden face. An oversized hand with long, bony fingers reached out from the depths of the robe. The fiery projectiles stopped in midair and dropped to the ground, shattering like glass. The creature laughed, making a horrible buzzing sound unlike any sound that human vocal cords were capable of making.

"Iss thattt theee beesst youuu ccaaann doooo, Kkkkaaate?"

Kate's eyes went wide at the sound of her name being so horribly pronounced, and stood frozen in place.

Luca struck again, this time concentrating all his energy into his swing. Before he had only swung with brute force. This time, he brought all his magical power to bear as well. He hit his mark, cutting halfway through the creature's neck before hearing Kate let out a bloodcurdling scream.

He turned to find her with her hand clamped down on her neck. Blood gushed out from between her fingers, and she fell to her knees. He turned back around to the statue, to find a deep, watery stain had appeared at the base of the neck. Exactly where Kate was bleeding from. He withdrew his blade and rushed to Kate. He cradled her in his arms, covering her wound and healing it.

While Luca was so indisposed, the thing, whose neck had refrozen in place, counterattacked. It turned its head in the direction of the handheld weapons hanging along the walls. They quivered, and came loose from their moorings. Swords, axes, maces, and a barrage of arrows went flying in all directions, aimed at the hearts of those running for cover all over the armory.

"Use the shields!" Allistair shouted, as he hid his family behind a catapult. He donned a nearby shield and helmet, then ran back into the line of fire to help others reach safety. A large portion of the weapons were aimed at Kate, who was still recovering from being almost decapitated by magical proxy.

Luca batted the weapons away with his sword. The statue tilted its head at Luca and spoke to him, sounding like a glacier cracking.

"Iiii tthooooughhttt yyouuu werrre ssstayyying beeehiiiinddd."

Luca narrowed his eyes. He lunged forward, but touched only mist as the creature drifted away. It stopped in front of Kate, who was still crouched on the floor and breathing hard.

She looked up at the statue towering over her. Before Kate could react, the thing stretched out its arm and grabbed her by the throat, pinning her up against the indentation in the wall where it had once resided, smashing the back of Kate's head into the architecture and breaking her back.

Luca tried to run to her, but was stopped by a thick wall of clear ice that reached all the way to the ceiling. Through the glassy blockade he watched Kate writhe and groan in pain, attempting to wriggle free.

Kate ceased her fruitless, painful struggle, and closed her eyes. Her body encased itself in a white-hot ball of flame, its black borders flaring around her form like a ring around a sun. The hand clutching her slipped, its thinning fingers dripping and cracking from the scorching fire. The creature's back became more solid, and the force pinning Katelyn to the wall grew insurmountable.

Through the glass shielding them, Luca could hear a faint crackling sound emanating from deep within Kate's psyche. She groaned as the tips of her clothing began to smoke. She was burning out. She couldn't see that the brighter she burned, the more invincible her foe became.

You're making it stronger. Stop! Luca cried, his voice bellowing between her ears.

〜

KATE SNUFFED OUT THE FIRE INSTANTLY.

The icy figure chipped and crackled as its free hand reached for the robe obscuring its face. Kate tried to flail her legs in desperation, but her limbs were useless. She could barely move.

The thing removed its hood and revealed its face to Kate. The statue's features were pale and icy, devoid of any color, including the eyes, which shone a flawless white. But they were unmistakable.

Kate's eyes went wide at the sight. She cried out in sheer terror, closing her eyes and trying to avert her face. But the grip around her neck forced her to stare forward as she sank into madness. She began muttering.

The creature plunged its semi-corporeal hand into Kate's chest, and she screamed. In the palm of the creature's hand, Kate's medallion glowed brilliantly. The thin layer of sanity that remained in Kate sensed that the thing was trying to grasp the medallion from her neck.

With her last ounce of courage, Kate stared straight into the creature's face. In a moment of unbridled daring, a single word began to form on her lips.

The icy giant released its grip. Kate plummeted to the floor in a broken heap.

"KATELYN!"

Luca shouted at the top of his lungs, and blasted through the ice barrier separating them. The creature dissolved into an icy mist and disappeared, leaving a large thin disk of ice where it had last stood. Luca raced his hand along Kate's back, realigning her vertebrae and giving her control of her limbs once more. She grabbed onto him, pulling herself up onto his lap.

"Luca," she whispered weakly, her mind still in chaos.

"Shh, don't worry, my love, I'm here." He placed his hands over her ears and began mending her brain. Kate's siblings watched nervously as her pupils slowly returned to normal, reflecting their beloved sister.

"By the gods, Kate, are you all right?" said Ted, holding her hand in his. "Talk to me, Kate. Are you okay?"

She blinked several times. Luca had restored her sanity, but he couldn't erase what she had seen. The face of the robed figure was permanently etched on her psyche. She rolled over onto her stomach, planted her face in her hands, and wept.

"Kate," Allistair said, stroking the back of her blood-covered head. "Kate, darling, what did you see?" She only sobbed in response. Allistair took a deep breath, and asked the question on everyone's lips. "Who is the Unnamed?"

She looked up at her brother, a broken woman. "It's me."

"What do you mean, it's you?" Ted cried, confused.

"Maybe you were mistaken?" suggested Allistair.

Kate screamed at him. "You think I don't know my own face! It was me goddammit! It was me…" her voice trailed off, choking on a sob.

"Okay, let's everybody calm down," said Ted. "We really need to figure out how to kill the other Kate."

"Don't call it that," Kate said brusquely.

"Sorry. But we all saw what happened when Luca attacked it," Ted replied.

"Yeah, I almost lost my head," Kate commented dryly and rubbed at her neck, still slick with blood. Ted ripped off a part of his shirt, to help Kate wipe herself off.

"I am so sorry," Luca said. He had nearly killed her.

"You didn't know."

"We need to go to the troll without delay," Luca said, his voice urgent. "We need answers, and we need them now. We have to find a way to destroy that thing without killing you."

"If that's not an option, my life is a small price to pay for saving the world from destruction."

"No, that's not going to happen," Luca growled. Why would she even suggest it?

"There has to be another way to destroy it, and this is our best bet of finding that out."

"Agreed," said Allistair. "Rest up, take what you need, and be as fast as possible."

"Yeah, we'll do what we can here," said Ted. The people of Icarya needed comfort.

Luca went to lead Kate away to the beds to let her lie down. After he turned his back, Allistair grabbed hold of his arm.

"Protect her," he pleaded.

"I will."

26

THE VAMPIRE PRINCE PACED THE LENGTH OF THE SEASIDE CAVERN, crossing back and forth in front of the icy cocoon that had burst open earlier that day, never venturing too close to the treacherous writing lining the cave's maw. Though its image had been erased by the incessant slushing of tides, the directive Kate had marked at the opening retained its vigor.

The puddle he had just stepped in froze, creating a layer of ice as he lifted his foot out of it. The ice grew taller, letting off a freezing mist until it towered above him. He turned around.

"Where's my son?" Dracula demanded.

"Ffeeed mmeee." It swirled around itself, hovering over the legend like a cloud.

He stood in silent defiance.

"Ffeeeeed mmmeeee!" the cloud screamed. But without vocal cords, it sounded more like water freezing over than words. It encircled Dracula as he reluctantly drew blood from his wrist, ripping it open with a single long fingernail. The cloud was stained red as it absorbed Dracula's life blood, and it took the shape that Kate and the others had seen.

It had lost its metallic aspect, and looked like an ethereal woman cloaked in robes and shrouded in a sparkling mist. Her eyes were clear and cold, her skin and hair white and almost transparent. It wore a sadistic expression on its face. On Kate's face.

"Katelyn is dead, I presume? It took you long enough."

"Nnnnoottt yyyeeettt."

"Not yet?!" Dracula thundered.

"Thhheeerrrre wwwweeeere cccoooommplicaaationssss."

The vampire's eyes burned red. He had waited long enough for this ice creature to hatch, and was not about to drag his feet at the crucial moment, when all of Icarya trembled in fear.

"You were charged with one task. My patience with you is thin!" Furious, he ripped the hood from around the creature's head. "Shielding yourself is not necessary," he growled.

"Iiit scccaarress tthemmmm," the creature explained.

It knew everything that Kate knew, and used the memory of the shadowy figure to gain a psychological advantage. It had deliberately forced them into the armory, so it could make use of the etching on the wall. "Sssheee haaaass tthe medalllliiiooonnn."

"Just kill her and take it! Now!"

"Sssheee wiilll uuuuse iiiittt. Ssshhe mmuuust giiive ittttttooo mmeee fffreeelyyy."

Dracula laughed. "I wouldn't count on that!"

"Iiii mmmuuuusst haaave iiiit."

"I am your master. You owe your rotten half-existence to me, and I will have my satisfaction first!"

"Iiii haaaave nnooo mmmaasterrr," the thing with Kate's face retorted. It grew, extending its height until it loomed over the undead lord, casting him in deep shadow.

"You think you can threaten me?" Dracula shouted. "I, who have survived millennia, who created you and provide you with your form? You *will* obey!" His eyes shone bright red.

As he hypnotized the creature, its mist slowly receded, maintaining a small but distinct aura. It shrank back down to size. Dracula smiled with cruel satisfaction.

"Now," he commanded, collecting himself. "You will kill Kate, and bring Luca to me. No more delays."

The icy eyes stared blankly at him. As he continued to look it straight in the face, its empty expression filled with hate, he felt a shiver down his spine.

Suddenly, the creature lunged at him, capturing him in its aura, which had ballooned again. He struggled with all his supernatural might, but could not break free. His near depletion of blood and aversion to water sapped him of his strength, and undermined his full abilities. The mist became thicker and more solid, making it difficult for the vampire to breathe.

"Dddooon'ttt tthreeeatennn mmmeee agaaaiiin," the thing sneered as it released Dracula, dropping him to his knees.

He had underestimated the power of this creature because of its age. In reality, it was as cunning as Kate, and had no intention of being subdued.

Dracula was livid, but cautious. He had lost this battle of wills, but he intended to win the war. He sighed, calculating his next move, contemplating how he would destroy his creation once it fulfilled its purpose. If he had the time.

"Then, I guess I'll have to wait," he said calmly as the ice creature retreated to the far corner of the cave, thinking of how to draw Kate into the open.

27

"I don't need to rest," Kate insisted. "I need to go right now."

Luca said nothing, just continued leading her to the beds.

"Luca, I'm fine!"

"You just saw yourself as the face of the apocalypse. You are not fine."

"So what if I did, what difference does it make? I'm not going to waste one more minute being selfish, when I could be out there doing something about this!"

"Selfish?" Luca was puzzled. Kate plopped herself onto the bed in a sitting position, feeling dejected. She covered her face in her hands.

"This is all my fault," she murmured. "If I didn't practice magic, none of this would be happening."

"How do you know that?"

"I just do. You saw her, she's pure magic."

"I wouldn't say pure magic. She had a tangible form."

"Fine, *almost* pure magic. And she's made of ice. And has my face. And my brain. I should have stopped casting the minute I started experiencing side effects. If this thing is what I've been feeling, then I've got to stop it, before it kills everything I've ever loved. Which is why we should get going!" She stood up, preparing to leave, but Luca held onto her arms, stopping her.

"Hold on now. What do you mean, she has your brain?" he asked.

"I was able to read its thoughts, and I think she was able to read mine."

"And?"

"And she wants my medallion."

"Well, there'll be no more magic until we figure out what's going on."

"Obviously."

"Kate, I'm not sure that this is your doing, conscious or otherwise."

"How could it not be? Maybe I've created enough magical residue to sustain this thing."

"I don't think it was acting alone," Luca admitted as he started packing the blankets from the bed into a rucksack. Kate looked confused.

"What makes you say that?" Kate asked as they moved to the larder.

"When it saw my face, it talked to me as if it knew me. It said, 'I thought you were staying behind.' Clearly, it left someone behind."

"But that doesn't make any sense," Kate said as she filled a wineskin with water.

"I think," Luca said flatly, "it mistook me for someone else."

"How could that be? You don't exactly have a common look."

They exchanged glances.

"That would be really bad," Kate said as she and Luca traveled through the crowded space.

"Why would he do that? What purpose could it serve?" Kate asked.

"I have no idea." Luca cursed himself. "I was a fool to leave him there. But, you needed me. And I needed you."

Kate pressed his forearm, a small comfort.

"Gideon!" Luca called out, finally spotting the griffon's golden mane where the animals had set up makeshift stables. He was watching over Philip's little family in his absence.

"Hello, Luca. Kate, are you all right? I was too far away to see, but I heard what happened. How awful."

"Awful, yes. But I'm fine. Luca and I are leaving. We're going to see Drigory, to see if he can help us."

"Good idea. You want me to take you there?"

"It isn't the stealthiest mode of travel, but you're the fastest one here."

"Absolutely. We'll be there before it even knows we've left."

"I doubt that," Kate muttered under her breath.

"Is that going to pose a problem?" asked Luca.

"I hope not. But I imagine that if it wanted to stop us, it would do so at the door. And right now, from what I can tell, it seems…inactive. So, if we're going to go, now's the time."

THE GROUND BELOW WAS COVERED IN DEEP SNOW, MORE THAN ICARYA had seen in even its harshest winters. Kate wondered how many Icaryans had been snowed in without enough food, how many had been caught unaware in the storm. They didn't see a sign of life anywhere. Not a single bird flying through the trees, or a single set of footprints on the blanket of white covering the forest floor. Kate hoped it was because everyone was safely hidden inside their homes. She gripped Luca's arms to steady herself.

In the center of the pass leading to the Northern Mountains, there was a thin river. A bridge connected the banks that marked where the base of one peak ended and the next began. Gideon landed there.

"I'll wait here for you," he said as his passengers dismounted.

"If you see or hear anything unusual, head back to the castle without delay. Understood?" Kate asked.

Gideon nodded. "Be careful."

"Where are we going?" asked Luca.

Kate pointed at the shadowy spot of the river underneath the small bridge.

"Down," she answered. "The water is probably freezing. Are you ready?"

"Ready."

The water was like a liquid glacier, numbing their limbs so that they traveled as if through honey. After an excruciatingly long hour, they came to a circular metal door covered by a grate. Kate banged on it with all her might. The mouth of the door opened, and the pair swam in. The grate closed behind them, and they entered a second chamber. It drained slowly. Kate and Luca were able to plant their feet on the ground again, but the draft from being drenched in freezing water made Kate shake. Even Luca's teeth were chattering. Once the chamber was emptied, the door in front of them opened and they stumbled onto the carpeted floor of Drigory's study.

A middle-aged man rushed to them with thick blankets. He was an elderly troll with a distinguished, yet warm look, and a tawny-blond beard streaked with white that trailed to his knees. He wore an enormous dried-out mushroom cap as a hat, and a miniature red tunic and pants.

"Quick, quick," he said, "come near the fire. I have tea and coffee ready for you." The troll, who stood about half Kate's height, brought them both steaming cups made from hollowed-out tree trunks. The fire blazed, and the pair warmed up quicker than they expected. In only half an hour, their clothes and hair were dry, and they were once again able to speak.

"I've been expecting you for some time, now. So," Drigory said in a snide voice as he looked at Kate, "had enough magic yet? I told you this would happen."

"No, you didn't!"

"Yes, I did! I told you, this world was created by magic, and would be destroyed by magic. What did you think that meant?"

"I didn't think it meant I was the only being in creation that practiced magic," Kate countered.

"Oh please. You're not as naive as you pretend to be. You knew," Drigory said.

After several long moments, Kate finally spoke. "Please, Drigory," she sighed, "this is no time for a lecture. We came here because we need help. I need to know if there's a way to destroy the thing I've created."

"*Did* you create it?"

Kate was taken aback by the question. "Well, of course I did, I—"

"Did you feed it?"

"Feed it? What? I cast the magic, if that's what you mean, and what's left over seems to have coagulated into this thing."

"All by itself?" Drigory responded sarcastically. Kate didn't know how to answer.

"We think it may be working with someone," interjected Luca.

"Of course it is!" Drigory cried. "Kate, do you remember nothing that I taught you?"

Being scolded like this made Kate feel like a novice all over again. She had no idea what Drigory was expecting her to recall just then. He sighed in exasperation.

"You can't make something from nothing, and this thing didn't make itself. Your carelessness may have conceived it, but if you didn't feed it and help it grow, then someone else *did*."

"Then how come it has my face?" Kate questioned.

"Because it *is* a part of you. A very small part," the troll answered. "Your emotions are driving it. All the bad ones, anyway. And all the spells that you've cast give it its power."

"Great."

"Be grateful it came alive when it did. By my calculations, this was not meant to happen for quite some time, and it would have been invincible. But your linking up with Luca here put that off course."

"Wait just a minute," Kate interjected, incredulous. "Are you telling me that I would have summoned this thing?!"

"I'm saying that you would have become this thing."

Kate shuddered. "Jesus Christ."

"What did you just say?"

Luca flinched at Kate's utterance. The hair on the back of his neck stood on end. Kate looked at him, observing that he looked unusually uncomfortable. She guessed the reason why.

"It's a name. One I haven't thought about in a long, long time."

"I don't like the sound of it."

"You wouldn't." She looked unsurprised. Luca's expression was puzzled, but she dismissed his query with a shake of her head. "Another time. We have more pressing matters now."

"Your magic alone wouldn't cause this thing to come into being now," Drigory continued. "Someone helped it, someone very powerful. With very powerful blood."

"I can smell my father's hand in this," Luca said. "Somehow, he followed me here."

"Why did he do that?" said Drigory. "Don't you want to kill him?"

How would he know that? Luca asked.

Kate shrugged.

"Yes," Luca said at last, "and that's exactly what I will do."

"Let's solve one problem at a time," Kate insisted. "How do we kill it? When Luca attacked it, I suffered the injury as well."

"That's because it's connected to you," Drigory explained. He pulled a thick tome from the solid oak bookshelves that covered the walls. He flipped to a page that he had thumb-marked the day before. "It's carrying a small piece of your soul around with it, acting as its consciousness. If she gets cut, you get cut."

"So if I die," Kate said, "she dies."

Luca didn't like where this was going, but Drigory cut him off.

"I'm afraid it's not that easy, Kate," the troll said.

"What do you mean?"

"If you die, it will suffer heavy damage, but that won't be enough to destroy it. It's made up of too much magic."

"Perfect. So what *will* kill it?"

"This." The troll turned the book in front of him around to face the pair.

"The bloodstone?" Kate questioned.

"What's the bloodstone?" Luca asked, fingering the aging page of the book. He studied its strangely beautiful illuminations.

"The bloodstone is a stone forged from the blood of the first Icaryans. It was crafted by the Great Magician who created Icarya. If the person who possesses the stone speaks a single magical word, known only by a select few, that person is given the power to destroy this world and create a new one. One that fulfills that person's every desire, good or evil."

"That's what it wants," said Kate.

"How do we know it can use it? If it doesn't know this magical word..." Luca reasoned.

"It does," Kate said with certainty.

Luca looked at Kate, who was staring at the floor.

It knew the word because she knew the word. It's what she had almost said before the creature retreated.

"Where's the stone?" Luca asked.

"It used to be passed down through the old ruling family, but it disappeared in the great civil war that left this dear one on the throne with her siblings," Drigory said.

He and Kate looked at each other.

"How does that help us? We don't want to destroy the world, we just want to destroy this thing," Luca said.

"The bloodstone can be weaponized," Drigory answered, again staring squarely at Kate. He pointed to a block of foreign-looking script on the page. "If you cut the stone open and smear the blood on a blade, that blade takes on the power to destroy any creature, when plunged through the heart."

"Would that kill Kate in the process?" Luca asked.

"Yes."

"It's a good thing we don't know where it is then, because that's not an option."

"What if it's the only option?" Kate asked, dead serious.

"No."

Kate blistered with the tremendous amount of pain and fear that lay behind his answer.

"Do you have any *other* ideas?" Drigory asked.

Luca thought for a moment. "If this thing has been feeding off my father, what would killing him mean for the monster?"

"Without blood to sustain its corporeal form, it would be reduced to simply magic. An icy cluster. It would be much less powerful. That might make it vulnerable enough."

"Vulnerable enough for what?" asked Kate.

"I can create a seal that could trap it. It wouldn't harm anyone, and it wouldn't cause your death. And shrunk down to size," Drigory added, "you would not feel its presence. You'd feel complete, like the you you've always been. But you'd have to stop casting."

"I'm willing to do more than that, if that's what it takes," Kate declared.

"That sounds like a plan," Luca said, satisfied by this alternate solution.

"And what about Dracula?" Drigory asked. Luca was startled at first by this offhand expression of knowledge, but he let it pass.

"Leave him to me." Luca once again felt the burning urge to destroy his father. He had threatened the only thing he had ever held dear. He would protect Kate, and Icarya, at all costs.

"What are you going to do?" Kate asked, her voice full of concern.

"I'm going to kill him."

"Can you win?" she asked after a pause.

"I have to."

"Luca," she said, her eyes filling up with tears. "I don't want to put you in danger."

"He wouldn't be here, threatening our entire world, if not for me," he said as he drew Kate closer to him.

"*Our* world?"

"Yes, Katelyn. In my heart, I am an Icaryan. I'll do whatever it takes to protect the place that has given me a home. And the woman who loves me." He bent his forehead to hers.

I have to do this, Luca insisted.

She closed her eyes in acknowledgement. They shared one last passionate embrace. Kate kissed him like she might never kiss him again.

I've loved every minute with you, she pressed.

"I'll come back, Kate," he said as he caressed her hair. "I won't be gone long."

"Please be careful. I want you back in one piece."

"I promise."

"You can use Radha," Drigory said, gesturing to the giant vulture resting in its chamber down the hall. "She will take you wherever you wish to go. Gideon will take Kate back to Castelmor."

Luca nodded, looked one more time at Kate, and disappeared down the hallway. Kate and Drigory sat back down at the table. Kate wiped at her eyes.

"He'll be fine, child. But you're not going to wait to find out, are you?" Drigory asked.

Kate looked him in the eyes, and shook her head.

"Will Hercules come in time?" he asked.

"He has to. Everything depends on him."

Drigory nodded. "Then we'll have to get this thing's attention. But before we do, let's work on blocking it from reading your mind, or else all is lost. Oh, and by the way…"

"Hmm?"

Drigory smiled. "Congratulations."

LUCA HURRIED TO DRACULA'S SEASIDE PRISON. THE VULTURE LET HIM down on the snowy beach before the cave. Sword drawn, he ignored the searing pain as he stepped over the seal that he had started but which Kate had finished. The cave was cloaked in darkness. It appeared to be abandoned. The first thing Luca saw was the broken icy shell that had once housed the magical being that now wore Kate's face.

As he scanned the space, he saw a figure emerge from the shadows. A cruel smile spread upon Dracula the elder's lips.

"I've been waiting for you," he said.

Luca didn't reply. He only advanced, raising his sword.

"You have no words for me? Only the end of your blade?" His father's deep voice was sadistically playful, and cocky.

Luca remained silent. He had nothing to say. He needed only to act.

"So be it. I've waited a long time to test your skills for myself." As Dracula said this, an icy cloud billowed between them.

Luca took a cautious step backward. Dracula meant for Luca to square off with the ice creature. Luca knew he had to be careful not to inflict any serious damage. The icy mist materialized, taking a more tangible form than Luca had seen in the armory. With the exception of the skin's bluish-white hue and the miniscule mist that continued to float around it like a halo, the creature seemed human.

It was as Kate had said. Though the creature's features were identical to Kate's in all but color, Luca observed how different its countenance was, lacking the love and warmth that Kate's true face exuded. This was nothing more than a shallow copy.

Its eyes glared at him, full of hate. The creature attacked, swinging high with a flat blade aimed at his head. Luca bent backward, avoiding the blow and blocking the next with his own sword. It fought double-handed, with short blades reflecting those Kate wore at her hips. It twirled and struck at him from both sides with impressive speed and strength. Its form was perfect.

Is this Kate's level of skill? He wondered, dodging its blows and circling around it. If it was, he had a newfound appreciation for his lover's martial ability.

"What's wrong, Luca?" Dracula sneered. "Don't worry, she will be dead soon enough. Though I must admit, the one small taste of her I had was delectable. When this is all over, I may take her for my own."

"Leave her alone," Luca growled. "This is between us."

"Is it?" Dracula retorted. "Enough, I tire of this." He pulled the ice-Kate back, standing off against Luca and drawing his sword. "This is what you came for, isn't it?"

Their blades clanged together. Dracula gave the fight his all. They fought for over an hour, neither so much as drawing blood, two dark phantoms circling each other. Luca matched his father in skill and ability and more.

All the while, Dracula continued to needle his son.

"Only a spurned woman could teach you to hate me so much."

Spurned?

"I believe the word you're looking for is *raped*," Luca said as he faced off against his father, trying to overtake Dracula with his strength alone.

"Ha! Is that what she told you?" The Count grabbed his son by the wrist, pulling Luca's face within inches of his own. "You know just as well as I do," he said, an arrogant grin spreading across his face, "I've never had to rape *any* woman."

Luca pushed this to the back of his mind, not allowing his father to break his concentration. Dracula's arrogance, like so many of his children before him, would be his downfall.

Luca finally gained the advantage and pressed it until the great vampire was backed into a corner, the tip of Luca's blade pointed at his heart. Dracula laughed.

"I knew you wouldn't fail me, Luca. You must truly love her."

Luca narrowed his eyes. "What is she to you?" he demanded.

"She is nothing. A means to an end."

As father and son were conversing, they took no notice of the change coming over the ice creature. It closed its eyes, stretching a hand up to its forehead.

Luca sensed that his father's muscles were no longer tensed. He had dropped the façade of putting up resistance. Dracula finished his thought.

"My end." He grabbed the tip of Luca's sword, and held it steadily over his undead heart.

"Drive it home. Fulfill your destiny."

"My destiny?"

"The destiny of all sons—to destroy their father."

Luca hesitated. "You've been there, haven't you? So close, but just out of reach. Testing me. Manipulating me. Even now." Luca's grip on his weapon tightened.

Dracula glared at his son. "You've always known that. I couldn't exactly kill your mother at a distance, now could I?"

"What?" Luca failed to suppress his shock.

"She wouldn't have stopped until she destroyed you. I did it to protect *you*." Dracula sighed. "I've tried this a million ways. I tried not to involve you. You're the only one who can do this. You are my true heir. And now, you're finally ready."

Luca raised his head slightly, breaking the intensity of his killing stance. He swallowed hard, burying his patricidal lust.

"You've caused me nothing but torment, and you expect me to give you peace?" Luca took a step backward, sheathed his sword, and turned to leave.

"Get back here and finish what you started!" Dracula roared.

Luca kept walking.

"You think you can turn your back on me?! I will haunt you to the end of your days, which we both know will be a very, very long time!"

Luca disappeared from the entrance, climbing back onto Radha and heading straight for Castelmor.

Dracula shook with rage. His excitement at reaching the culmination of his millennia-long plan had caused him to reveal his hand too early. Even so, he never expected his son to simply walk away. After all, he had come to save the woman he loved, and he had accomplished nothing. Just to spite his father.

"Impudent whelp!" he screamed, turning to look for the other Kate. "What are you waiting for? After him! Bring him back here now! He's going to regret crossing me!"

"Iiii dddontt tthiiinkkk sssssoooo."

"Excuse me? That wasn't a request. That's an order!"

"Yoouu've ouuutllivvved yyyyouuur uuusefulllnessss," the creature creaked as it approached Dracula, enclosing him in its mist.

"What are you doing, you overgrown snowflake!? Wait—I said stop!"

The ice maiden continued to stare at her creator cruelly as she trapped his feet in ice, then his legs.

"You don't know what you're doing! This won't kill me, it will only—"

"Preeeeccccissseelyyyyy," it said, emitting a horrible crackling sound meant to be a laugh. It had caught him at the precise moment when he was too drained, too weak to fight back.

"No! *No!*"

"Oohhhhhh, onnne laaaasstttt tthinnggg..." The figure bared its oversized fangs and bit Dracula's neck hard before he completely froze over, becoming encapsulated. The creature inhaled. As it did so, the crystalline, broken nature of its vocal cords restructured themselves.

"Ah, much better," the other Kate said, speaking in the deep masculine voice that belonged to the Count.

"And now, to attend to business." It dematerialized, leaving the cavern deserted, save for one tall, icy stalagmite that, upon close inspection, vibrated almost imperceptibly, as if someone was pounding at it from the inside.

LUCA SOARED BACK TO CASTELMOR ASTRIDE DRIGORY'S VULTURE. IN THE air, his mind raced.

How will we trap the creature if he remains at large?

Though he had been full of determination leaving the cave, he still worried if the decision he had made was the right one. He wanted desperately to speak to Kate, to receive her counsel and beg her forgiveness for failing her. He had allowed the threat looming over Icarya to remain. He felt her, but faintly.

Luca...

Kate called out to him, but he couldn't decipher from where. The distance between them felt insurmountable.

Where are you? What are we going to do? He pondered as he landed near the entrance to the armory where he and Kate had left from before. Kate was not waiting for him at the door like he expected.

"Kate? Kate!" he called out her name as he searched for any sign of her.

"Luca!" Allistair was the first of Kate's siblings to catch sight of him.

"Allistair,. Where's Kate?"

"She's supposed to be with you."

"No," Luca corrected. "We parted ways after seeing Drigory. She should have been here hours ago." They both realized the gravity of the situation.

"Are you telling me Kate never made it back here?" Luca cried.

"No one has seen her since you both left," replied Allistair. "Good god, if that thing has her—" He wrung his hands.

"I'm going back to Drigory's right now!" shouted Luca, not waiting for Allistair to respond. He moved through the crowd milling about the armory like a phantom, and caught up to Radha before she took off.

"I'm coming with you," Luca declared as he climbed back onto the vulture's back.

Kate, what are you doing? He sensed that he was being blocked, but he couldn't determine the source.

...I'll love you forever...

When he reached the submerged dwelling, he didn't waste a single second, calling out for Kate the minute his head was no longer underwater. He burst through the door as it opened, nearly ripping it off its hinges. The blood boiling in his veins prevented the frigid waters from affecting him the way they had before.

"Where is Kate?!" Luca demanded as the troll approached him.

"Now just calm down—"

Luca lifted the troll off the ground, bringing Drigory's eyes to meet his, blazing red in a mix of anger and fear as the water dripping from his hair and clothes began to freeze.

"Where is she?!"

Drigory was frightened by Luca's outburst, and promptly poured his heart out.

"She's gone to kill the monster, where else? Put me down!"

Luca dropped the troll unceremoniously. Drigory quickly rearranged his ruffled clothes.

"How could she, without the bloodstone? Kate's not stupid!" Luca cried.

"No, she isn't. The bloodstone didn't disappear, so much as it was hidden."

Luca's heart raced. He knew Kate. He knew she blamed herself for all of this, and that she would sacrifice everything to save Icarya. His only hope was to beat her to the stone before she could use it.

"Where?" he roared.

Drigory took a deep breath. "In plain sight." The volume Drigory referenced earlier still lay open on the desk. Drigory turned the page. "I trust you recognize this?" he said, studying Luca's face for his response. Sure enough, Luca's visage became one of shock. On the following page was an illustration of the bloodstone, set into an intricate necklace made of gold.

The medallion. She's had it the whole time.

"Kate has surrendered herself to the creature," Drigory explained.

Luca's heart broke, lost in fear, anger, and an overwhelming sense of loss and betrayal.

She's on a suicide mission... How could you do this?

He opened his lips to say something, but his voice was overpowered by that of his father's, which thundered across all of Icarya.

"Citizens of Icarya. You are called upon to witness the death of your beloved queen. Gather at the Ancestor's Mound. Then look upon her no more."

Luca turned quickly to the troll. "Where is the Ancestor's Mound?"

"It's the burial place of the old queens. Radha knows the way. You must hurry. Save her, Luca, the way only *you* can."

THE MIDDAY SUN BEAT DOWN ON THE ANCESTOR'S MOUND, CASTING A bright reflection in the snow covering the grass hill that housed the queens of old. From above, Luca spied Kate's family at the front of the congregation that was rapidly forming at the base of the mound from every direction. It seemed to Luca that everyone had in fact been safe inside their homes as Kate had hoped. People were lazy and carefree most of the time, but many remembered darker times when they had had to be more diligent. They had called upon those old senses to protect them during the storm, almost by instinct. Ted was the first to approach Luca, accosting him before he dismounted.

"What's this all about, Luca? Where is my sister?"

Luca didn't know what to say. He didn't want to burden Ted with the knowledge that threatened to crush his own heart, but he didn't want to lie.

He didn't have to. Before Luca could say anything, a gale wind blew across the mound, swirling snow in every direction and stealing everyone's breath away. As the snowdrift cleared, the ice creature became visible, casting a towering shadow in the snow and causing the crowd to erupt in screams. She pulled up her robes, and out fell a bruised and battered Kate. She was bound by her neck and her hands, which were tied tightly behind her back. Through the distance and the cold, Luca could smell the blood oozing from her wrists.

The ice witch yanked on the rope around Kate's neck, pulling her to her feet. The queen of Icarya stood up as proudly as she could, upturning her nose slightly. Her mouth was set in iron. As she came to her feet, Luca saw the medallion hanging down her neck, thumping against her chest. At the sight of their queen thus mistreated, Icaryans reacted on every side, attempting to rush up the hill to her defense. They were knocked back by an icy gust, some blown several feet in the air.

"Get back! Those who surrender now may be allowed to live as slaves."

Not a soul moved.

The creature scoffed, tugging at Kate's neck. "Your precious queen has surrendered at the first sign of danger, begging me to spare your lives." It paused, its hateful expression becoming mixed with pain as it addressed the world it meant to destroy. "I have spilled oceans of blood to protect you, blood I can never wipe clean. I have given you my life, my very soul. And you can't even swear your loyalty to me?" She turned to face Kate. "What exactly are you trying to save?" the creature cried, its voice bitter.

Kate stared numbly ahead, a single tear staining her cheek before melting into the snow at her feet. She turned her head, looking her demon in the face. Her blank stare became filled with self-loathing.

Luca, eyeing the pair, saw Kate's eyes flicker. The separation between Kate and the creature faded in that moment. His heart ached for her, as he observed her struggle to retain her sense of self.

The creature grinned, and lowered her voice to speak to Kate in private. But Luca continued to listen.

"I appreciate your rage." It inhaled, breathing in Kate's hatred with satisfaction. "I would have you with me," it said. The two stared at each other. Kate turned her head forward, saying nothing. The creature seemed surprised, and disappointed. "You deserve them," she retorted. "In a moment," she whispered, leering at Kate, "you will be gone and I will have everything. You have sacrificed all, and gained nothing!" The creature trembled in laughter, her icy aura exuding a shrill twinkling sound.

Out of the corner of her eye, Kate spied movement. Two figures weaved slowly through the crowd below, stopping only when they realized they had drawn her attention. She stared in disbelief as she saw the man she knew to be her father standing next to Meryn. She didn't know how it was possible, but seeing them standing side-by-side, she understood their relationship to each other. And to her. They stared back at her. It steeled her will.

"A waste of a life, all for a mantle that was never yours anyway," the creature mused.

Kate held her head higher, and whispered a retort. "Yes it is."

Kate turned her gaze to Luca, holding his stare.

He fought to free himself from the icy bonds keeping his feet planted to the floor. But it was hopeless. Even if he broke free, what could he do? The sound of his father's voice suggested to him that Dracula had met his end at this creature's hand, and yet here it was, at the height of corporeality and overflowing with magical power. Kate's way was the only way. And they both knew it. Tears streamed down Luca's face as he continued to stare at her. He already mourned her, and the death of all the hopes her love had instilled in his heart. The world became silent, and he heard Kate's insistent voice ringing in his head.

Bring me back.

〜

As the creature laughed demonically, Kate broke the bonds around her wrists with sheer force. She ducked, avoiding the creature's icy clutch as the rope around her neck tightened. In a split second, she grabbed the blade she had convinced the icy shadow she wasn't hiding at her leg and cut the cord around her neck in a single motion. The other Kate moved to protect her chest. In a brilliant, shocking move, Kate plunged the dagger into her own heart, piercing the bloodstone right through the center.

"Auugh!" Kate let out a loud groan as the creature screamed, reeling at Kate's unexpected maneuver. In tandem, Luca felt the blow. He collapsed as their connection was nearly severed.

All of Icarya shouted in unison: "Kate!"

She pushed the blade in deeper, until only the hilt was sticking out of her chest. The creature's head rolled back, and she shattered to the ground, reduced to a fine glassy powder. A ray of sunshine emerged from the clouds, melting the powder and causing it to run down the hill as Kate fell to her knees, coughing up blood through shallow breaths. She reached up and pulled out the knife she had buried in her chest. She dropped it on the ground as she shuddered at the sudden gush of blood. She grabbed her lower abdomen, and lay down in the grass.

The ice blockading Kate's family softened. Luca rose and smashed through it, and they all rushed to her. Luca arrived first, coming upon her as her eyes began to roll into the back of her head.

"Kate," he sobbed, "Kate, hold on." His hands were covered in her blood as he tried desperately to heal her. But the wound she had inflicted with the bloodstone was too powerful, even for him.

"Pl-please," she could barely form the words. "I'm n-not ready t-to die." She grabbed him, and used her last ounce of strength to pull him to her neck.

Luca trembled with hesitation and grief. He inhaled the scent of her blood. He allowed it to seep into his brain, and succumbed to her desire, and his own. Just as Kate's eyes began to glaze over, Luca bit down as hard as he could, tears streaming from his face. He choked on his sobs as he swallowed mouthful after mouthful.

～

WHEN KATE'S FAMILY REACHED THE SUMMIT, THIS WAS THE SIGHT THAT filled their eyes. They stood immobilized at a short distance as Luca crouched over their sister, splayed out on her back, unresponsive. Her brothers clung to each other for support. The sun attacked the anomalous snow, leaving behind only wet earth and tiny white patches. At the base of the mound, the puddle of water that had moments before been Kate's split soul evaporated into the air and was gone.

The flash of white that streaked across the sky above their heads went unnoticed by all.

～

KATE CRIED OUT.

Luca pulled his mouth away, and looked at Kate's face. His anguish multiplied as he saw a red blood light shining from her once beautiful brown eyes, and two fangs poking out of what used to be her delicate mouth. Seeing her like that, so close to his own nature, a strange emotion stirred deep inside his heart. In that moment, he found her more endearing than he ever had before, and his attachment to her was only intensified.

"Luca, is that you?" Her consciousness was in transition, and she was temporarily delirious. Once the change was complete, she would become more like her old self.

She'll never be the same again, Luca lamented. *But I'll love her forever.*

"Yes, Katelyn, it's me," he said quietly.

She moaned. "I'm so thirsty." His face twisted up in sadness and pain. Brokenhearted, he leaned over her once more, leaving his neck exposed within inches of her mouth. At the same time, he became aware of the quickening pace of his heartbeat, racing with joyful anticipation. Not until this moment had he realized how badly he truly wanted this. If only it hadn't come so soon.

"You smell so sweet..." she whispered. Luca closed his eyes as he felt her teeth brush against his skin.

∾

"HOLD IT RIGHT THERE!" HERCULES'S VOICE RANG OUT AS HE SPED UP THE mound from the opposite side. He grabbed Luca by the scruff of his neck, tossing him aside like a rag doll. He seized Kate by the jaw.

She snarled and snapped at him.

He jammed the contents of a small vial down her throat.

She gagged as if he had poured acid in her mouth, then lurched onto her side.

∾

"WHAT ARE YOU DOING?" LUCA SHOUTED AS HE GOT TO HIS FEET.

"Saving her, what does it look like I'm doing?" Hercules shot back.

"You're a little late for that!"

"No," Kate said, in her normal voice. She turned onto her back again, and revealed dark brown eyes. "He's just in time." Hercules crouched over her and placed his hand on her shoulder. She clasped it. "Well done, hero."

"Kate?" Luca questioned, not believing his eyes. "Kate, are you all right? What-what's happened?"

"Our plan succeeded, that's what happened!" shouted Drigory, making his appearance at the top of the hill.

"I-I don't understand. You were—"

"I was," said Kate, sitting up. Her clothes were soaked in blood, but the wound to her heart was healed. The slippery dagger lay on the ground beside her.

"You saved me. I knew it would come to that. But," she continued, stroking Luca's stunned, tearful face, "that wasn't enough. You've seen all I have done to keep Icarya happy. Did you really think I would disappoint the man I love?"

"Kate sent me after a rare flower," Hercules explained. "A flower used in a potion that cures all unwanted conditions. Including—"

"Vampirism," Luca answered. The plot Kate had formulated unfolded in his mind.

"If you don't want me that way, then how could I live with myself, knowing that I'd forced you into it?" she asked.

Luca's expression softened, and he pulled her close. "I'll always want you, Kate. Always." Luca was utterly relieved that Kate was alive. But he also knew that he would fulfill what he now realized was their mutual desire. In time.

She smiled at him. He clung to her, squeezing and kissing her until she couldn't breathe.

"I love you, Kate. Thank you. Thank you for loving me."

"It has been my absolute pleasure," she said, burying her face in his strong chest, heaving with emotion.

"But don't ever do that to me again."

"I'm sorry. I never meant to hide anything from you. I wanted to tell you what I was planning so badly, but," she hesitated as she snuggled close to him, "Drigory was convinced that you wouldn't agree, and that if Hercules hadn't gotten to me before I...before I..."

Kate couldn't bring herself to say out loud that she had almost fed off Luca. He brushed an errant strand of hair out of her face as she collected herself and as he reflected on how his own reaction to seeing her that way had surprised him.

Kate continued, "Before I turned completely, he thought that your spell over me would be too powerful, even for his potion. The timing was everything, and I just couldn't risk a single thing not going right."

"He was right," Luca answered. "And so were you."

Kate rested her head on his chest again.

"What should I do with this?" Hercules asked, pulling out a second vial.

Luca eyed it carefully, taking the bottle from Hercules and rolling it in his fingers. He went to put it to his lips.

Kate stopped him.

"No," she said, lowering his hand. "You love me the way I am. I love you the way you are."

"But—"

"How many times have you helped me, healed me, rescued me, and you still don't realize your worth? I told you before, I want you—*all* of you."

Luca looked at her and sighed. He handed the vial back to Hercules.

"I'll take that," Drigory said, spiriting it away into the hidden folds of his sleeves.

"Are you sure?" Luca asked as Kate's family crowded around them and smothered them both with hugs.

"Absolutely. Besides," said Kate, smiling coyly, "someone has to teach my baby to control its power."

Luca cocked his head. Kate's family perked up at their sister's offhand announcement. They jumped for joy and issued their congratulations.

The shock sunk in. "Your baby!" Luca shouted.

"Well," Kate took Luca's hand and placed it across her stomach. "I should say, our baby."

Luca's fingertips tingled. He sensed a small, fast heartbeat. His eyes gleamed, and his chest puffed up with fatherly pride.

"Kate," he gushed, "you're pregnant."

She beamed. "Apparently."

"Been pregnant for weeks!" Drigory exclaimed. "Over three hundred years old, you'd think if she got knocked up, she'd know it."

"Hey! This is new for me," she defended her ignorance as she stepped deeper into Luca's outstretched arms.

Luca smiled.

LATE THAT NIGHT, KATE SAT CROUCHED ON THE EMBROIDERED RUG IN her chamber at Castelmor. A robe of black silk with lace embellishments was draped over her skin as she gazed silently into the hearth. Her utility belt was splayed across her lap. The fire whistled and screamed as she placed each of her magic orbs into the fire, one by one. The flames roared with each new addition, and Kate watched until each sphere had melted, its contents consumed by the blaze.

Luca, enrobed in crimson silk, came out of the washroom and sat beside her, placing his hand on her shoulder.

"It's late," he said, his voice soft as velvet.

"I'm almost finished," she said, not breaking her concentration.

"Kate, you died today. You should get some sleep. The rest can wait until morning."

"No," she said, her voice firm. "I don't want them for one more minute."

Luca sighed in resignation and kissed the base of her neck. "How are you feeling?" he asked.

"Like you said, I died today," Kate answered. "How do you think I feel?" Her tone was even and steely.

Luca slipped his hand under her robe, caressing her belly. "That's not what I meant."

Kate sighed, realizing that she was taking her sour mood out on Luca, and for no good reason. She put her hand over his, and craned her neck to the side to lean her head on his shoulder.

"Sorry. I'm okay."

"Are you sure? Drigory said you're a few weeks along and, well... you've been through a lot in the past few weeks."

"I know. He's assured me that everything is fine."

"Okay," Luca whispered.

"I saw her," Kate replied in a dreamy voice, remembering her vision of the princess's coronation. "*We* saw her." She closed her eyes, the curves of her unborn daughter's face flashing in her brain as she committed them to memory.

He kissed the top of Kate's head, sharing her acknowledgement. "Are you okay though? When that ice creature dropped you from under her robes, you didn't look too good. What did she do to you?"

Kate remained silent for a long time, staring into the fire. Luca waited as he saw her eyes get glassy.

"She trapped me in my darkest memories, reliving them over and over again without end. It wasn't the whole me, but it was me. My fear, my anger, my guilt. That's all it knew. And trapped in that cloud, that's all I knew." Kate closed her eyes and breathed.

Luca held her close.

"I had a hell of a time trying to concentrate on something else," she finished, opening her eyes again and rummaging through the pouches on her belt.

"And I saw Meryn in the crowd today," she continued. "And my father. My real father. They were there, and then they weren't. I looked for them after, but I couldn't find them."

Luca sensed her disappointment.

"Why didn't they come to me?" she asked. "I have so many questions..."

Luca kissed her shoulder. "If they want to see you, they know where to find you. Put it out of your mind."

Kate pursed her lips.

Luca sighed, knowing full well that she wouldn't rest until she'd found them. He knew that feeling all too well. But she knew she wouldn't be searching alone, and she smiled.

"What was it?" Luca asked.

"What was what?" Kate said as she flung the final orb into the fire.

"The something else you thought of."

Kate's smile warmed, and she looked up at him. "Your eyes. The way they glowed when you made love to me for the first time."

Luca gazed at her. "You really do love me the way I am, don't you?" he said, holding her cheek in the palm of his hand.

"I've been saying that for the longest time," Kate answered coyly, "is it just now starting to sink in?" She nuzzled his nose, and said quietly, "Finished."

She laid her belt, now much lighter, to the side as Luca picked her up in his arms and carried her over to the bed. She wrapped her arms around him, holding his gaze as he placed her gently on the mattress. Luca kept his eyes locked on Kate. She reclined on the bed, staring deep into his eyes. Deep enough that she didn't notice him pull something small out of his robe and tuck it under the pillow as he joined her on the bed. When he blinked, Kate regained her senses, not realizing she had ever lost them.

"Hey," she said, as if just remembering something, "how did things go with Dracula?"

It was Luca's turn to be a bit more solemn. "They didn't. He was using me. He wanted me to come, wanted me to kill him."

"Had enough of living, I guess."

"I walked away."

Kate raised her head in surprise. "You did what?"

"I didn't want to give him the satisfaction." Luca looked at Kate, his eyes sorrowful. "I just couldn't conceive of a scenario where giving him what he wanted was a good idea. But I failed to protect you. All because of him and his cruel machinations. I hate him." He paused. "I hate them both. Because of them, I let you down."

Kate shook her head. "I've never been prouder of you." She took his full lips in hers.

"He'll come back. He always does."

"We'll deal with it. Together." She returned her head to his chest. "I'm sorry about your family," she whispered.

Comforted by her acceptance, Luca's sadness dissipated, and was replaced with pride. He wrapped one arm around Kate's shoulders and the other around her lower abdomen. "I've got my family, right here."

Kate beamed, and kissed him again before stretching her limbs in preparation for sleep. Luca rolled onto his side to face her, propping his head up with his hand and stroking her belly.

"Kate?"

"Mmm?"

"Are you happy?"

She tilted her head. His head turned down. "Are you happy with me, as the father of your child?"

She took his head in her hand, and brought his eyes to meet hers. "I would have no other."

"I love you, Katelyn."

"I love you."

He bent over to plant a light kiss on Kate's stomach before returning to meet her gaze. His eyes twinkled at her, and he took several deep breaths before asking: "Marry me?"

Kate blinked, taken completely by surprise. "Luca, just because I'm pregnant doesn't mean we have to get married. I'm not expecting anything."

"You're my whole world," Luca said as he leaned over her, caressing her neck with his lips. "I want all of Icarya to know our lives are one. I'm yours, and you're mine. Forever."

Kate looked at him with purpose. "Forever?"

Luca understood her meaning, and the eternal weight of his words. He nodded.

Forever.

Her whole face brightened. He brought his mouth to hers, their tongues battling with each other as their mutual excitement grew. He pulled his mouth away from hers, resting his forehead on hers and breathing hard.

"Marry me," he whispered feverishly.

Kate wrapped her arms around him tighter. "I'd be honored."

Luca smiled. He tucked his hand under the pillow and retrieved a dazzling sapphire housed in an elaborate and delicate setting of white gold, which gave the appearance of a stone set in lacework.

"I had this made for you," he said.

Kate's mouth opened in astonishment. "Luca!" she cried.

"Do you like it?"

"It's gorgeous! Thank you," she said.

"I used the money you paid me when we first met."

"That was the best money I ever spent," she joked. Kate admired the ring as she slipped it on her finger. She turned to look at Luca as realization set in.

"You didn't just ask me to marry you because of the baby, did you?"

Luca smirked at her, and shook his head.

Her eyes sparkled at him.

In that moment, the couple was happier than they had ever been before.

"Kate?" Luca asked, his tone flirtatious.

"Yes?" She knew what was coming as he inched closer to her.

"If you're pregnant, does that mean we can't—"

"Absolutely not."

He grinned. "Good."

Kate laughed into his shoulder as he climbed on top of her, being careful not to press against her stomach.

"What happened to me getting some rest?" she chided.

"Oh, you'll sleep. Tomorrow."

Kate grasped at his hair as his lips caressed her collarbone. "I'm gonna hold you to that," she whispered as she closed her eyes, sighing in the pleasure of Luca's embrace.

EPILOGUE

HAYDEE FLED INTO THE DESERT, CARRIED ON THE SHADOWS BY AN infernal wind that howled between the buildings of Likhan and out to the Burning Sands. She quitted the shadows as night fell, collapsing onto a dune that slid under her weight until she reached a flattened area surrounded on all sides by wind-whipped mounds. Her breath was ragged, and she gasped for the clean air of the night. The smell of her own seared flesh filled her nostrils and invaded her lungs, choking her. She raised her fingers to her cheek, straining against unseen bonds to confirm what she already knew. The flaming fetters had ruined her face, and would not abate until they had dug down to the bone and turned her skull to ash. Her silk robes lay in scorched tatters. Haydee rolled onto her side and screamed, piercing the far-reaching silence. Countless grains of sand had entered the channels furrowed across her once-proud cheeks, nose, and chin as her face had touched the shifting ground. They bit into her wounds, multiplying her agony.

Haydee felt the last traces of life seep out of her skin, swirling and hovering in the night sky like midnight tentacles, hungry for their promised feast. She lay with her eyes turned skyward, and allowed her hatred to coil around her charred heart. Hatred for her parents. For Reza and Mehmnet, for Darien. For the Icaryan queen. She felt the shadows snake and swirl around her limbs, pulling her apart. The sky shifted in its blackness, and she saw the night shudder with the darker shadows of the dead realm. At last, she could see both as they were, and would see neither evermore. She exhaled, welcoming the shadows until her flesh was devoured. Nothing remained, as though she'd never been there, had never been at all. The obsidian cloud thundered, charged with violence. With vengeance. The cloud spread outward, stretching and billowing until it became a thick blanket over the desert floor. The heavy storm rumbled above the sand, tracing a path that carved through the desert and back toward the pulsing rhythm of life—toward the city.

~

Thank you for reading! Did you enjoy? Please add your review because nothing helps an author more and encourages readers to take a chance on a book than a review.

And don't miss more from Kathryn Troy with THE SHADOW OF THERON. Turn the page for a sneak peek!

Also be sure to sign up for the City Owl Press newsletter to receive notice of all book releases!

SNEAK PEEK OF THE SHADOW OF THERON

It would have been a pleasant day, if not for the hanging.

The sun glistened off the newly constructed gallows—it was not often Lighura had a public execution—and people greeted each other in the square, staking out spots with a good view as they consumed their sweet buns and boiled eggs.

Lysandro was not hungry. He couldn't see how good people could be content to stuff themselves before a man was set to die, before the stench of a man expiring in his own piss filled their nostrils. He could smell it already.

Kato brushed against his elbow.

"You'll be able to see better from here, Don de Castel."

"I can see all I care to from here, thank you."

The innkeeper nodded. "As you say, Signor. But if you change your mind—"

Lysandro nodded and planted his feet on the ground, fists clenched at his side.

The crowd snapped to attention as the door to the magistrate's office opened. Lysandro's stomach soured at the sight of Marek. He exuded a sense of utter disinterest in the events of which he himself was the director. But Lysandro saw the glint of malice in Marek's eyes that he was unable to hide. He relished the power over the life and death of the wretch behind him, his broad chest inflated with self-importance. In short, Lysandro loathed him.

His attention turned to the bound man following the magistrate. Two of Marek's officers stood beside him and another behind, forming a diamond around the condemned. It was clear this man would not go easily to his death.

He writhed and twisted his body to get away from the men holding him, one at each elbow, kicking and flailing his legs out in a childlike tantrum. He was so focused on trying to escape their grip that only inchoate groans passed his lips. When they ascended the steps to the platform, the man's struggling became more desperate, more violent. The crowd gasped when the man wrangled one arm free and it looked like he might escape. But he fell to the ground as two of Marek's men fumbled after him, fighting to keep him in their grip. They forced him to his feet again.

Without saying a word, Marek turned to face his underlings. They redoubled their efforts, squeezing the prisoner tight between them until his feet barely touched the ground. The man's struggling didn't cease, but his range of motion was now severely restricted. The captive's eyes went wide in fear, showing the whites of them like a man held in the throes of a hysterical fit.

Drop back, Lysandro thought. He couldn't stop his mind from racing through all the ways the man might free himself. It he could just loosen their hold on him again, he could run. But he'd never make it. Not without help.

When Marek turned his face to the crowd, his eyes had narrowed to murderous slits, and his jaw was tightly clenched to preserve the façade of a smile that he wore there. He lifted his chin and addressed those who had gathered:

"People of Lighura—Jair Oreyo is guilty of killing Don Aldo Carras, who caught him stealing silver. His crime was discovered by his widow, Doña Sofia Carras, who tripped over her husband's body when responding to his screams."

Lysandro heard the gasps of those around him as Marek recounted the grisly details. Marek was either too stupid or too cruel to show more consideration for Carras's family. They stood huddled together in a tight circle, their faces pointed at the ground, while Marek expounded on the way Don Aldo's brains had been bashed against the stairway of their own home and turned the entryway slippery with blood. The women and children who congregated in the square turned their heads away from the platform as if to shut out Marek's words and shield themselves from the nightmares such lurid descriptions were bound to produce.

Lysandro could feel his face flushing hot. A good man's guts were being strewn about with words. That he couldn't stifle them turned him livid.

Seemingly sated by his talk of violence, Marek shifted to patting himself on the back for a job well done. He turned to his officers and beckoned with a small gesture for the prisoner to be brought forward. His men accomplished it, but with great difficulty.

"Any last words?" he asked in a cool, collected tone.

Jair was foaming at the mouth. Lysandro could see the veins on his neck bulge as his face went purple with rage, and he lunged at Marek.

"Liar!"

Lysandro's ears pricked up. Alarm bells rang in his head like the one in the temple tower—a full-throated clang that deepened his suspicion.

"Murderer!" Jair shouted. "You're just as guilty as me!"

He pled with his captors, who rammed the noose around his neck. "Don't listen to him, he's a liar! *Stop*, or he'll do the same thing to you!"

The knife tucked up Lysandro's sleeve prodded him at the wrist. He calculated the distance and the force it would take to sever the rope swinging from the beam.

He could do it. Avoiding notice, though—that would be another matter entirely. But something else stopped him from sliding the hidden blade into his hand.

You're just as guilty as me.

Jair was a murderer; he just wasn't alone.

The corner of Lysandro's mouth twitched as the officers tightened the noose around Jair's throat, but his fingers remained loose at his side.

The blood in Lothan Marek's veins hissed in fury as his brothers dragged Jairo, kicking and screaming, toward the noose. He was being ridiculous. It was one thing to steal from the poor, and another to murder a pillar of the community and think no one would notice. Lothan had no choice but to act. And Jair had the gall to call him out in front of the whole village.

His behavior worked in Lothan's favor. He was acting like a lunatic with his hair on fire, and Lothan expected people to discount his exclamations as the ravings of an almost dead man. Jair's outrage was Lothan's shield, so long as he kept the anger from his face.

Jair had been effective at his job; his taste for brutality had served him well on occasion. He was perhaps the strongest among them, excepting Lothan himself, and it was a bitter shame to kill him. Almost.

All those who shared his blood were a greedy, groveling, worthless waste of a power that should have been his alone. Today brought him one step closer to the magic scattered across their veins being made whole.

Lothan quashed his annoyance as Jair squealed and squirmed to the last minute, wriggling like a worm until the floor gave way beneath him and silence reigned over the square, heralded by a definitive, satisfying crack. Jair's latent power shivered up Lothan's spine. The surge of energy buzzed through him like a current, crackling at his fingertips and the ends of his hair. It was delicious. But not nearly enough.

Lysandro was grateful for the silence; it was infinitely better than a roar of cheers would have been. The Carras family remained clustered together as the knot of onlookers unfurled itself, and people returned to their routines to try to forget what they'd seen. Lysandro made his way toward them. Marek approached at the same time, holding a large wooden box in his hands.

"Doña Carras," he said, presenting her with the recovered silverware.

He looked so pleased with himself.

Don Aldo's widow stared at him, then took the box into her hands with a dumb expression on her face.

Lothan furrowed his brows. "This *is* your stolen silver, is it not? I imagined its return would bring you some comfort." He had to fight to keep the bite out of his voice.

Lysandro could hold his tongue no longer.

"Perhaps she'd be more grateful if you'd preserved her husband's dignity, rather than turn his final moments into a spectacle."

Marek looked up at him, his eyes bright with challenge.

"Or perhaps they'd have been grateful if you had arrested Jair weeks ago, after he'd already been accused of thievery by the blacksmith. Granted, his family's possessions are humbler than this fine collection," Lysandro continued, gesturing at the box of silver, "but had your justice been swifter—"

The widow sobbed, and Lysandro let his accusation hang in the air.

"The blacksmith's account was not reliable. He was not as—"

"Worthy of your attention?" Lysandro offered. His mouth set into a hard line. "I shouldn't need to remind you that the office of magistrate is bound to protect *all* of Lighura, not just its wealthier citizens."

Lothan scowled.

"What did you lie about?" Lysandro asked.

"Excuse me?"

The abrupt turn took Marek by surprise. Lysandro lifted his gaze over Marek's shoulder to the hanged man. "With his last breath, he called you a liar. What did you lie about?"

Marek huffed through his nose and shifted on his feet like a bull in a pen.

"He called me a murderer too. Do you also accuse me of that?"

Marek fixed him with a venomous stare. Doña Sofia's hand flew to her mouth, and her younger children hid their faces in her voluminous black skirts.

Lysandro didn't flinch.

He waited for an answer with feigned curiosity. Marek had walked into the trap himself. Lysandro wasn't about to help him out of it.

Marek's gaze slid to the widow. "I did my duty here today. No one can say I didn't." He turned his back on them both and left.

Doña Sofia let out a sigh of relief. "Thank you."

"Someone had to say something."

She looked down again and brushed her fingers against the grain of the box Marek had given her as her children came out of hiding. Lysandro smiled at them and ruffled the younger boy's hair before turning his gaze back to their mother.

"Is there anything you need?" he asked.

"We'll be all right. Thank you again."

Lysandro nodded and looked to her eldest son. "Take good care of them."

The young don was a strapping teenager, who tried to act older than he was by appearing to be unmoved by the whole affair. He was managing it badly. The boy's eyes darted from one end of the square to the other, not finding an answer to the question forming on his lips.

"There's so much to go through. So many papers. I don't even—"

"There's nothing that can't wait a few days' time," Lysandro interrupted. "I'll come see you soon, help you get everything sorted. Let's see if we can't make any sense of it."

"Thank you."

"It's my pleasure," he replied. "Take care."

Before departing from the square himself, Lysandro spared one last look at the hanged man, cast in silhouette by the sun's rays as Marek's officers worked to cut him down. Lysandro wondered at all he might have inquired of the dead man—all the questions he could never ask.

The cheerful weather was wasted on the somber mood that hung over the dusty little village until nightfall. Lysandro called on his father for a late supper, having finally found his appetite after a full day's abstinence. He greeted the doorman genially.

"Good evening, Diego."

"Good evening, Don Lysandro. You'll find him in the dining hall this evening."

"The dining hall?" Lysandro asked. "Does he have guests?"

"No, Signor. He simply said he longed for some formality."

Lysandro raised an amused eyebrow. He thanked the man and headed through the familiar hallways of the house in which he had grown up and found his way to his father. Don de Castel the elder was already seated at the head of a long wooden table in an elegantly papered room of cream and burgundy. Cheeses, warm bread, and a stiff fortified wine lay fanned out before him.

"Standing on ceremony today, Father?" Lysandro asked, seating himself at his father's right hand and pouring himself a drink.

"Indeed," Elias answered, not looking up from his plate as he tore off a piece of bread from a larger loaf and soaked it in a spiced olive oil.

"In your dressing gown?" Lysandro asked.

Elias grunted in the affirmative. "It's my best one."

Lysandro smiled and took in the image of his father. His robe was one of fine fabric, luxurious and warm against the chill in the air coming off the sea. The wine-colored gown was elevated by an intricately embroidered scroll pattern, with golden threads woven into the cuffs and collar. His father's face was thin, but sharp, and marked by an imposing chin and a well-kept, respectable beard of silver to match the hair smoothed back on his head. Yes, Lysandro thought, his father looked every ounce a don.

"Marek hung Carass's murderer today," Lysandro said.

"Mm."

"How *he* got to be magistrate I'll never know."

"That's easy. You didn't try for it."

Lysandro sipped at his wine. "Surely there are other able men in this village."

"There's so much influence you could wield, if only you would. There's no one sitting on the Andran Council now for Lighura."

"I doubt the Council would take kindly to my views."

"You still think you should give up all your land, and have it owned by the peasants who live there?" Elias asked.

"I clearly can't manage it on my own. Why *shouldn't* they own the fruit of their labors?"

"Without their rents you would be impoverished."

"I've known many men poorer than I who lead much happier lives."

Elias reclined in his high-backed seat and studied his son's reserved expression. "The social season starts in a few days. Will you attend the opening ball?"

Lysandro's heart constricted at the mention of it. He tried to dodge the question by digging into the slice of pork loin on his plate, but his father's expectant stare was unwavering.

"Why?" Lysandro asked, swallowing. "So I can mix with ladies almost ten years my junior and talk about the latest fashions?" Women saw his wealth and his title, and little else.

"That problem will get worse the older *you* get without choosing a bride. You're almost thirty."

"I seem to have exhausted my prospects."

"You only need to choose one."

If only there was *one*, Lysandro thought. *Just one.*

"You ask too much," Elias said.

"I just want what you had with Mother. Is *that* too much?"

Elias's eyes softened. "No. Maybe some travel would be in order. You've always longed to see Mirêne for yourself."

"Perhaps." Though Mirêne was more attuned to the Goddess's loving and more artful face, and better reflected Lysandro's own inclinations, he couldn't leave Lighura now—not after what had happened. There was a tension in the air, a sense of trouble brewing into something darker. More sinister.

He returned home and descended into the cavernous rooms carved out from underneath his estate. The space was sparsely furnished, with only a small dresser and a low bed covered in soft, dark furs. Wax puddled at the bases of the wrought-iron candelabras that flanked the corners of the room and lent it their dim light.

Lysandro considered what his father had said. He might find more in common with the people of Mirêne, but his heart belonged to Lighura too. Lysandro couldn't leave the fate of its people in the hands of Marek. Lysandro's belief that he was a thief and a murderer was stronger than ever. But he needed proof to remove him. Proof that might finally be within reach.

The trading ship that had quit the port yesterday had left heading north, rather than back the way they'd come. It would be easy for them to round to the other side of the coast unseen, rather than out to sea.

He stripped down to his skin and donned much simpler attire, dyed black to blend with the coming night. The worn fabric often felt more familiar and reassuring to him than the fine clothes he wore in the daytime. Too fancy an outfit would give him away and would more than likely get in his way. He didn't wear any metal or ornamentation that might glint in the moonlight; he had to be able to weave in and out of the darkness unseen. He completed his ensemble with a broad hat, leather gloves, and a sword honed to a fine point. He wrapped a strip of black cloth tightly around his face, revealing only his eyes, and tucked his long hair, kept in an older, more distinctive style, tucked inside his shirt.

Lysandro abhorred violence. In the full light of day, it went against the example of kindness he worked so hard to set. But the edge of a sword carried a certain sense of rightness. So he sought justice from the shadows.

～

Lighura's coast was too small to be a true harbor. It could only manage two ships at once, three in an emergency. Tonight, as most nights, the port was empty, leaving the water to creep slowly up the narrow beach without disruption. The only sounds for miles were the breaking of the surf and the call of gulls. But Lighura had pride of place in Andras. Aside from its beautiful coast, it was reputed to be the birthplace of the hero Theron, though exactly *where* he had lived had been lost to the passage of time.

As Lothan made his way down the sloping path to the shore, past the grass-covered dunes and toward the thin strip of sand, he spied the merchant vessel he sought approaching from a distance. They were still too far away for Lothan to tell if they carried any genuine relics aboard. If they truly possessed what they claimed, he would know—just as the work of Argoss sang in his veins, the lingering sense of the goddess sent his skin crawling. The only thing he felt in that moment was the blade pulsing against his abdomen. Under his coat blossomed the scent of fresh blood—a river's worth of it.

The drums of the broken metal shard's magic beat furiously between his ears. It was perhaps the only proof in the whole world that the goddess had failed—Argoss may have lost his life, but his sorcery was beyond her ability to destroy. A hot determination overcame Lothan as he brushed his fingers against the makeshift handle at his belt, drenching them in gore. What the goddess's whores insisted did not exist was his birthright, to bend and shape to his will. It had eluded him until now, with no clean or clever way to adhere the bleeding metal to the handle of his cheap knife, no symmetrical point or edge to pull them neatly together. But Jair's energy had come to roost in him, and he willed the broken fragment to cling to the grip. This time, it had obeyed.

The flow of blood racing along its jagged edge made him sticky, lapping at his skin like a wonton lover. It turned his blood feverish, and made his mouth run dry. He licked his lips as a distraction.

The sense of triumph he had first experienced when the shard had come into his possession had waned. What good did it do him if he couldn't find a way to salvage what remained of the once-mighty Blood Sword? It was so small. And he was not a blacksmith or a sorcerer. At least, not in the true sense of the word. He'd managed to find its locations, and had it transported from the farthest edges of Andras without raising suspicion, but that had been accomplished through instinct and sheer luck. The "why" of it eluded him. It was a constant source of frustration. When Lothan jabbed it through the air for the first time to test it, blood didn't fly off the edge in a venomous spray, which was a bit of a disappointment. But this was only one piece—Lothan consoled himself with the prospect of finding more, and one day wielding the full blade without squandering its power as Argoss had.

He had half a mind to slay his brothers right where they stood and take back from them what was his. But he was tied to his post, and much of what he craved lay beyond his grasp. He needed them. Although at this particular moment, the furtive glow of the lanterns on the beach was infuriatingly stationary. Lothan quickened his steps, and almost barreled into Jenner.

"What are you doing just standing there like an idiot? Spread out! Who do you have on the cliff?"

"That was Jair's job, Lord Lothan."

Lothan stared at him, and the man's legs nearly buckled as he spun on his heel and hurried to do the job himself.

They scattered at his command, taking up their positions as the ship made land.

Lothan was incensed by the illicit goods as they received the smugglers. They had only trinkets to offer— illustrated pages and "blessed" bits of junk, useless things that allowed deluded fanatics to feel nearer to the goddess and their hero—but nothing that bore the mark of Argoss. They had promised him more. They had promised him the Cerulean Key. Lothan did not take kindly to being lied to.

He turned to the man standing at his left and whispered in his ear.

"Get Gorin down here."

His brother retreated up the cliff face to recall the lookout. The more of them Lothan had nearby, the quicker he could dispatch the two-faced captain and his crew.

Lothan was still waiting for the pair of them to come back down when Jenner handed the captain his money. The captain in turn handed it to his second, who scurried up onto the boat. Lothan shot a piercing look to ·the cliffs, but neither man was anywhere in sight. He'd just about lost his patience when a single head popped into view.

"He's gone!"

"What do you mean, gone?"

"Like he's just vanished into thin air."

Lothan's skin prickled. Then he heard a scream, and a splash. That's when he knew they were not alone.

The sailors aboard the ship drew their swords, but it was useless against an invisible enemy. One man came flying in their direction and landed face-first in the mud. Another two, from Lothan's vantage point, seemed to disappear entirely, as if the floor had opened up from under them. Pandemonium erupted on the small vessel, but no one could discern the cause.

"It's him!"

"It's the Shadow of Theron!"

Marek's men watched but made no move to help, their eyes round in the lantern light. They grew skittish, wavering in place like horses ready to bolt.

He screamed at his men —better they fear him than some impostor who styled himself after a ridiculous excuse for a god. But his raging was drowned out by another voice that echoed across the sea.

"Ho, there! Looking for this?"

The Shadow of Theron appeared out of the darkness. He stood balanced on the thin outcropping of the ship's prow, with the sack of coins Jenner had just given over to the captain dangling from his hand.

The realization that he'd snuck past the lot of them without so much as a ripple out of place seized Lothan with a fit of rage. For too long, the Shadow had plagued him. Whenever he had come close to achieving even the smallest of his aims, Theron's Impostor had been there; he always knew the precise moment to strike, and always came away laughing—leaving Lothan chasing after him like an empty-headed fool. He reached for the bleeding dagger at his belt.

Not this night.

"Get him!" the captain shouted.

Jenner lunged for the chest, but the captain kicked the lid shut with his boot and caught him by the hand.

"No money, no trade!" The captain scooped up the ill-gotten treasure and sped back to the ship. The sailors seemed to have the Shadow cornered, stuck as he was on the thin bowsprit poking out over the water, but he batted their swords away with ease, their seething violence no more than a child's game to him. He pretended to lose his balance and flung the coins far out to sea.

A blood vessel in Lothan's neck threatened to burst; the smugglers howled in indignation. But when they charged him, he cut one of the lines connected to the foremast and used it to sail clear across the water to the stern. He bounded off the ship and landed on the beachhead with the grace of a jungle cat. He turned his back on Lothan, not showing a care in the world, and waved the ship off.

"Safe journey! Be careful of those rocks, they're trickier than they look!" Then he returned his gaze to the men on the beach, and grinned.

All Lothan needed was to get close enough to deliver one small slice.

But the Shadow was untouchable. He dodged Marek and his men with nimble steps at every turn, cutting through their number as he stayed always just a hair's breadth out of reach.

In a matter of minutes, Lothan's lieutenants lay sprawled flat in the sand, bloodied and unconscious. Lothan slowly worked to close the circle tighter and tighter as the Shadow danced around him. He was close enough now that the Shadow could see what it was that Lothan held; the broken blade shimmered brilliantly in the moonlight. The Shadow grew more careful, pushing Lothan to the brink of his endurance.

Lothan shot him a grim smile and tried to knock him off his balance.

"Was Theron himself such a coward in the face of great magic, or is that just you?"

But the Shadow was relentless, and deftly avoided his blows.

Lothan was rewarded for his patience. He thrust straight ahead, causing the Shadow to twist away to the side. But instead of righting himself, Lothan stepped into the dodge, leaving himself exposed, and retracted his arm back at rapid speed.

It was a shallow cut on the upper arm, nothing more. But Lothan felt the edge of the blade bite through the Shadow's sleeve, and the soft release as it rent open his flesh. The tang of blood filled the air as the tiny droplets joined the flood along the enchanted metal. The Shadow staggered backward, his chest heaving.

Lothan shivered in triumph. But he didn't stop. He struck again, aiming high for the head. The Shadow of Theron deflected the blow with more force than Lothan thought possible. But the power that pulsed at his fingertips didn't lie. Lothan stood grinning in the moonlight as the Shadow turned and ran for his life, although he was somewhat perturbed by the Shadow's speed. He shouldn't have been able to run at all.

The others were rising from the ground as his enemy shrank back into the shadows.

"Where did he go?"

"Should we go after him?"

"Let him be," Lothan said, a devilish grin on his face. Lothan was giddy, drunk with victory. "I cut him. With this." He held out the vermillion remnant of the Blood Sword of Argoss. His brothers gaped and dropped again to their knees, pressing their heads back into the sand.

"It may not be what it was. But if it has even a fraction of its old force...he won't live through the night."

~

Don't stop now. Keep reading with your copy of <u>THE SHADOW OF THERON</u>

Want even more from Kathryn Troy? Read THE SHADOW OF THERON and be sure to find her at kathryntroy.blogspot.com

∿

The powers of old are fading. A new Age is dawning.

Holy relics are all that remain of Theron's sacred legend.

Now those relics, the enchanted weapons forged by the Three-Faced Goddess to help Theron defeat the wicked Sorcerer Argoss, are disappearing.

Lysandro knows the village magistrate Marek is responsible, and he searches for proof disguised as the masked protector the Shadow of Theron.

But when Marek wounds him with an accursed sword that shouldn't exist, Lysandro must find a way to stop Marek from gaining any more artifacts created by the Goddess or her nemesis.

The arrival of the beautiful newcomer Seraphine, with secrets of her own, only escalates their rivalry.

As the feud between Lysandro and Marek throws Lighura into chaos, a pair of priestesses seeks to recover the relics and return them to safekeeping. But the stones warn that Argoss is returning, and they must race to retrieve Theron's most powerful weapon.

While they risk their lives for a legend, only one thing is certain. The three temples to the Goddess have been keeping secrets: not just from the faithful, but from each other.

∿

Please sign up for the City Owl Press newsletter for chances to win special subscriber-only contests and giveaways as well as receiving information on upcoming releases and special excerpts.

All reviews are **welcome** and **appreciated**. Please consider leaving one on your favorite social media and book buying sites.

For books in the world of romance and speculative fiction that embody Innovation, Creativity, and Affordability, check out City Owl Press at www.cityowlpress.com.

ACKNOWLEDGMENTS

Thanks to the team at City Owl Press for all that they do, and for my wonderful readers. You are the best.

ABOUT THE AUTHOR

KATHRYN TROY is a history professor by day, a novelist by night. She likes to write what she reads — fantasy, romantic fantasy, gothic fiction, historical fiction, paranormal, horror, and weird fiction. Horror cinema and horticulture are her other passions. When she's not writing or reading or teaching, she's either gaming, traveling, baking, or adding some new weird creepy cool thing to  her art collection. She is a Long Island native with one husband, two children, and three rats.

kathryntroy.blogspot.com

ABOUT THE PUBLISHER

City Owl Press is a cutting edge indie publishing company, bringing the world of romance and speculative fiction to discerning readers.

Escape Your World. Get Lost in Ours!

www.cityowlpress.com

facebook.com/YourCityOwlPress
x.com/cityowlpress
instagram.com/cityowlbooks
pinterest.com/cityowlpress

www.ingramcontent.com/pod-product-compliance
Lightning Source LLC
Chambersburg PA
CBHW020654030726

47498CB00002B/509